SECRET CODERS
Secrets & Sequences

GENE LUEN YANG
& MIKE HOLMES

First Second
New York

"It was this wonderful time between magic and so-called rationality."

–Wally Feurzeig, co-creator of the Logo programming language, on the early days of Logo

First Second
New York

Copyright © 2017 by Humble Comics LLC

Published by First Second
First Second is an imprint of Roaring Brook Press,
a division of Holtzbrinck Publishing Holdings Limited Partnership
175 Fifth Avenue, New York, New York 10010

Library of Congress Control Number: 2016938729

Paperback ISBN: 978-1-62672-618-5
Hardcover ISBN: 978-1-62672-077-0

Our books may be purchased in bulk for promotional, educational,
or business use. Please contact your local bookseller or the Macmillan
Corporate and Premium Sales Department at (800) 221-7945 x5442
or by email at MacmillanSpecialMarkets@macmillan.com.

First edition 2017

Book design by Rob Steen

Printed in China by Toppan Leefung Printing Ltd., Dongguan City, Guangdong Province

Paperback: 10 9 8 7 6 5 4 3 2 1
Hardcover: 10 9 8 7 6 5 4 3 2 1

Chapter

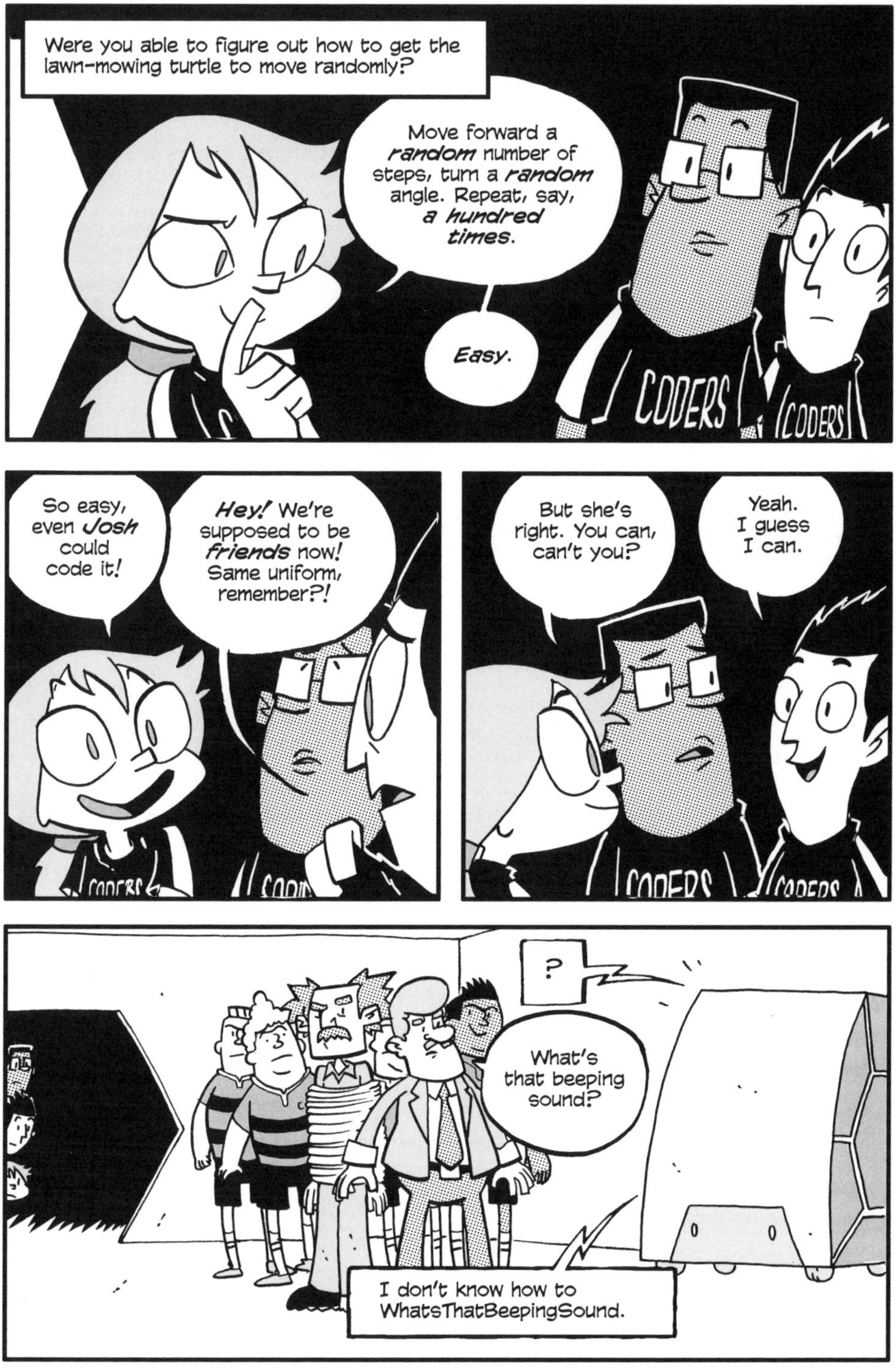
Were you able to figure out how to get the lawn-mowing turtle to move randomly?
Move forward a random number of steps, turn a random angle. Repeat, say, a hundred times.
Easy.
CODERS
CODERS
So easy, even Josh could code it!
Hey! We're supposed to be friends now! Same uniform, remember?!
But she's right. You can, can't you?
Yeah. I guess I can.
?
What's that beeping sound?
I don't know how to WhatsThatBeepingSound.

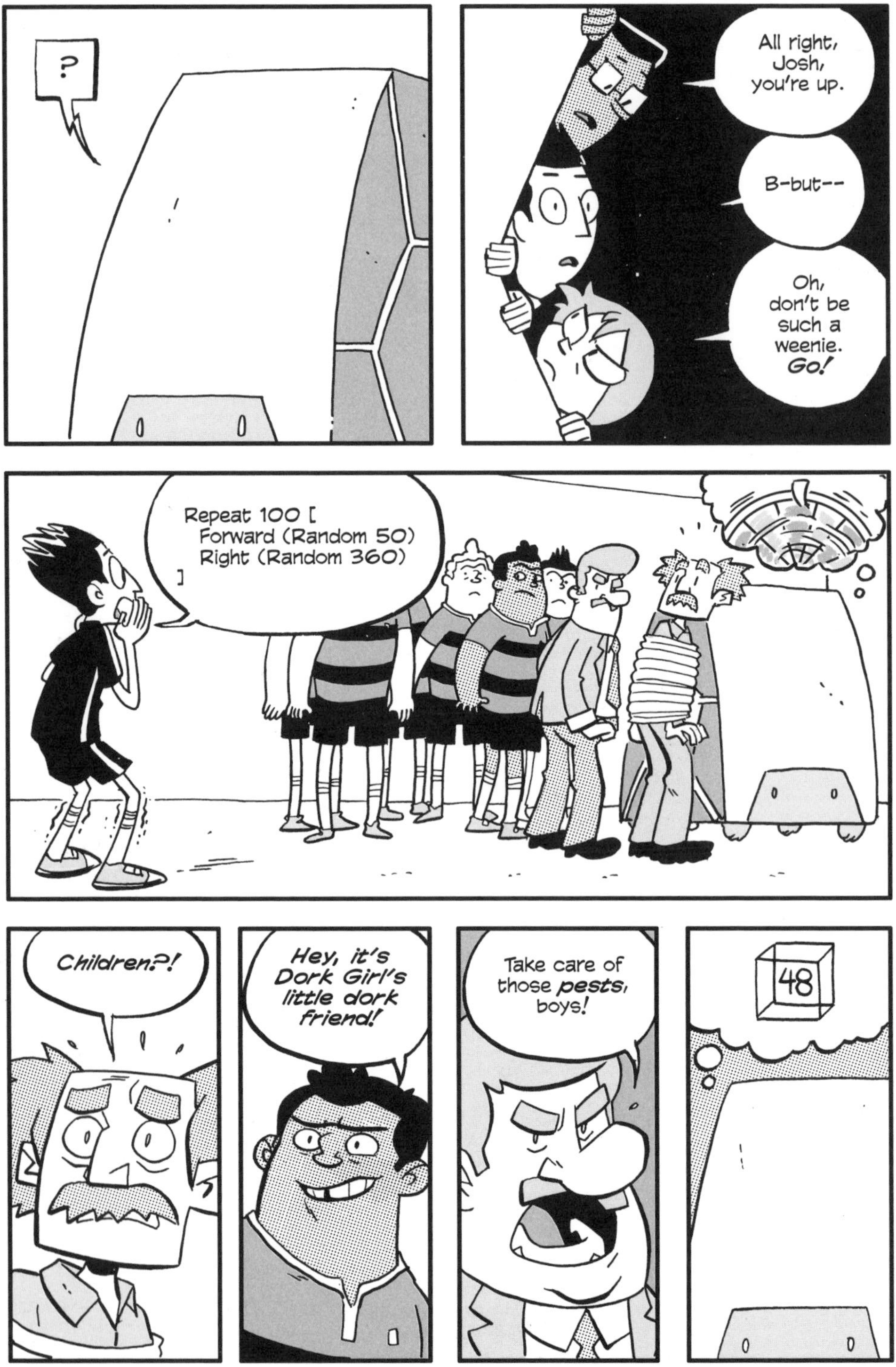
?
All right, Josh, you're up.
B-but--
Oh, don't be such a weenie. *Go!*
Repeat 100 [
Forward (Random 50)
Right (Random 360)
]
Children?!
Hey, it's Dork Girl's little dork friend!
Take care of those *pests*, boys!
48

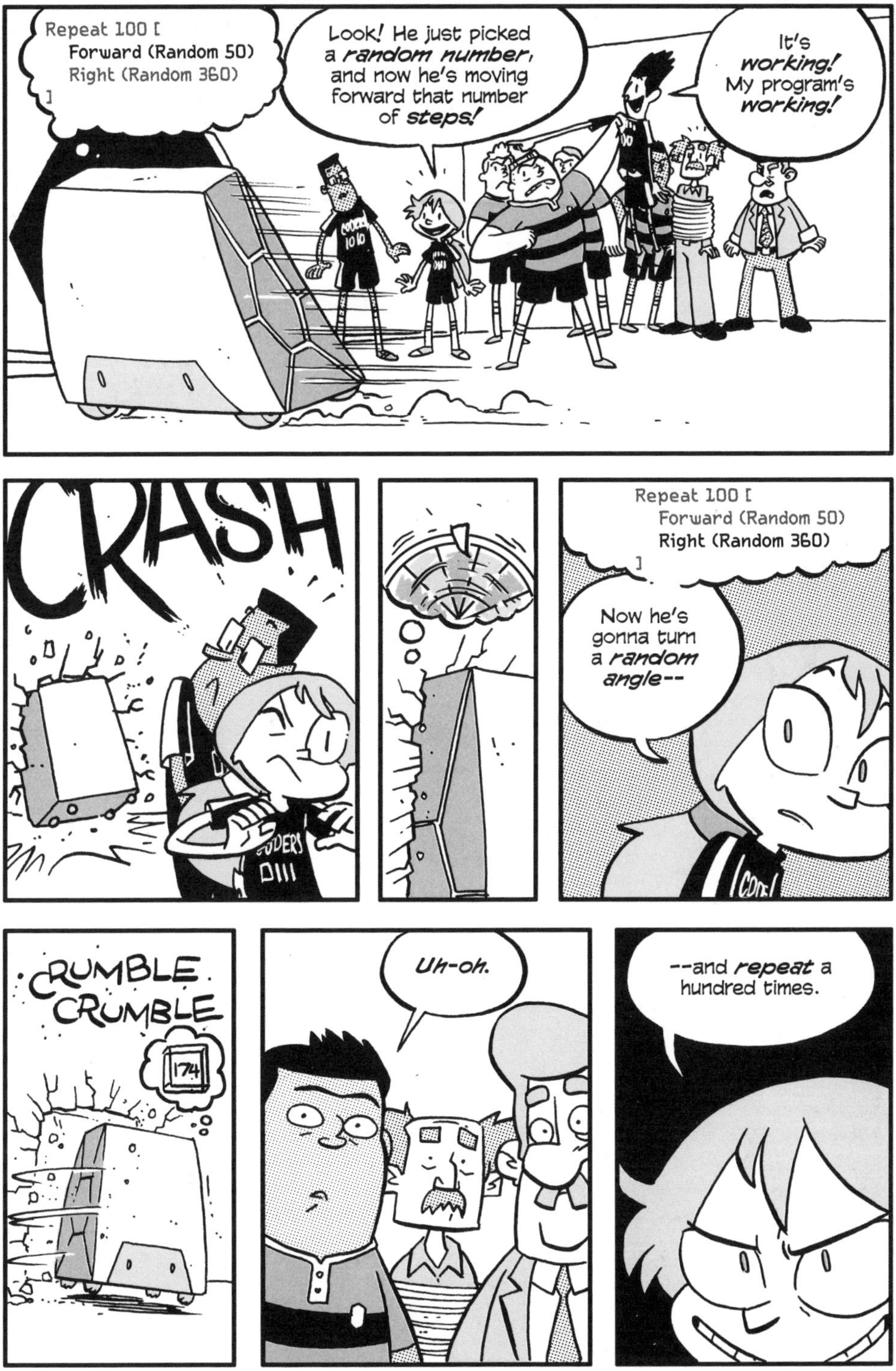
Repeat 100 [
Forward (Random 50)
Right (Random 360)
]
Look! He just picked a *random number*, and now he's moving forward that number of *steps!*
It's *working!* My program's *working!*
CRASH
Repeat 100 [
Forward (Random 50)
Right (Random 360)
]
Now he's gonna turn a *random angle--*
CRUMBLE CRUMBLE
174
Uh-oh.
--and *repeat* a hundred times.

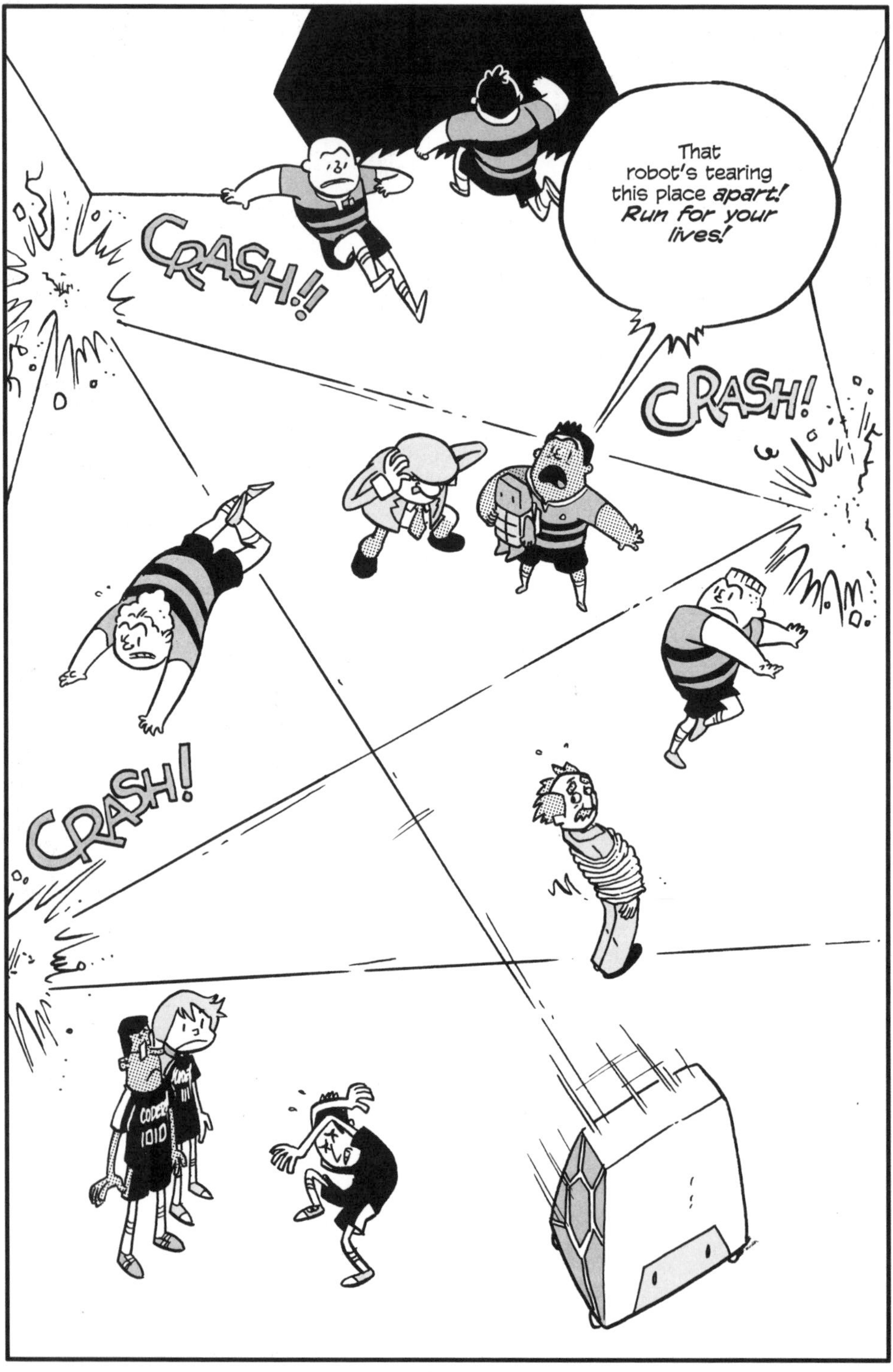
That robot's tearing this place *apart!* *Run for your lives!*
CRASH!!
CRASH!
CRASH!
CODER 1010

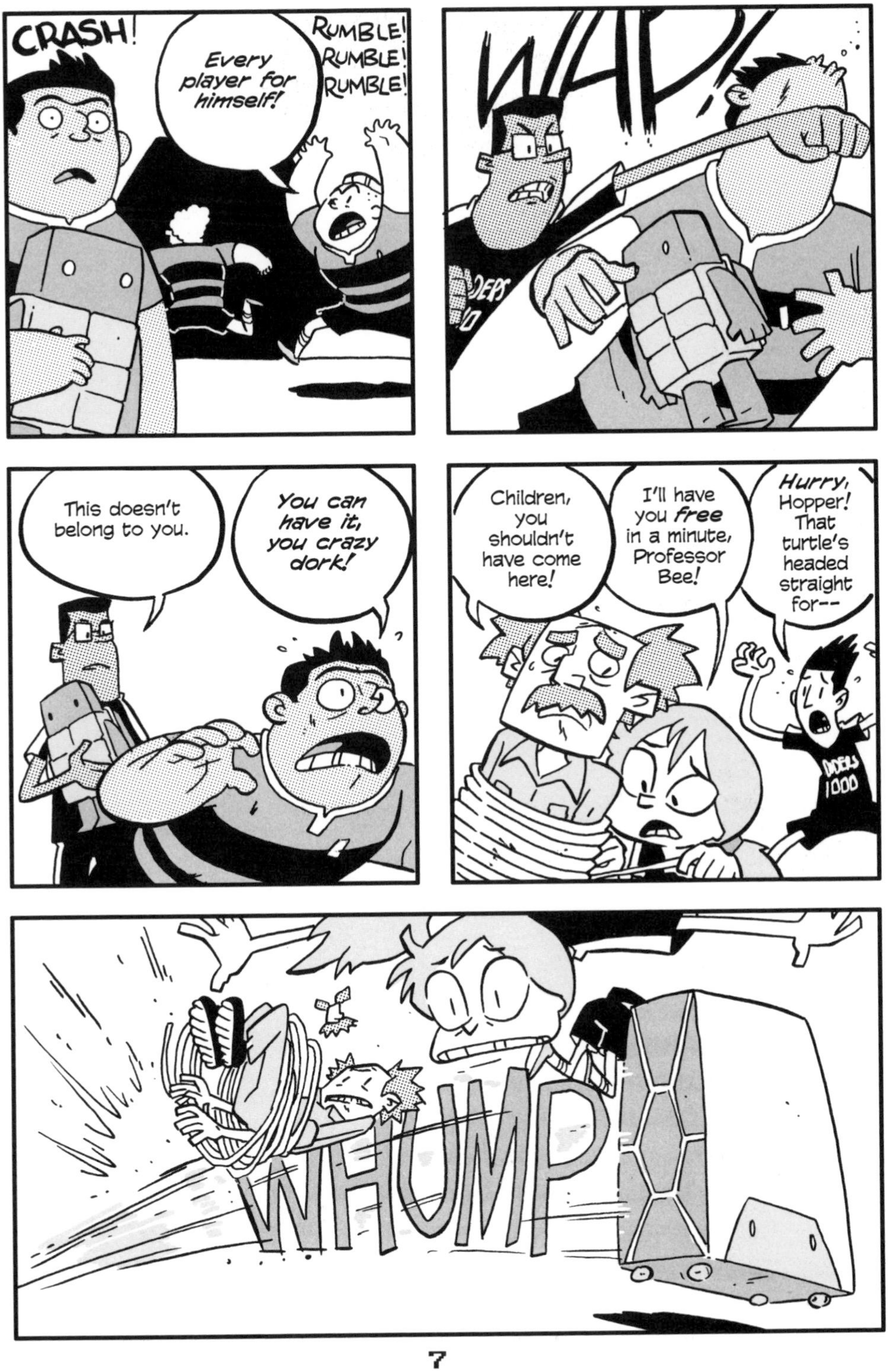
CRASH!
Every player for himself!
RUMBLE! RUMBLE! RUMBLE!
WAP!
This doesn't belong to you.
You can have it, you crazy dork!
Children, you shouldn't have come here!
I'll have you free in a minute, Professor Bee!
Hurry, Hopper! That turtle's headed straight for--
WHUMP!

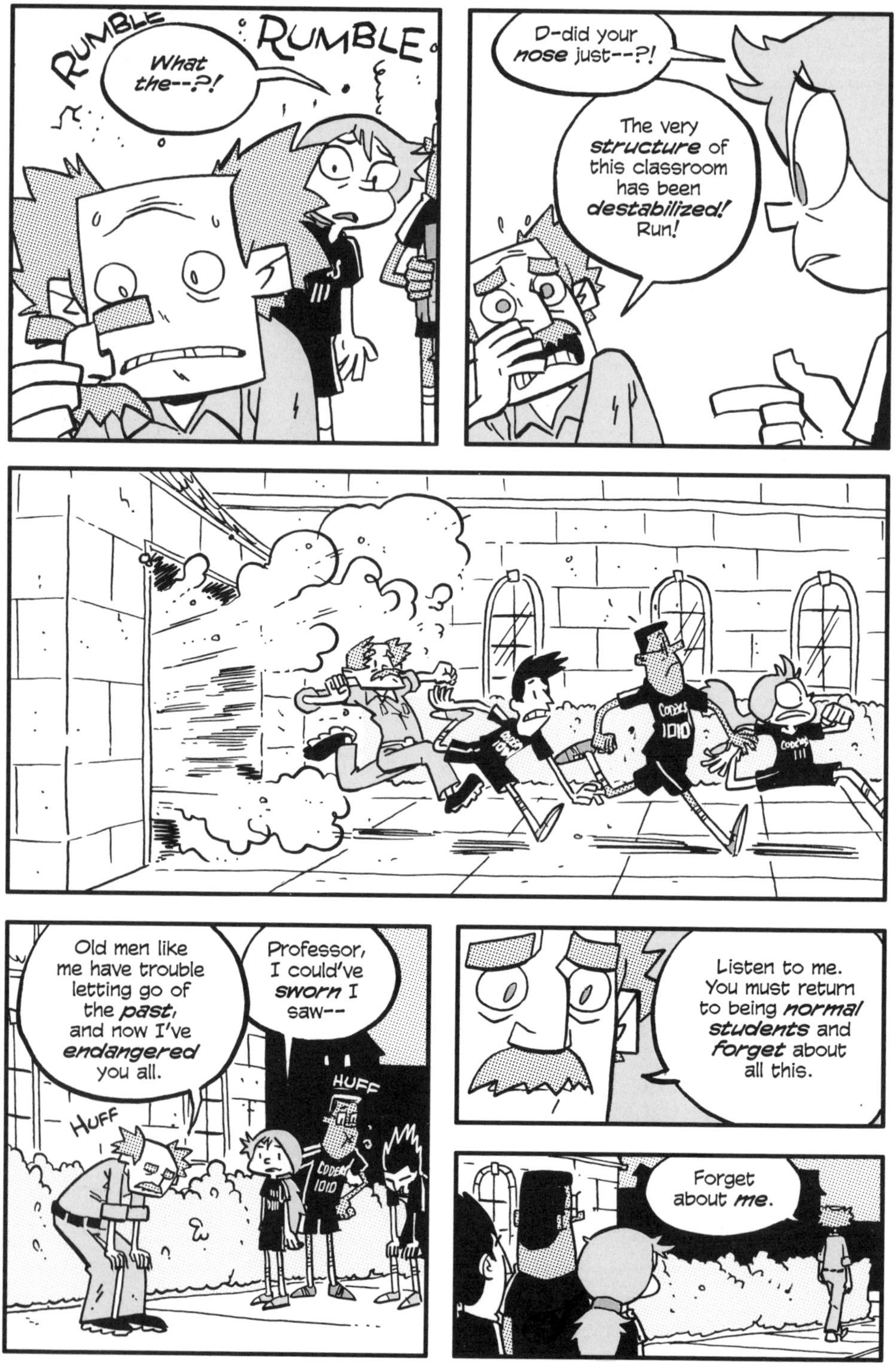
RUMBLE
RUMBLE
What the--?!
D-did your nose just--?!
The very structure of this classroom has been destabilized! Run!
Old men like me have trouble letting go of the past, and now I've endangered you all.
Professor, I could've sworn I saw--
HUFF
HUFF
Listen to me. You must return to being normal students and forget about all this.
Forget about me.

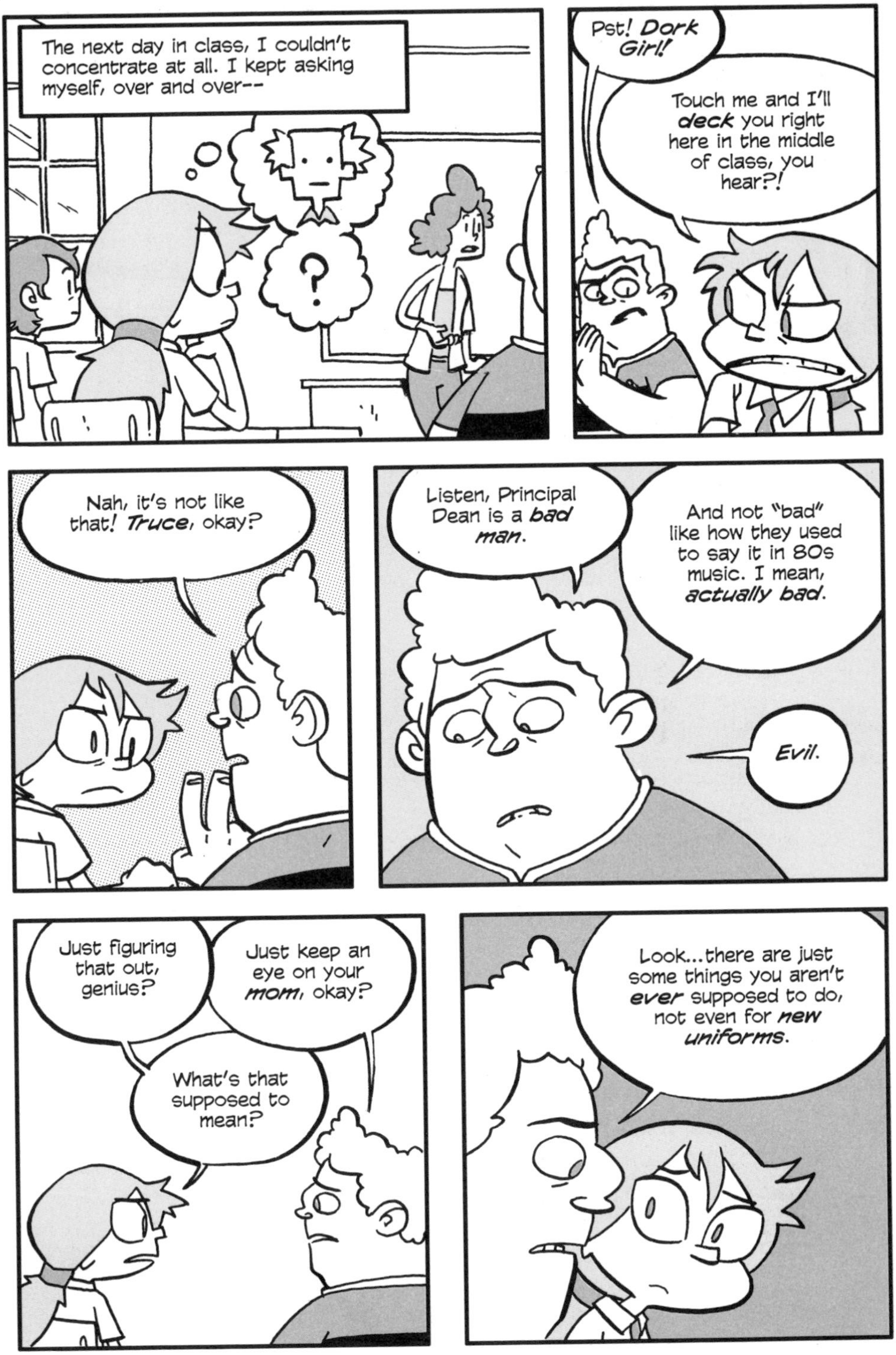
The next day in class, I couldn't concentrate at all. I kept asking myself, over and over--
?
Pst! *Dork Girl!*
Touch me and I'll *deck* you right here in the middle of class, you hear?!
Nah, it's not like that! *Truce*, okay?
Listen, Principal Dean is a *bad man*.
And not "bad" like how they used to say it in 80s music. I mean, *actually bad*.
Evil.
Just figuring that out, genius?
Just keep an eye on your *mom*, okay?
What's that supposed to mean?
Look...there are just some things you aren't *ever* supposed to do, not even for *new uniforms*.

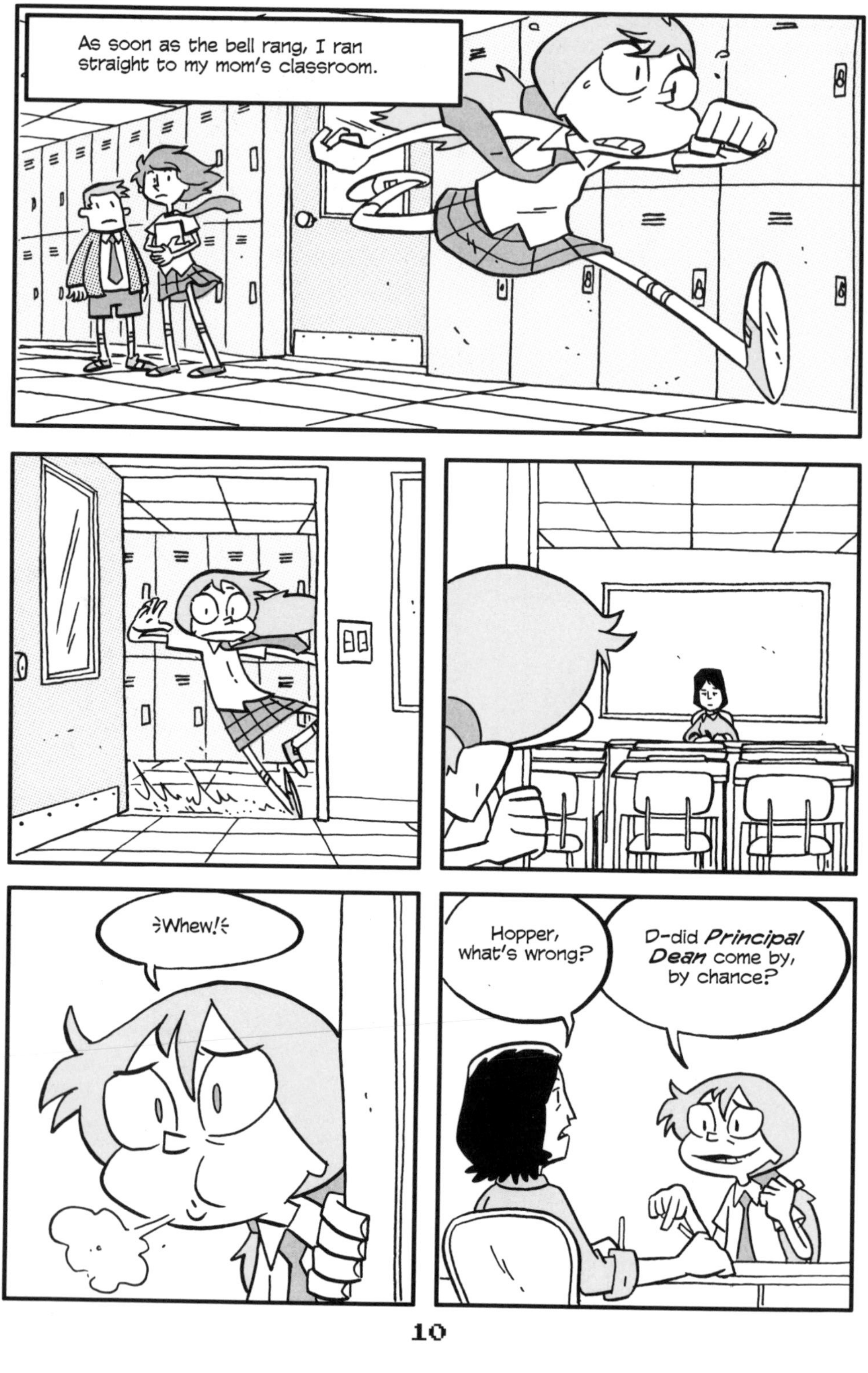
As soon as the bell rang, I ran straight to my mom's classroom.
Whew!
Hopper, what's wrong?
D-did *Principal Dean* come by, by chance?

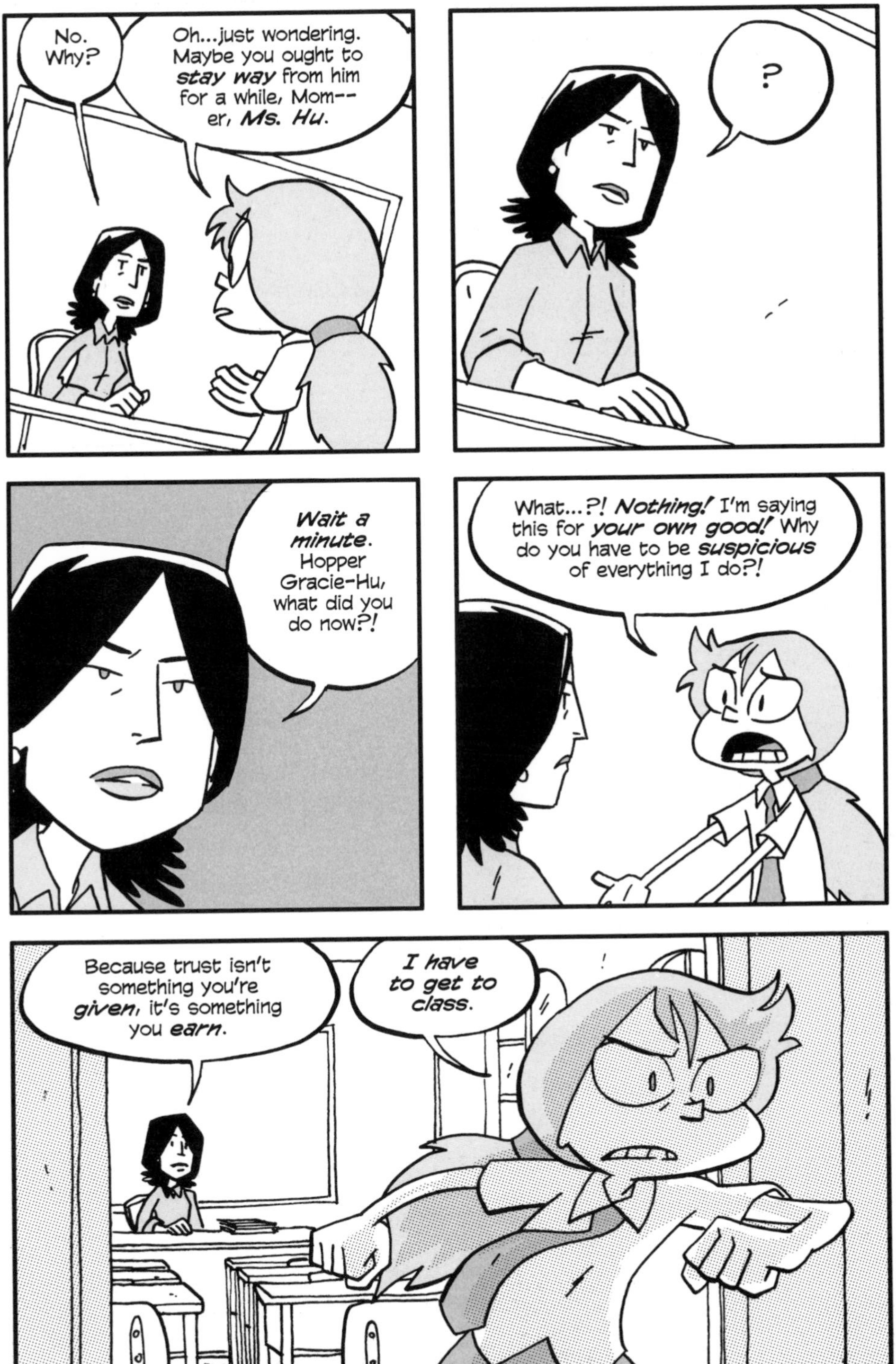

No. Why?
Oh...just wondering. Maybe you ought to stay way from him for a while, Mom-- er, Ms. Hu.
?
Wait a minute. Hopper Gracie-Hu, what did you do now?!
What...?! Nothing! I'm saying this for your own good! Why do you have to be suspicious of everything I do?!
Because trust isn't something you're given, it's something you earn.
I have to get to class.

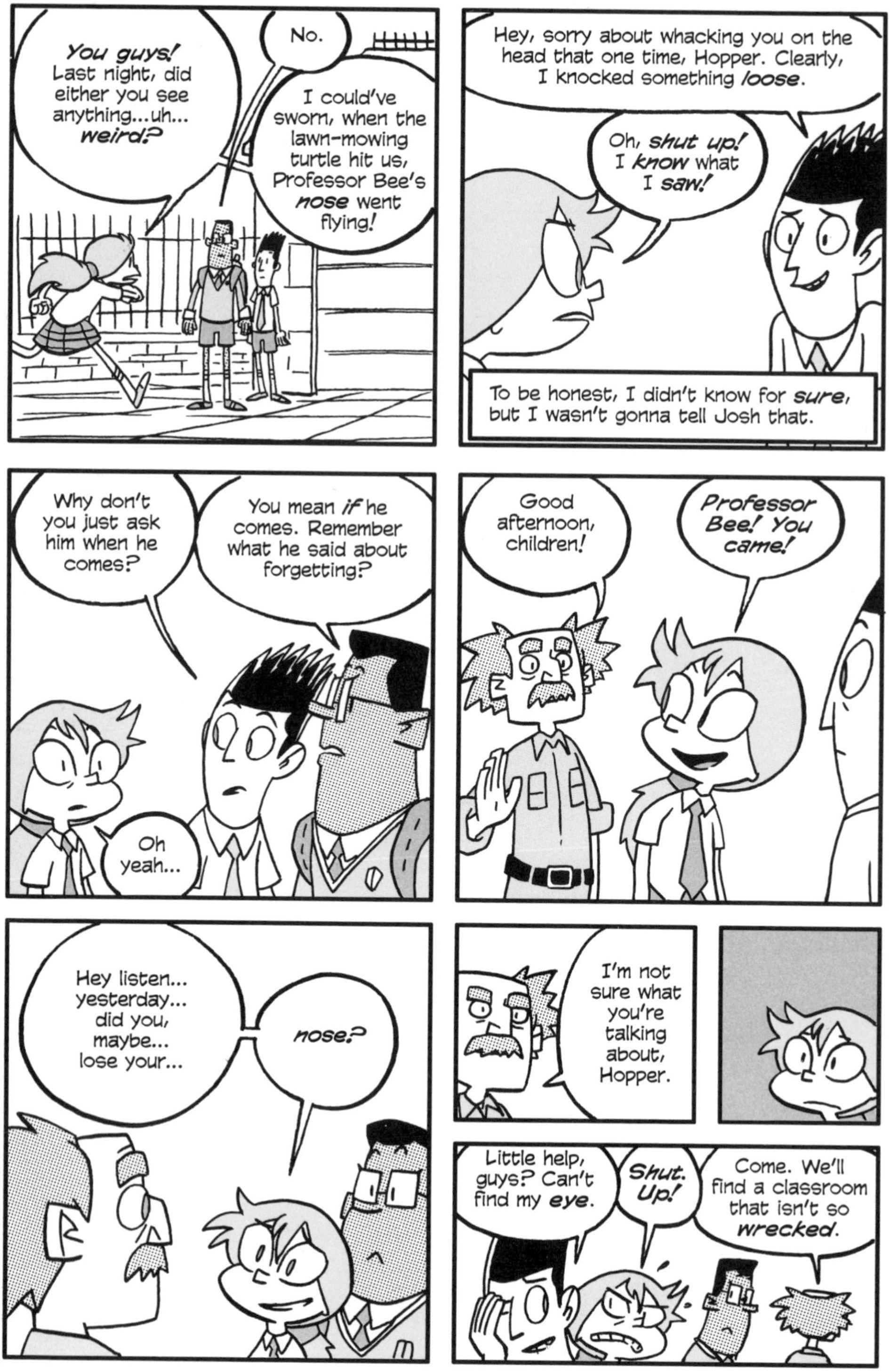
You guys! Last night, did either you see anything...uh... weird?
No.
I could've sworn, when the lawn-mowing turtle hit us, Professor Bee's nose went flying!
Hey, sorry about whacking you on the head that one time, Hopper. Clearly, I knocked something loose.
Oh, shut up! I know what I saw!
To be honest, I didn't know for sure, but I wasn't gonna tell Josh that.
Why don't you just ask him when he comes?
You mean if he comes. Remember what he said about forgetting?
Oh yeah...
Good afternoon, children!
Professor Bee! You came!
Hey listen... yesterday... did you, maybe... lose your...
nose?
I'm not sure what you're talking about, Hopper.
Little help, guys? Can't find my eye.
Shut. Up!
Come. We'll find a classroom that isn't so wrecked.

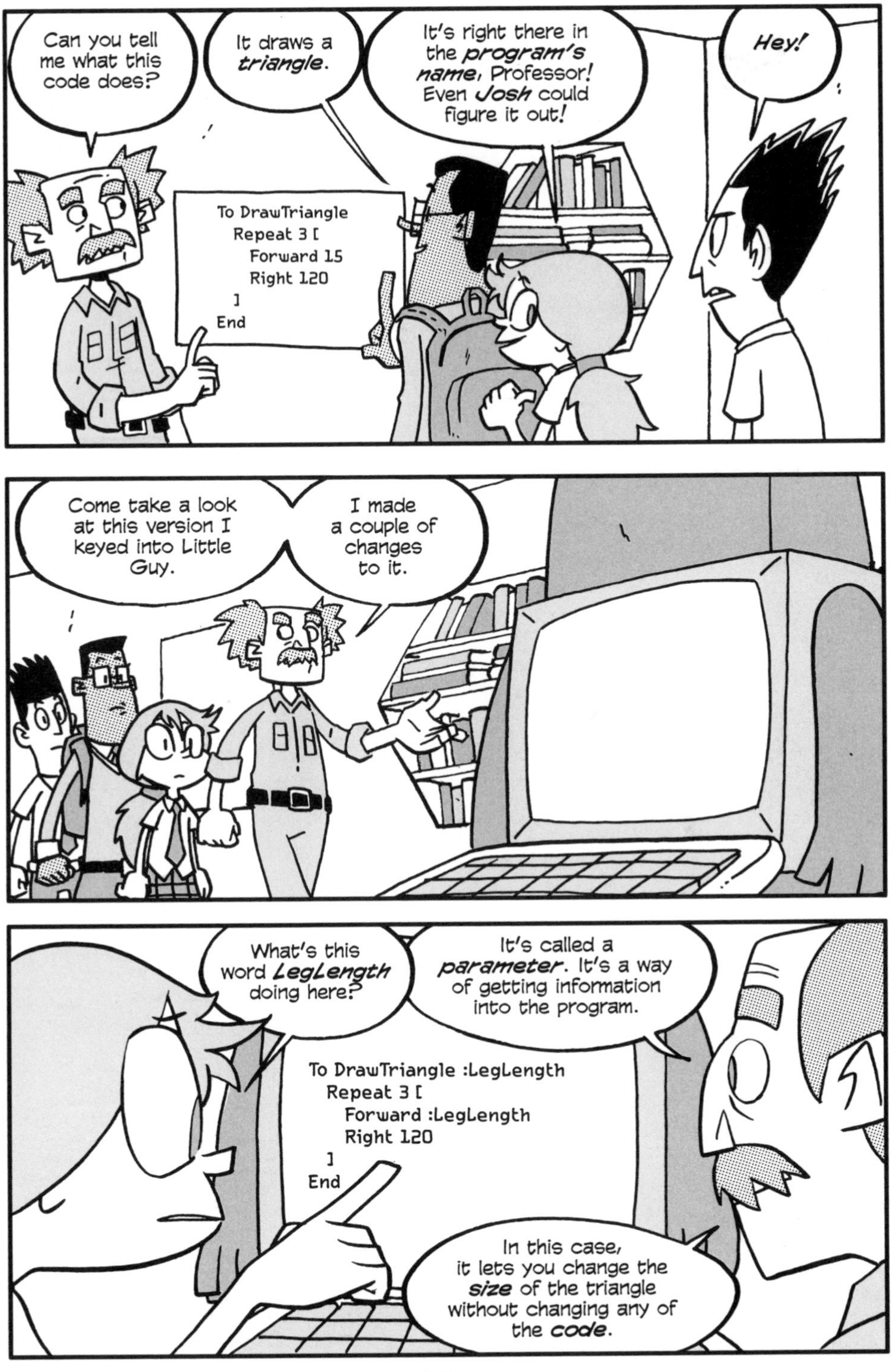
Can you tell me what this code does?
It draws a *triangle*.
It's right there in the *program's name*, Professor! Even *Josh* could figure it out!
Hey!
To DrawTriangle
Repeat 3 [
Forward 15
Right 120
]
End
Come take a look at this version I keyed into Little Guy.
I made a couple of changes to it.
What's this word *LegLength* doing here?
It's called a *parameter*. It's a way of getting information into the program.
To DrawTriangle :LegLength
Repeat 3 [
Forward :LegLength
Right 120
]
End
In this case, it lets you change the *size* of the triangle without changing any of the *code*.

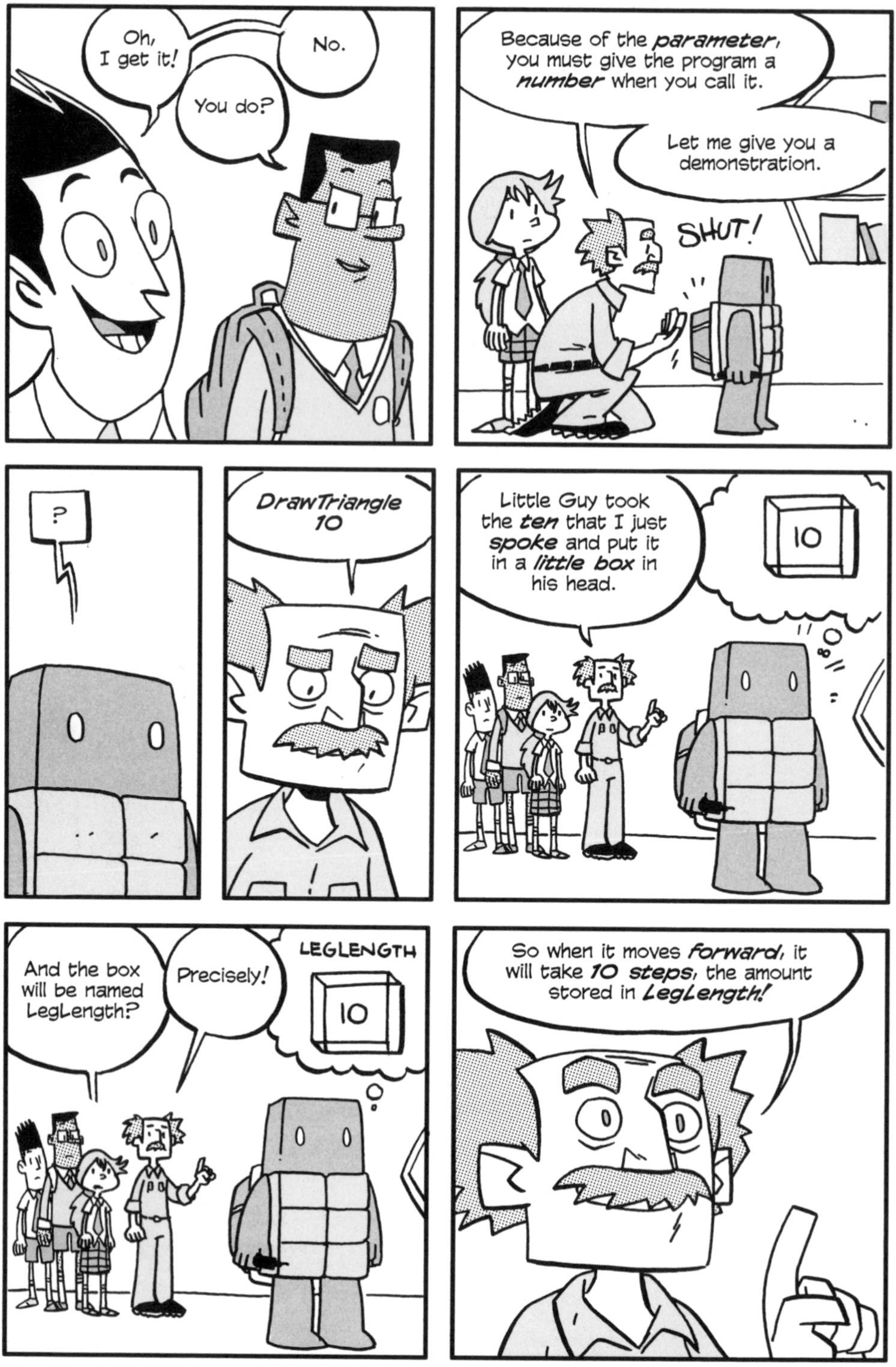
Oh, I get it!
You do?
No.
Because of the parameter, you must give the program a number when you call it.
Let me give you a demonstration.
SHUT!
?
DrawTriangle 10
Little Guy took the ten that I just spoke and put it in a little box in his head.
10
And the box will be named LegLength?
Precisely!
LEGLENGTH
10
So when it moves forward, it will take 10 steps, the amount stored in LegLength!

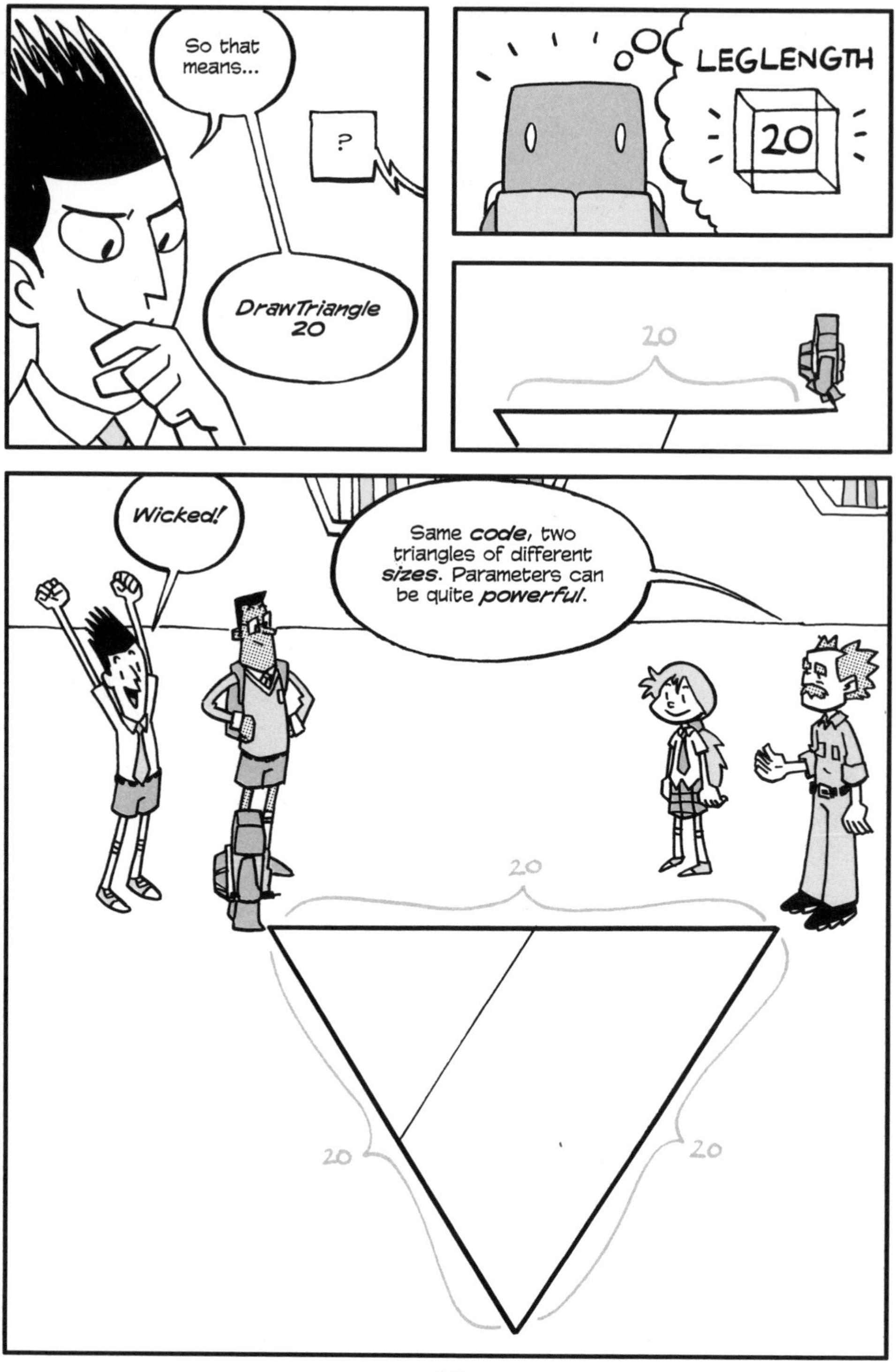
So that means...
DrawTriangle 20
?
LEGLENGTH
20
20
Wicked!
Same code, two triangles of different sizes. Parameters can be quite powerful.
20
20
20

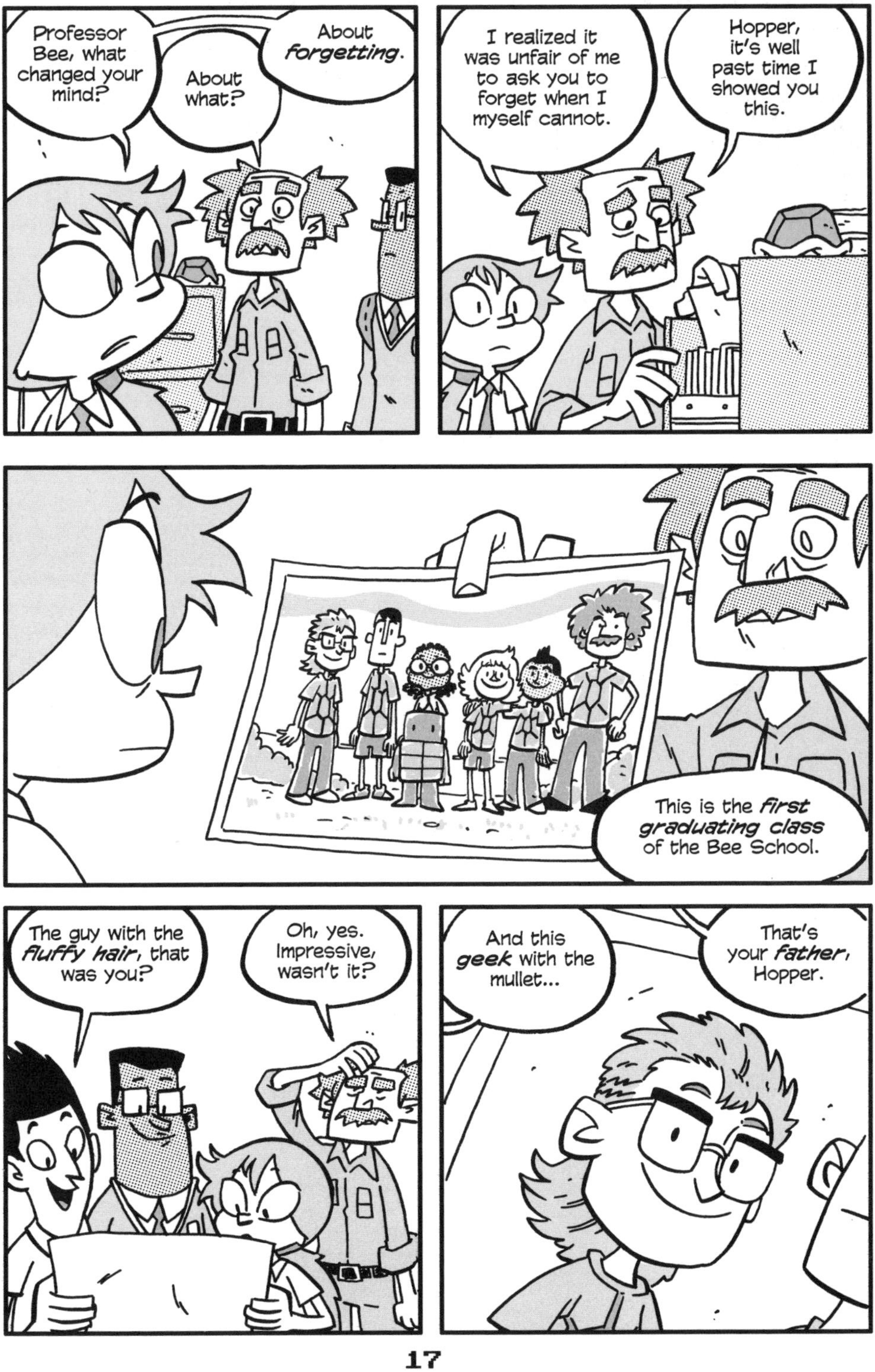
Professor Bee, what changed your mind?
About what?
About *forgetting*.
I realized it was unfair of me to ask you to forget when I myself cannot.
Hopper, it's well past time I showed you this.
This is the *first graduating class* of the Bee School.
The guy with the *fluffy hair*, that was you?
Oh, yes. Impressive, wasn't it?
And this *geek* with the mullet...
That's your *father*, Hopper.

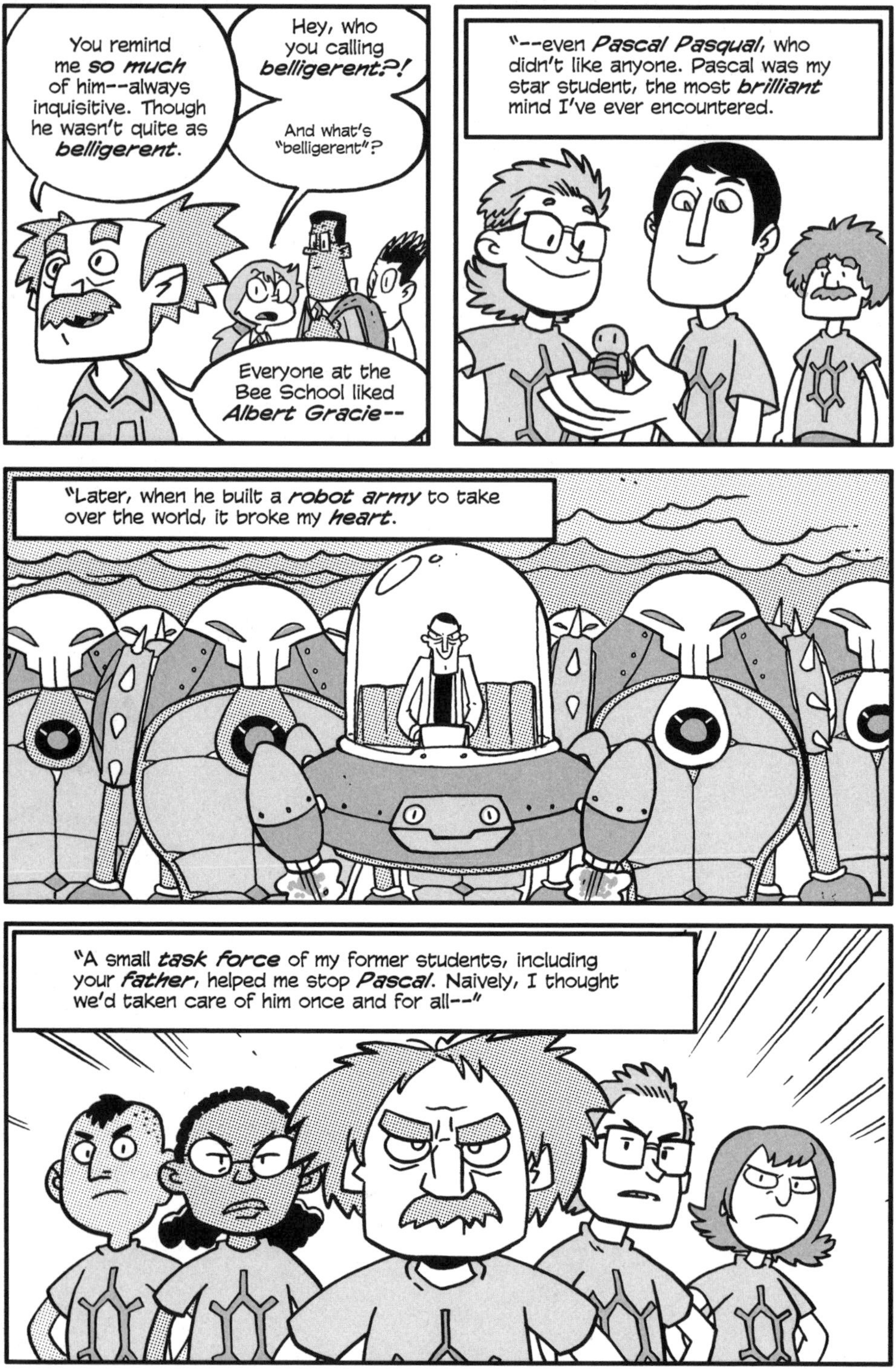
You remind me so much of him--always inquisitive. Though he wasn't quite as belligerent.
Hey, who you calling belligerent?!
And what's "belligerent"?
Everyone at the Bee School liked Albert Gracie--
"--even Pascal Pasqual, who didn't like anyone. Pascal was my star student, the most brilliant mind I've ever encountered.
"Later, when he built a robot army to take over the world, it broke my heart.
"A small task force of my former students, including your father, helped me stop Pascal. Naively, I thought we'd taken care of him once and for all--"

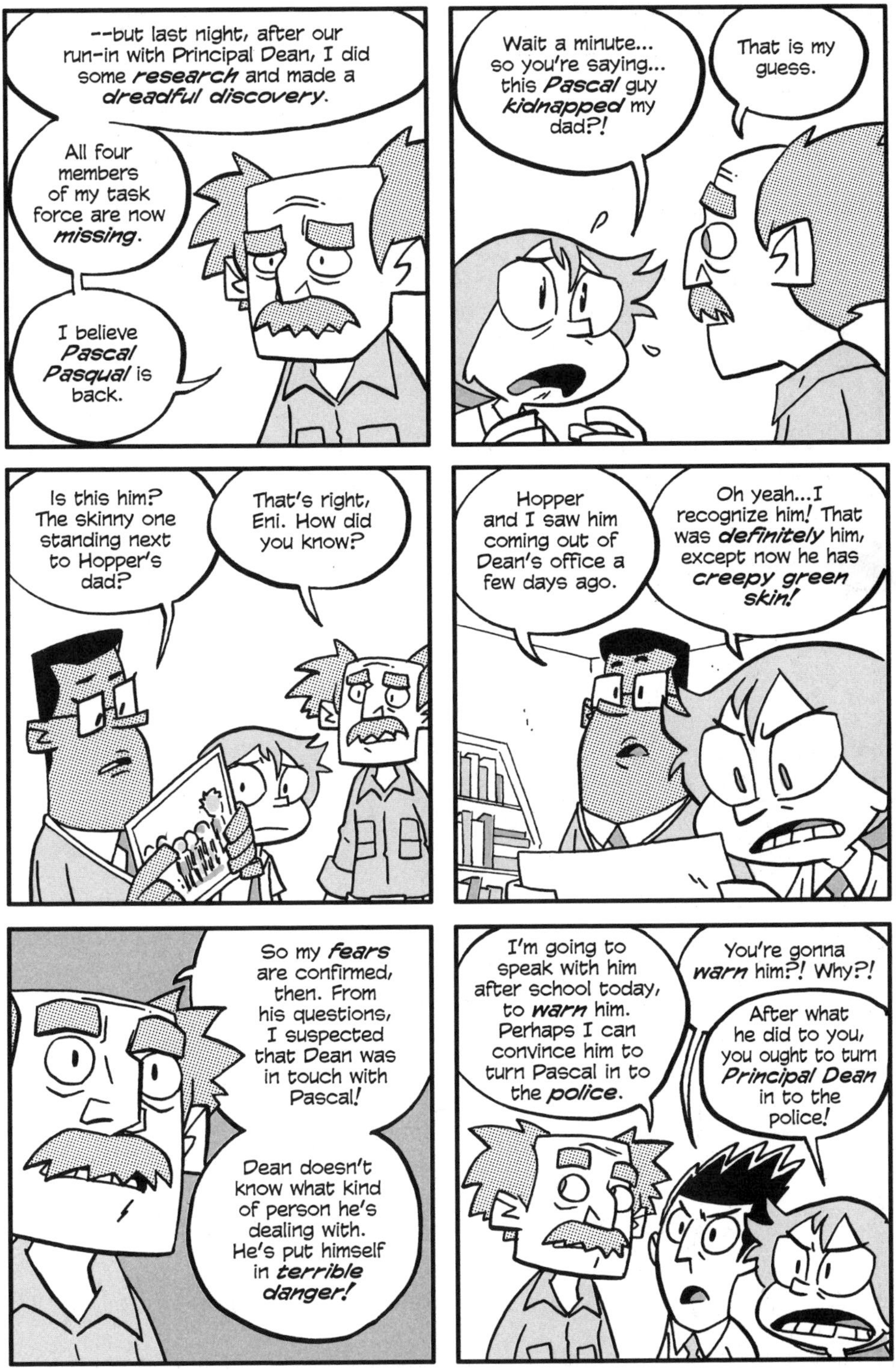
--but last night, after our run-in with Principal Dean, I did some *research* and made a *dreadful discovery*.
All four members of my task force are now *missing*.
I believe *Pascal Pasqual* is back.
Wait a minute... so you're saying... this *Pascal* guy *kidnapped* my dad?!
That is my guess.
Is this him? The skinny one standing next to Hopper's dad?
That's right, Eni. How did you know?
Hopper and I saw him coming out of Dean's office a few days ago.
Oh yeah...I recognize him! That was *definitely* him, except now he has *creepy green skin!*
So my *fears* are confirmed, then. From his questions, I suspected that Dean was in touch with Pascal!
Dean doesn't know what kind of person he's dealing with. He's put himself in *terrible danger!*
I'm going to speak with him after school today, to *warn* him. Perhaps I can convince him to turn Pascal in to the *police*.
You're gonna *warn* him?! Why?!
After what he did to you, you ought to turn *Principal Dean* in to the police!

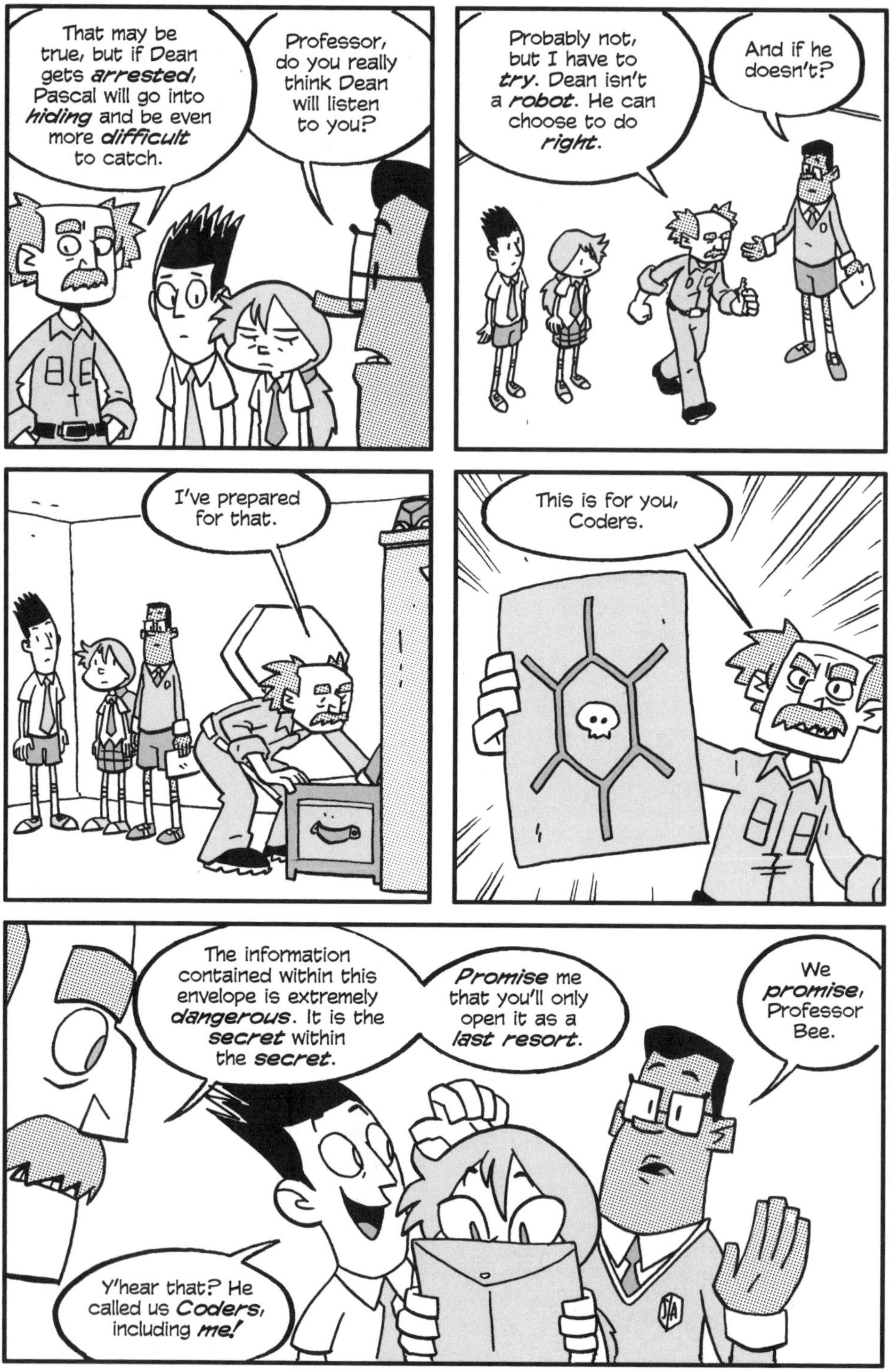
That may be true, but if Dean gets *arrested*, Pascal will go into *hiding* and be even more *difficult* to catch.
Professor, do you really think Dean will listen to you?
Probably not, but I have to *try*. Dean isn't a *robot*. He can choose to do *right*.
And if he doesn't?
I've prepared for that.
This is for you, Coders.
The information contained within this envelope is extremely *dangerous*. It is the *secret* within the *secret*.
Promise me that you'll only open it as a *last resort*.
We *promise*, Professor Bee.
Y'hear that? He called us *Coders*, including *me!*

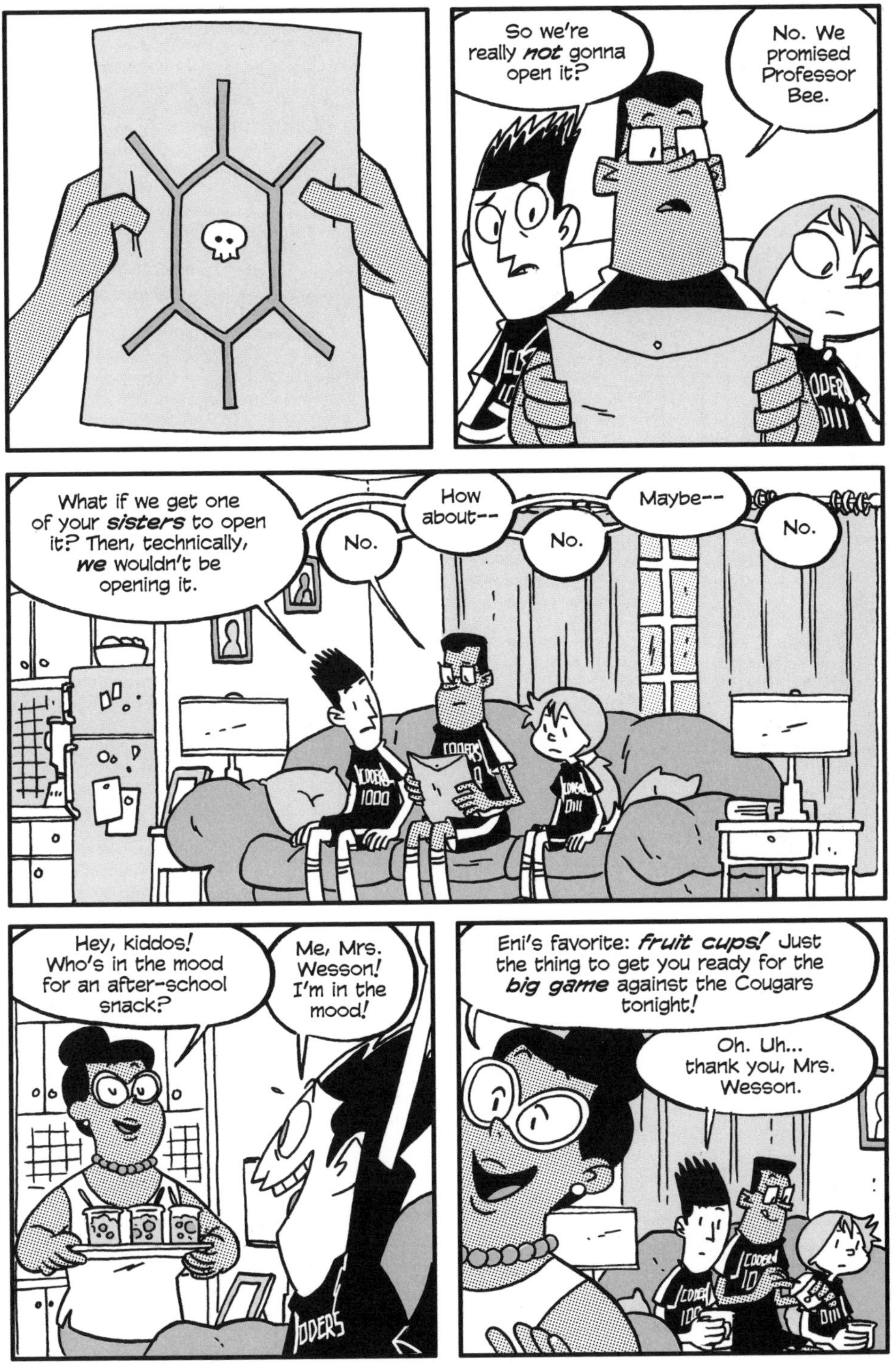
So we're really *not* gonna open it?
No. We promised Professor Bee.
What if we get one of your *sisters* to open it? Then, technically, *we* wouldn't be opening it.
No.
How about--
No.
Maybe--
No.
Hey, kiddos! Who's in the mood for an after-school snack?
Me, Mrs. Wesson! I'm in the mood!
Eni's favorite: *fruit cups!* Just the thing to get you ready for the *big game* against the Cougars tonight!
Oh. Uh... thank you, Mrs. Wesson.

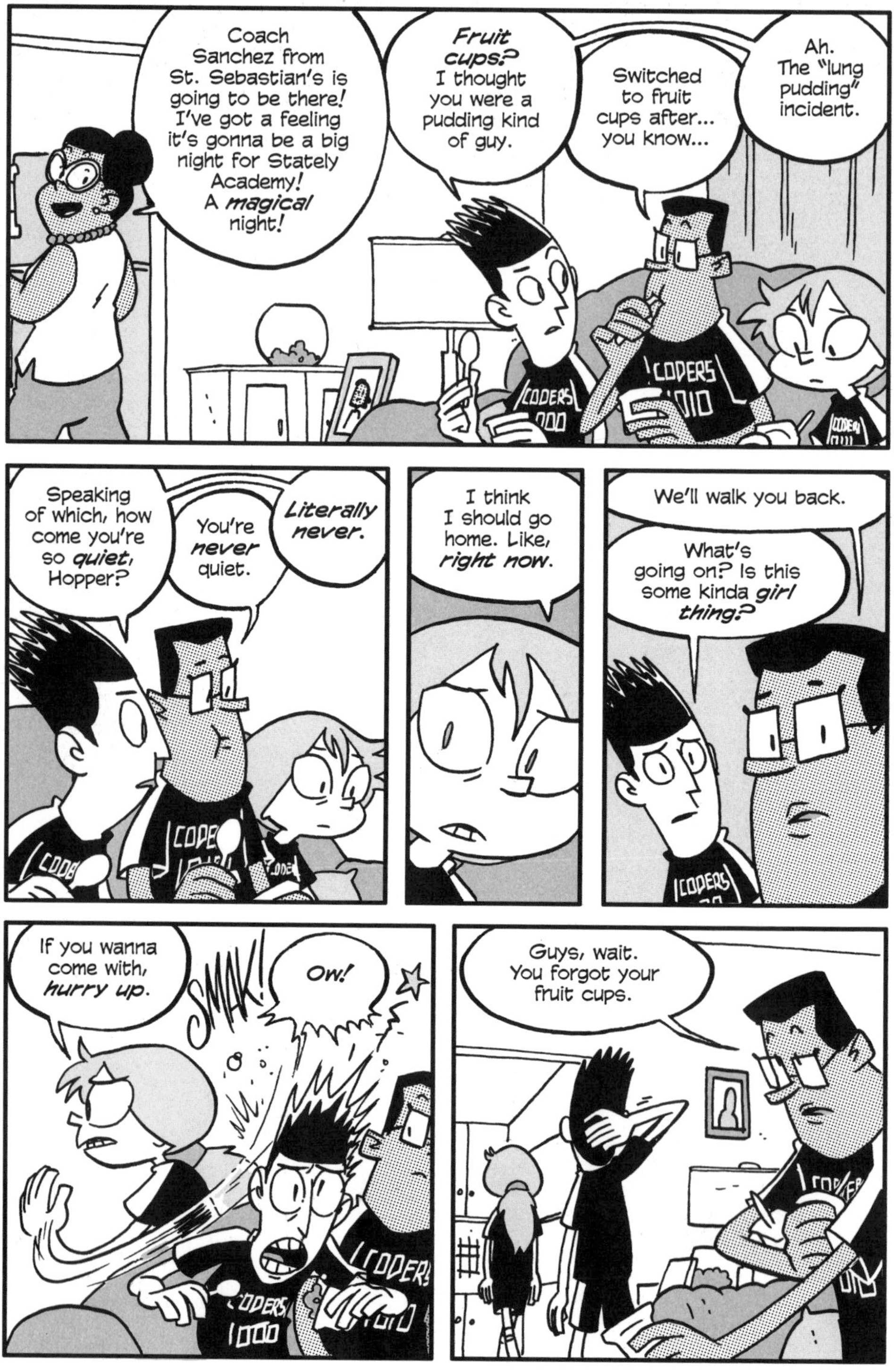
Coach Sanchez from St. Sebastian's is going to be there! I've got a feeling it's gonna be a big night for Stately Academy! A *magical* night!
Fruit cups? I thought you were a pudding kind of guy.
Switched to fruit cups after... you know...
Ah. The "lung pudding" incident.
CODERS 1010
Speaking of which, how come you're so *quiet*, Hopper?
You're *never* quiet.
Literally never.
I think I should go home. Like, *right now*.
We'll walk you back.
What's going on? Is this some kinda *girl thing?*
If you wanna come with, *hurry up*.
SMAK!
Ow!
CODERS 1000
Guys, wait. You forgot your fruit cups.

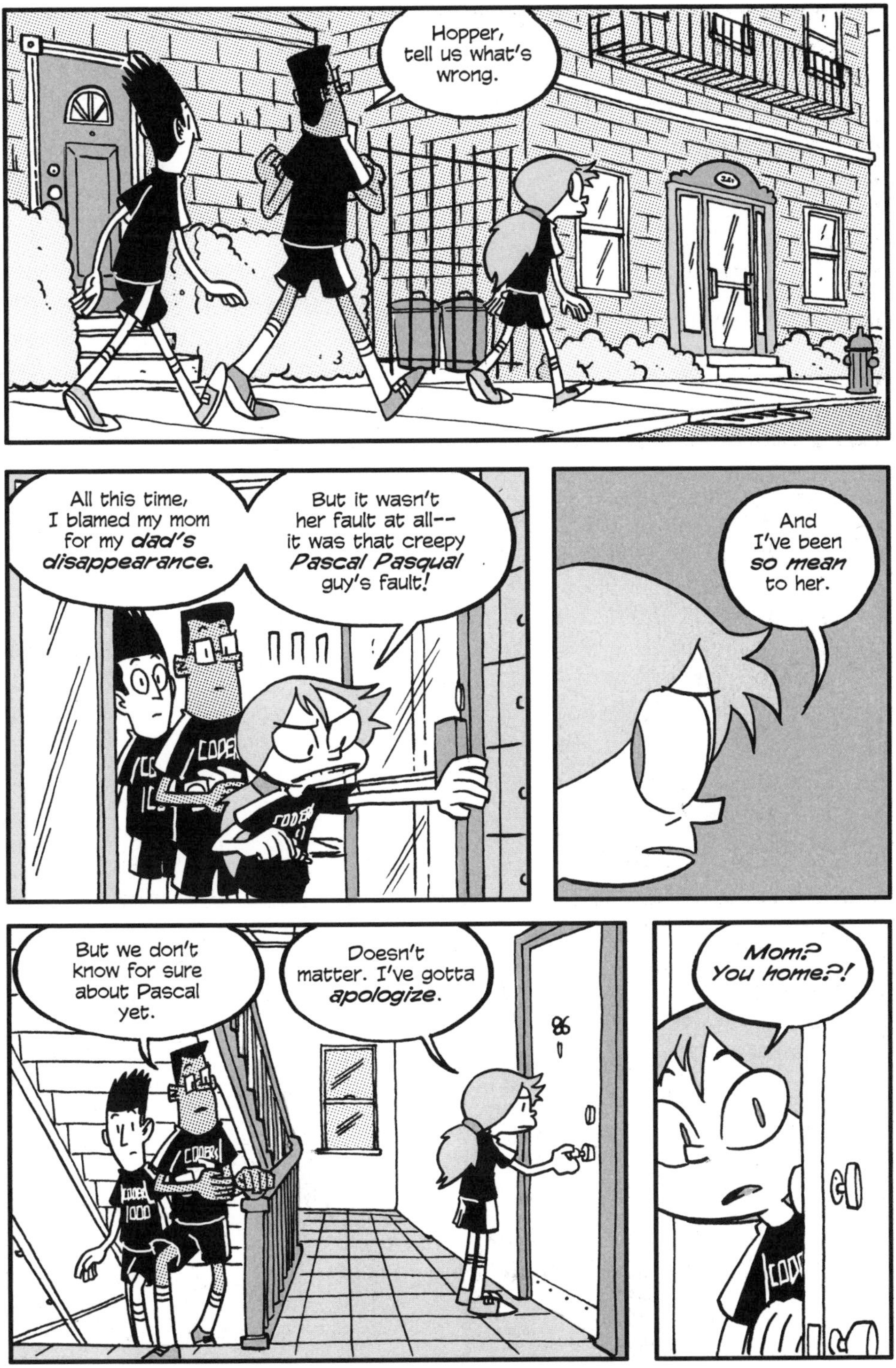
Hopper, tell us what's wrong.
All this time, I blamed my mom for my *dad's disappearance.*
But it wasn't her fault at all-- it was that creepy *Pascal Pasqual* guy's fault!
And I've been *so mean* to her.
But we don't know for sure about Pascal yet.
Doesn't matter. I've gotta *apologize*.
Mom? You home?!

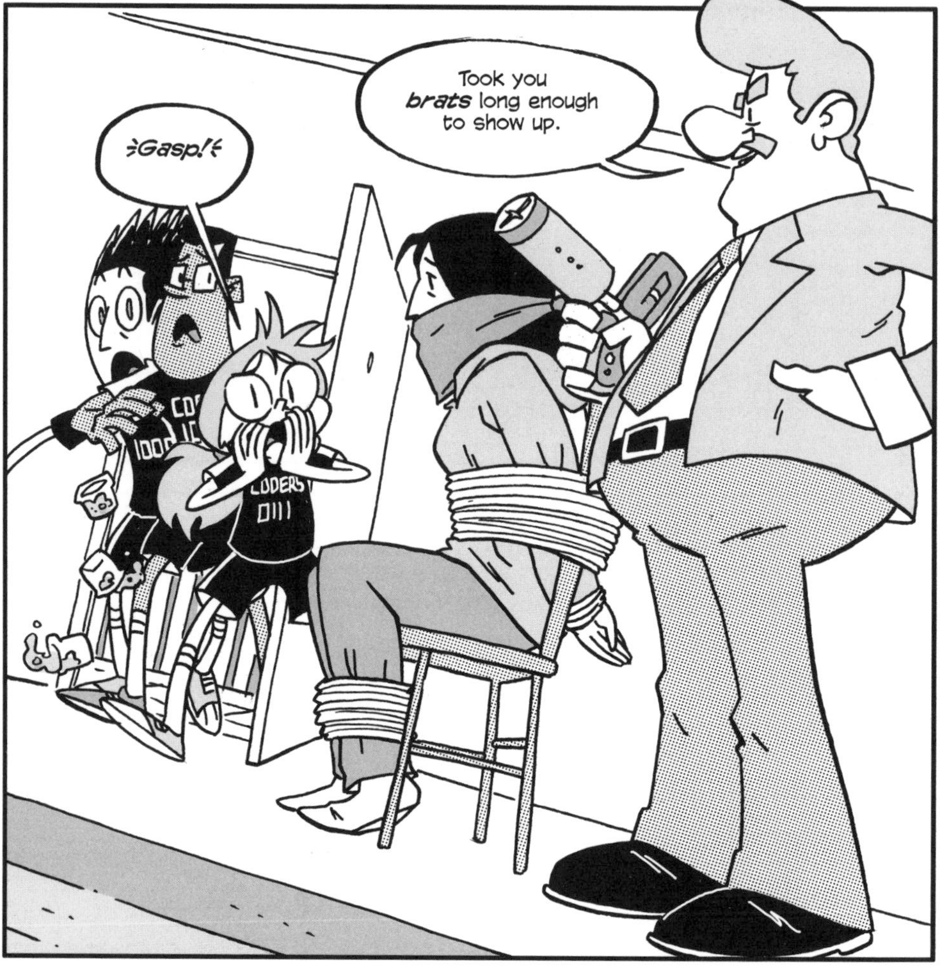
Took you *brats* long enough to show up.
Gasp!
CODERS 0111

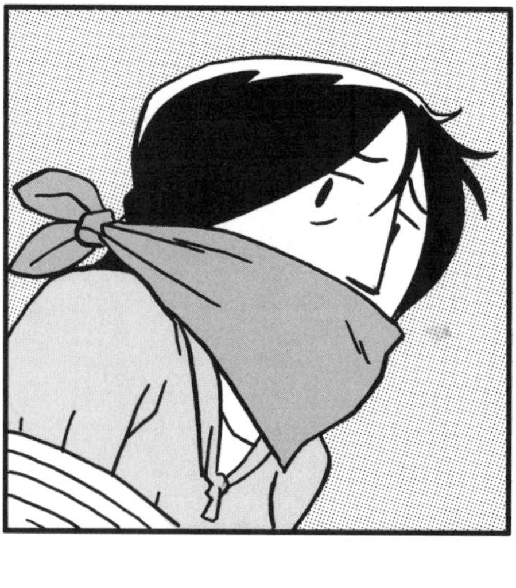

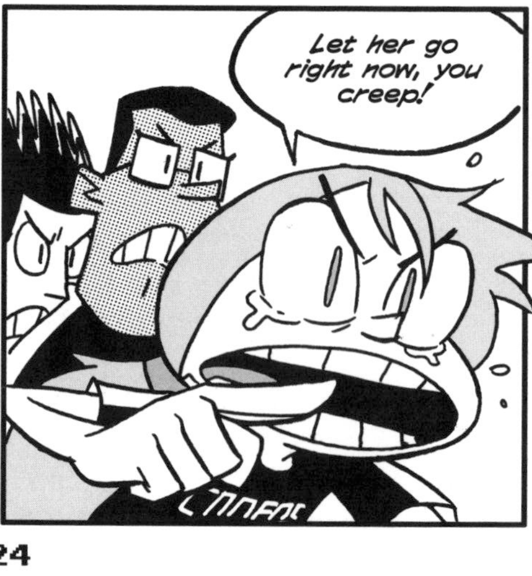
Let her go right now, you creep!

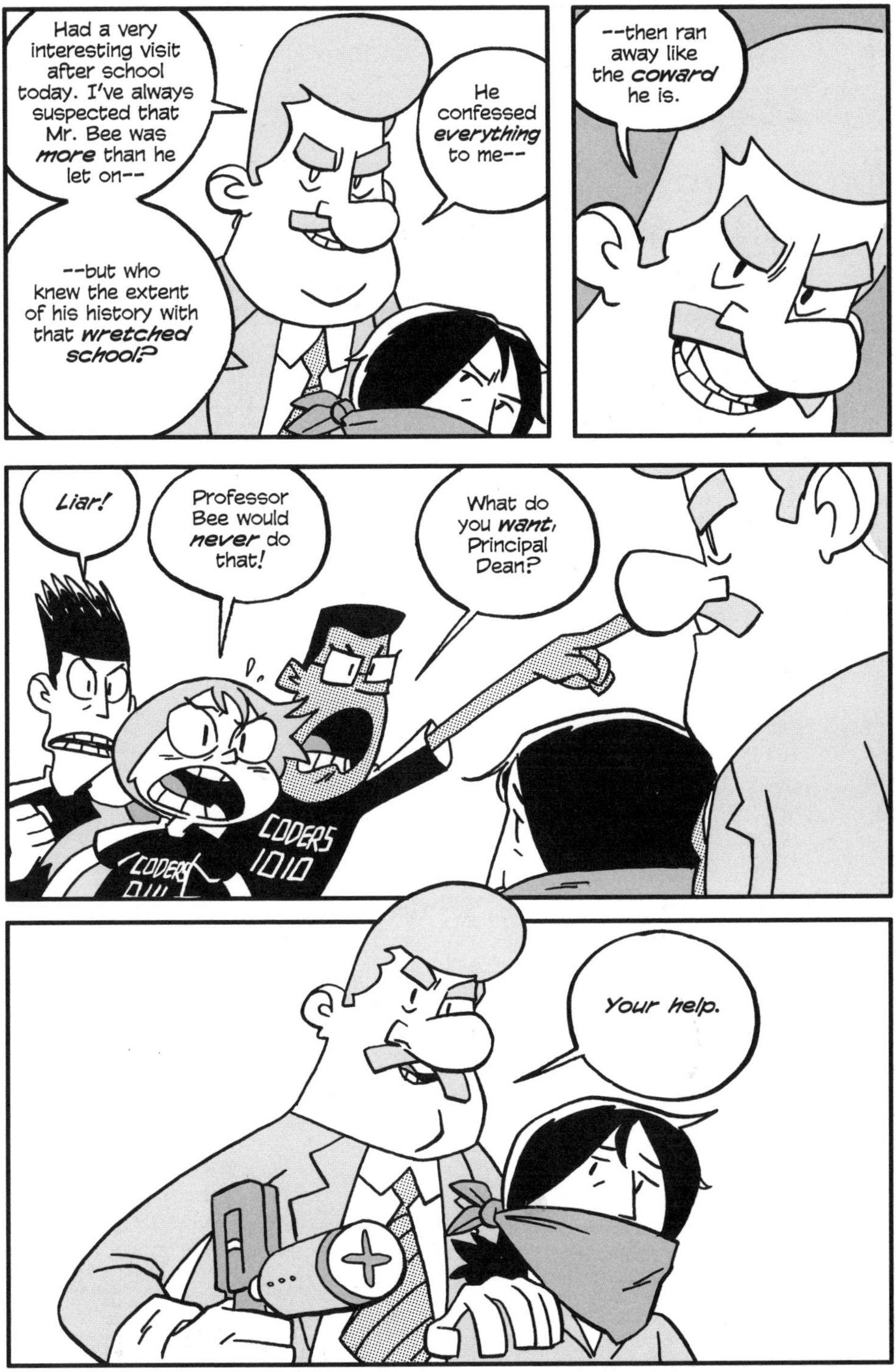
Had a very interesting visit after school today. I've always suspected that Mr. Bee was *more* than he let on--
--but who knew the extent of his history with that *wretched school?*
He confessed *everything* to me--
--then ran away like the *coward* he is.
Liar!
Professor Bee would *never* do that!
What do you *want,* Principal Dean?
CODERS 1010
CODERS
Your help.

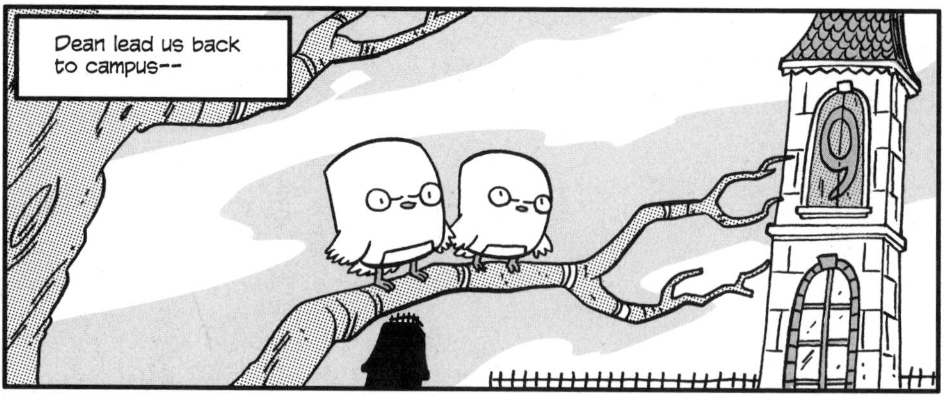
Dean lead us back to campus--

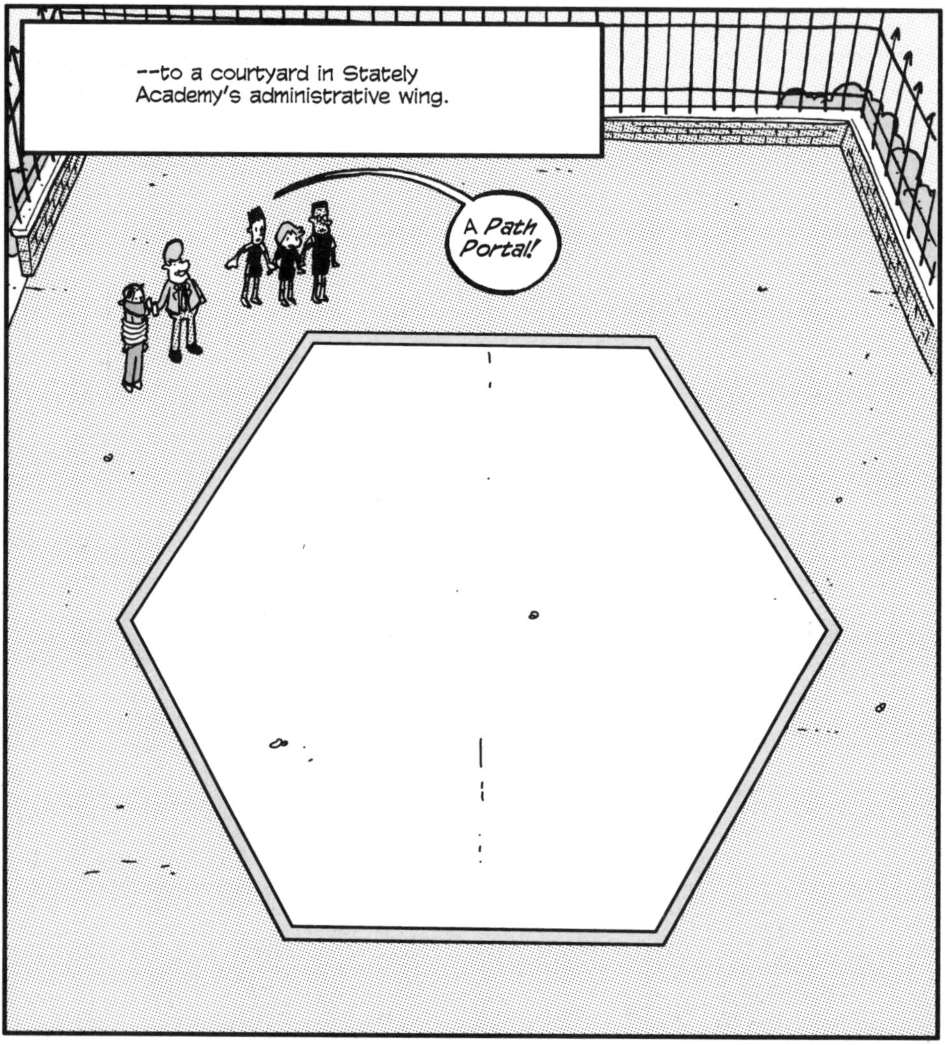
--to a courtyard in Stately Academy's administrative wing.
A *Path Portal!*

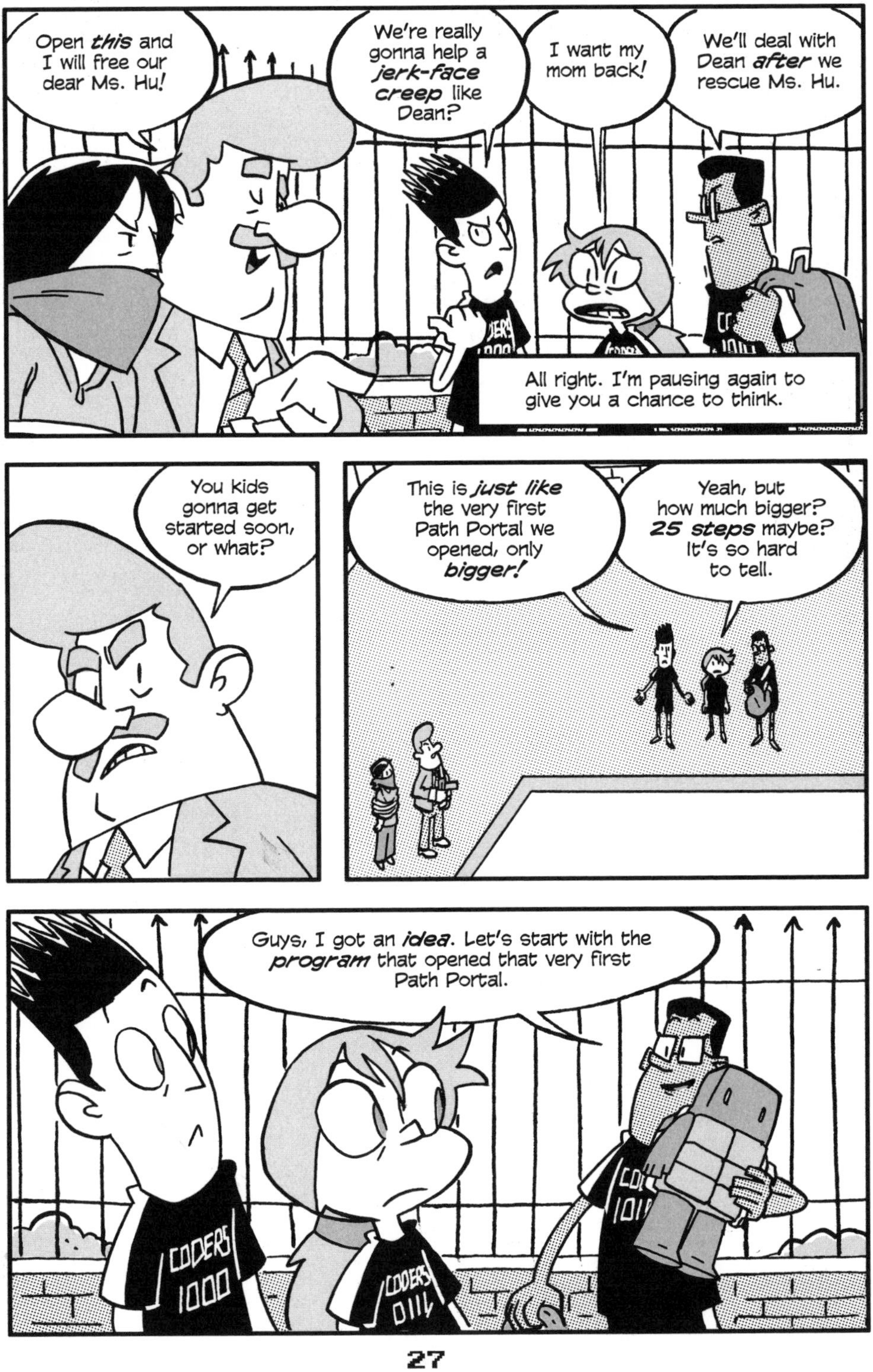
Open *this* and I will free our dear Ms. Hu!
We're really gonna help a *jerk-face creep* like Dean?
I want my mom back!
We'll deal with Dean *after* we rescue Ms. Hu.
All right. I'm pausing again to give you a chance to think.
You kids gonna get started soon, or what?
This is *just like* the very first Path Portal we opened, only *bigger!*
Yeah, but how much bigger? *25 steps* maybe? It's so hard to tell.
Guys, I got an *idea*. Let's start with the *program* that opened that very first Path Portal.

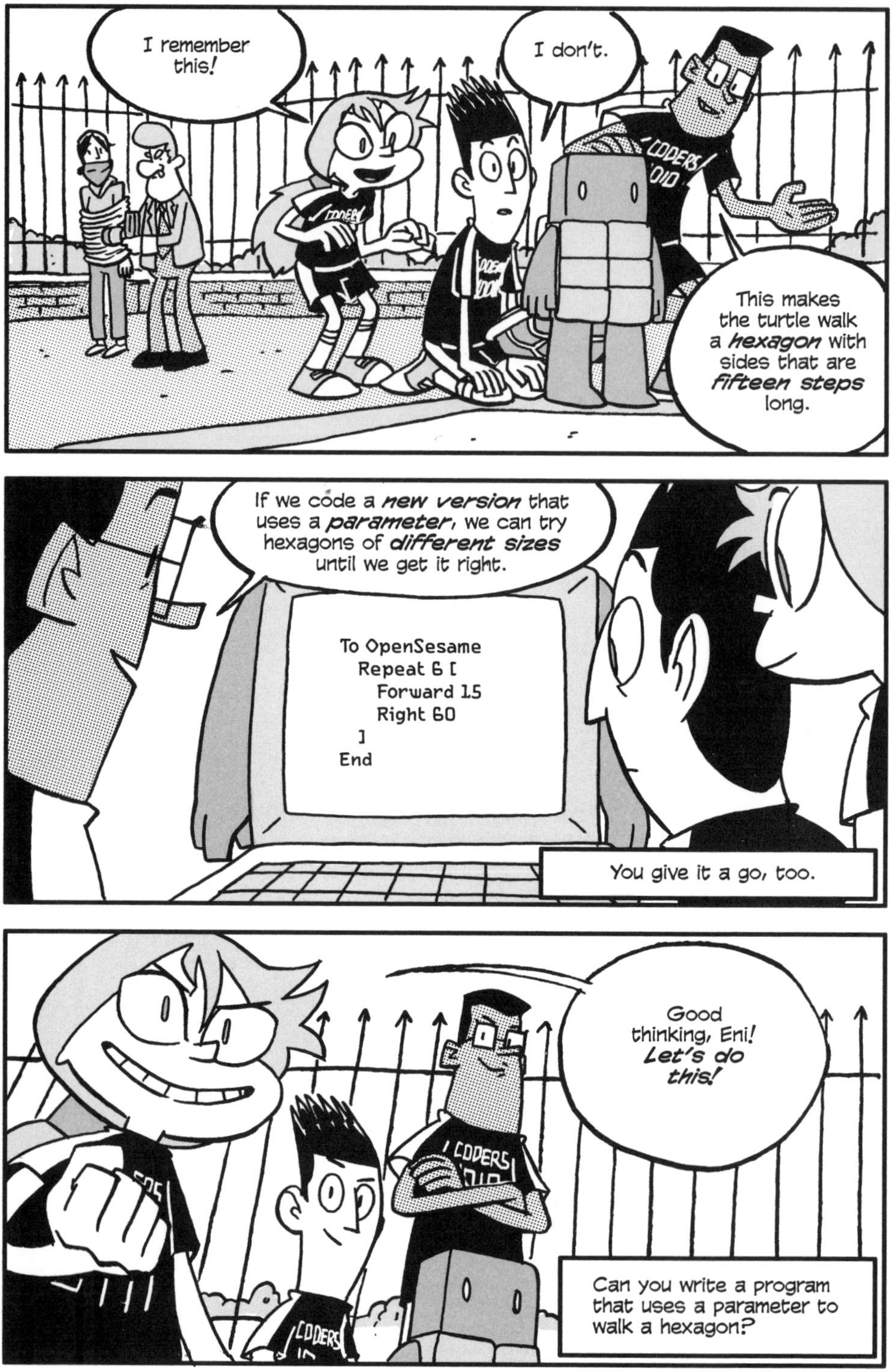
I remember this!
I don't.
This makes the turtle walk a *hexagon* with sides that are *fifteen steps* long.
If we code a *new version* that uses a *parameter*, we can try hexagons of *different sizes* until we get it right.
To OpenSesame
Repeat 6 [
Forward 15
Right 60
]
End
You give it a go, too.
Good thinking, Eni! *Let's do this!*
Can you write a program that uses a parameter to walk a hexagon?

Chapter

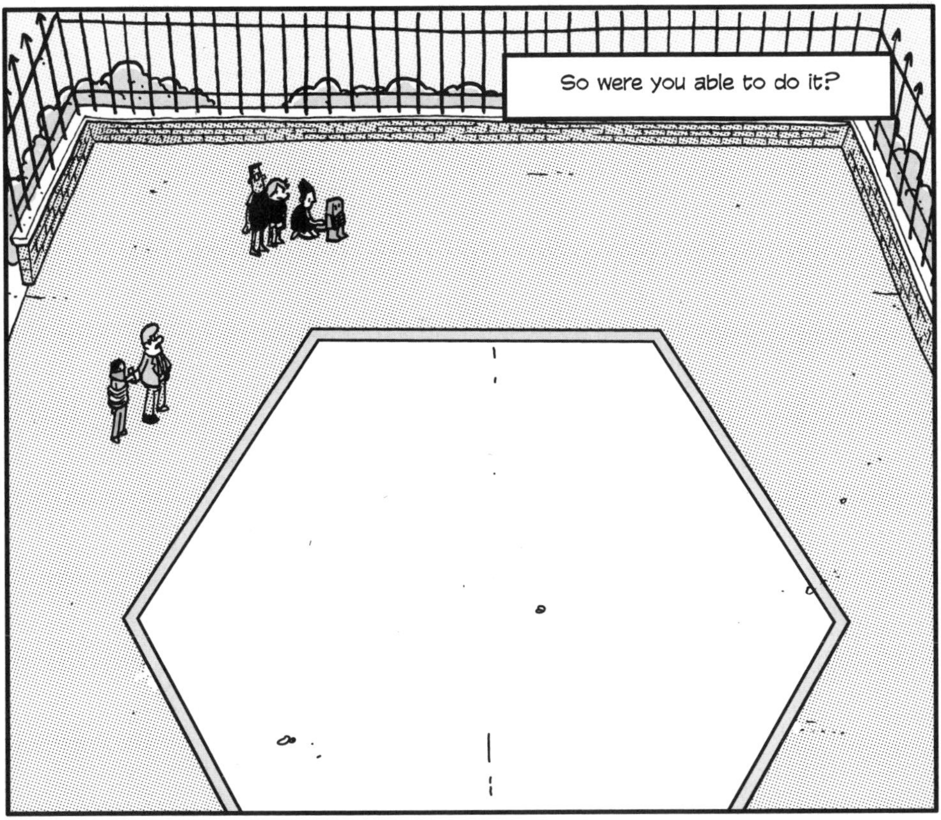
So were you able to do it?

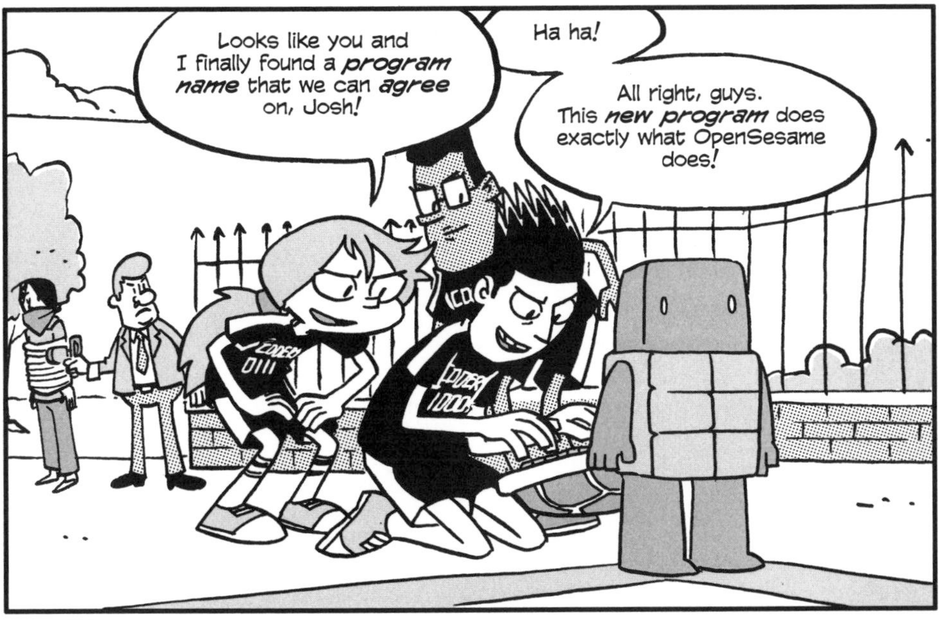
Looks like you and I finally found a *program name* that we can *agree* on, Josh!
Ha ha!
All right, guys. This *new program* does exactly what OpenSesame does!

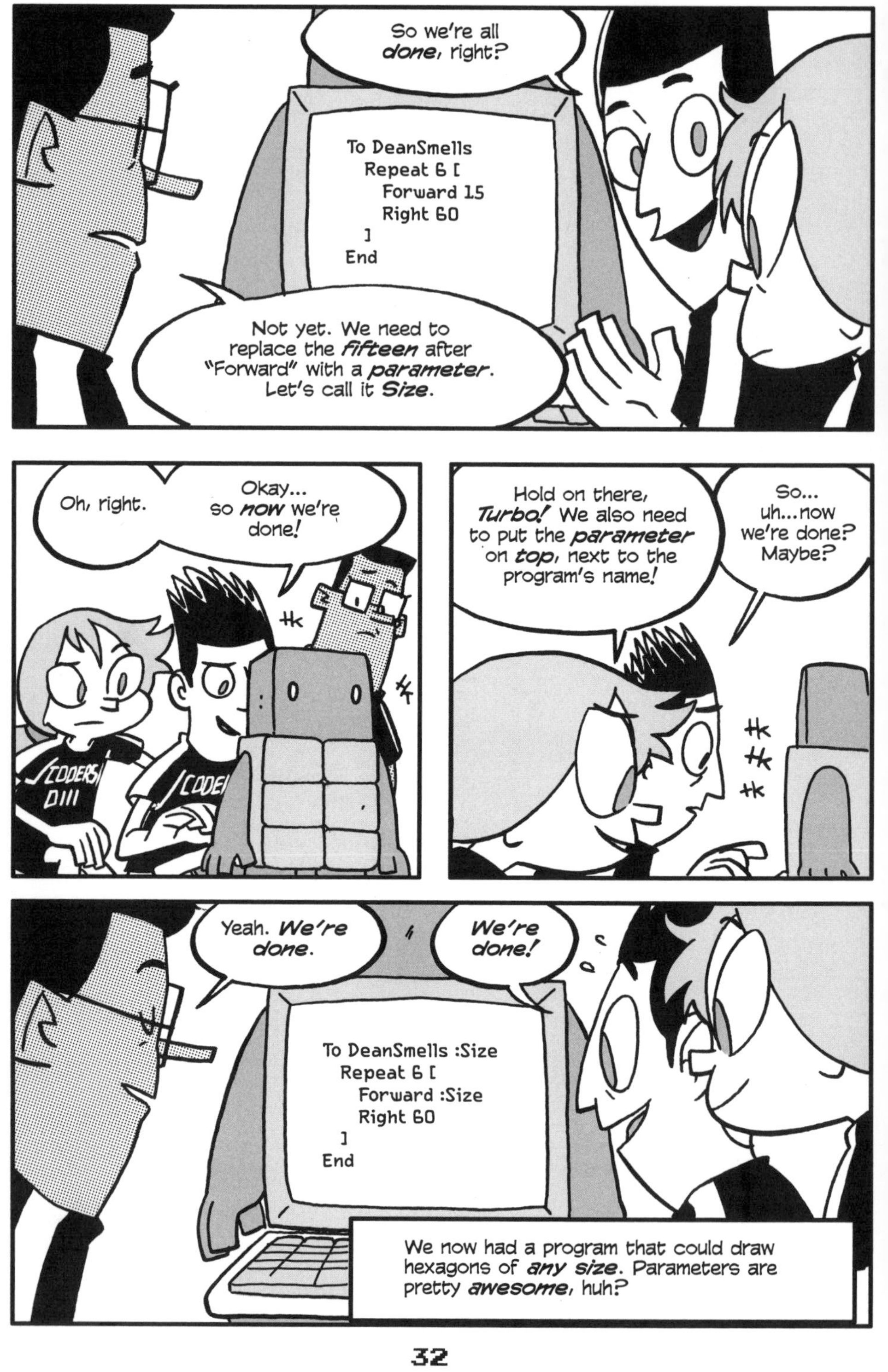
So we're all *done*, right?
To DeanSmells
Repeat 6 [
Forward 15
Right 60
]
End
Not yet. We need to replace the *fifteen* after "Forward" with a *parameter*. Let's call it *Size*.
Oh, right.
Okay... so *now* we're done!
tk
tk
Hold on there, *Turbo!* We also need to put the *parameter* on *top*, next to the program's name!
So... uh...now we're done? Maybe?
tk
tk
tk
Yeah. *We're done*.
We're done!
To DeanSmells :Size
Repeat 6 [
Forward :Size
Right 60
]
End
We now had a program that could draw hexagons of *any size*. Parameters are pretty *awesome*, huh?

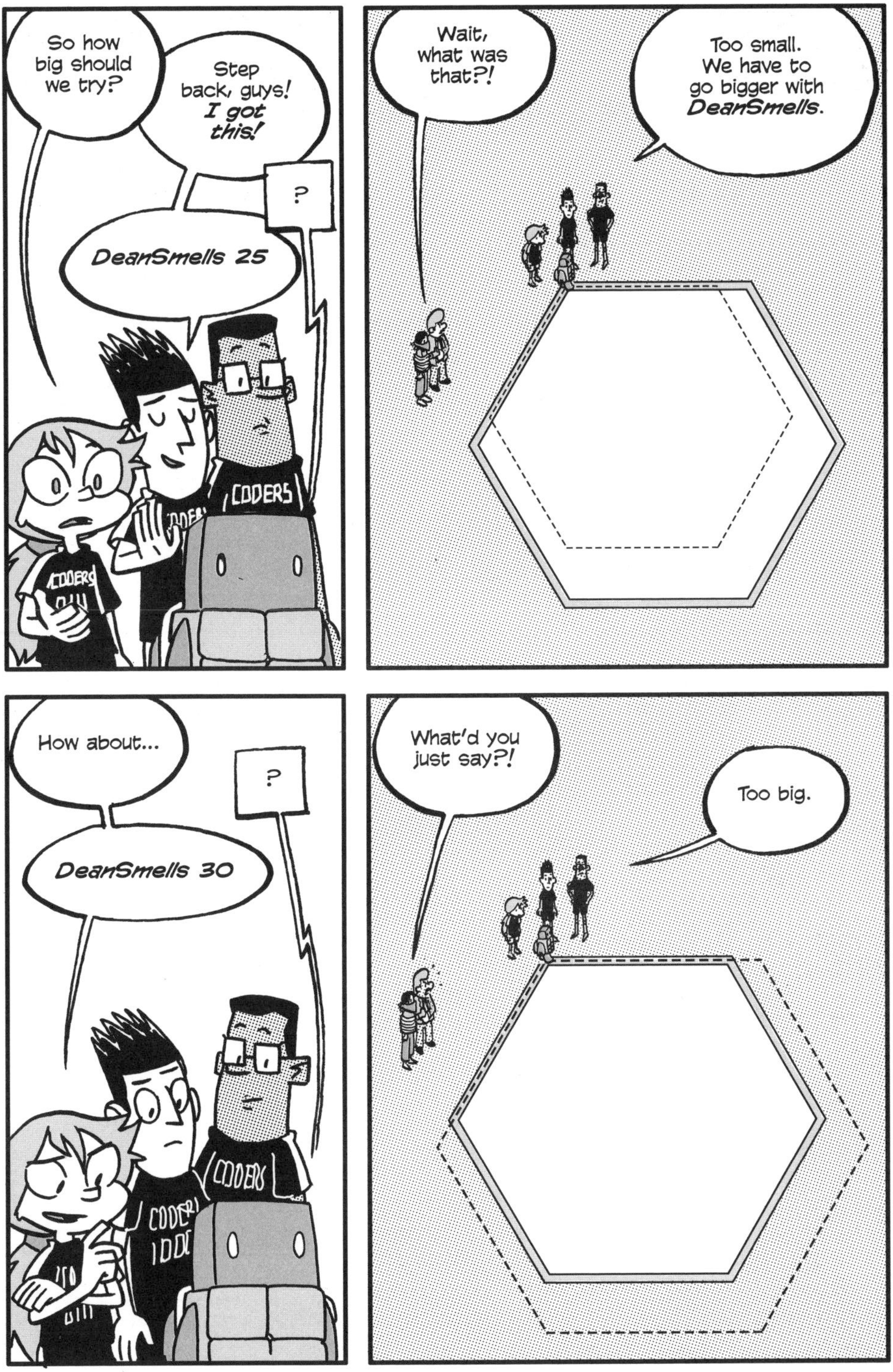
So how big should we try?
Step back, guys! *I got this!*
?
DeanSmells 25
CODERS
Wait, what was that?!
Too small. We have to go bigger with ***DeanSmells***.
How about...
?
DeanSmells 30
CODERS
What'd you just say?!
Too big.

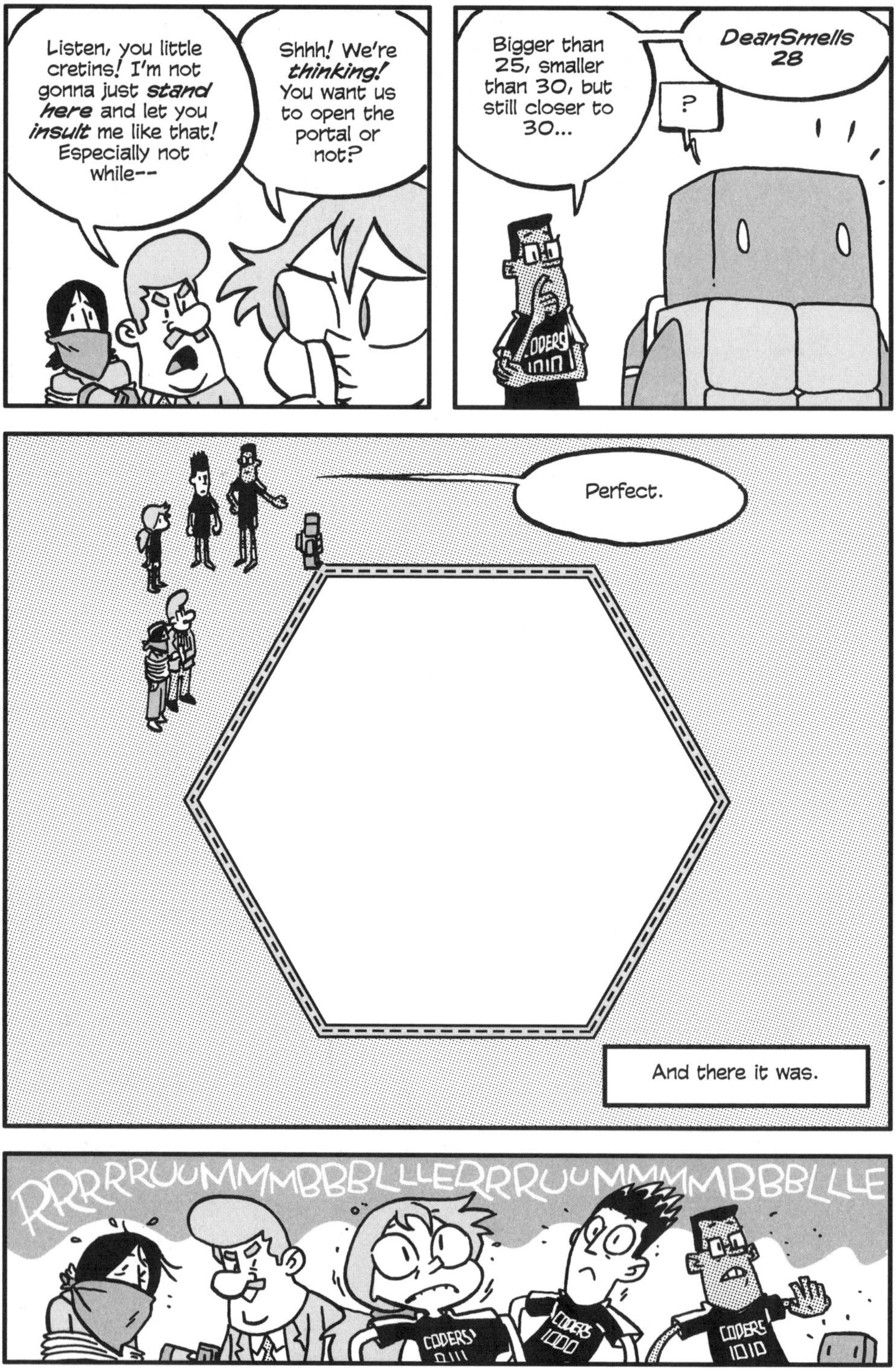
Listen, you little cretins! I'm not gonna just *stand here* and let you *insult* me like that! Especially not while--
Shhh! We're *thinking!* You want us to open the portal or not?
Bigger than 25, smaller than 30, but still closer to 30...
DeanSmells 28
?
CODERS 1010
Perfect.
And there it was.
RRRRRUUMMMBBBLLLERRRUUMMMMBBBLLLE

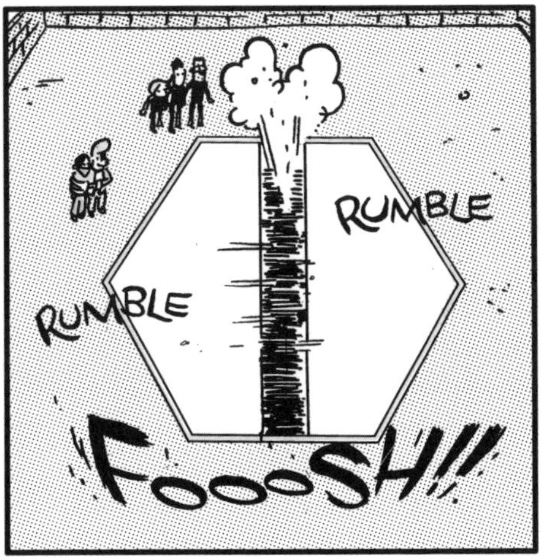
RUMBLE
RUMBLE
FOOOOSH!!

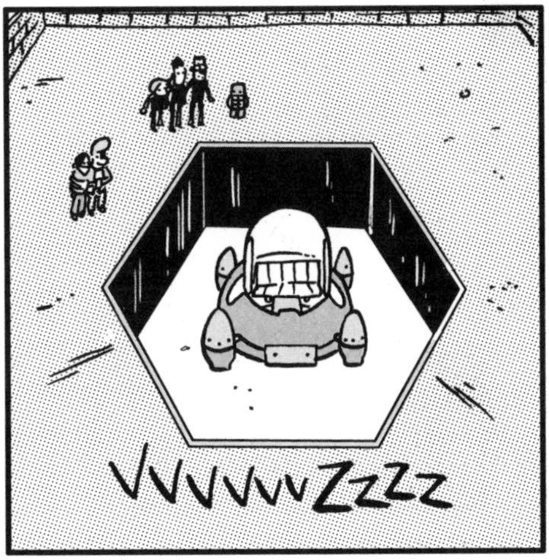
VVVVVVVZZZZ

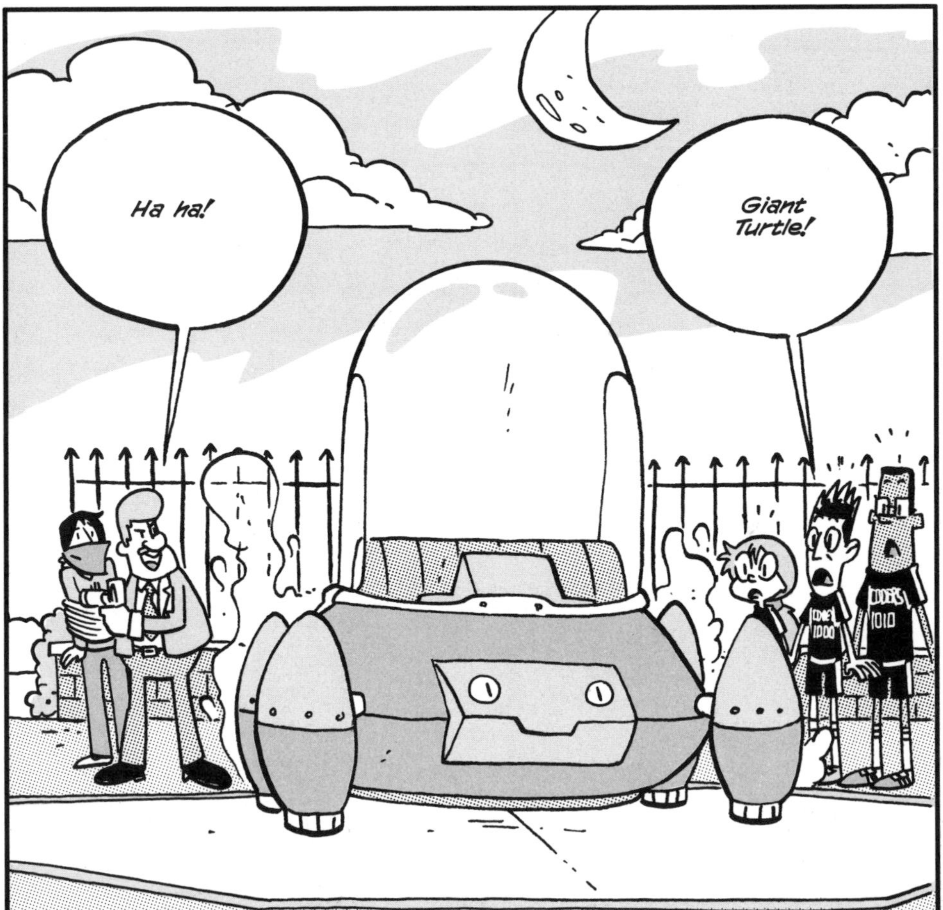
Ha ha!
Giant Turtle!

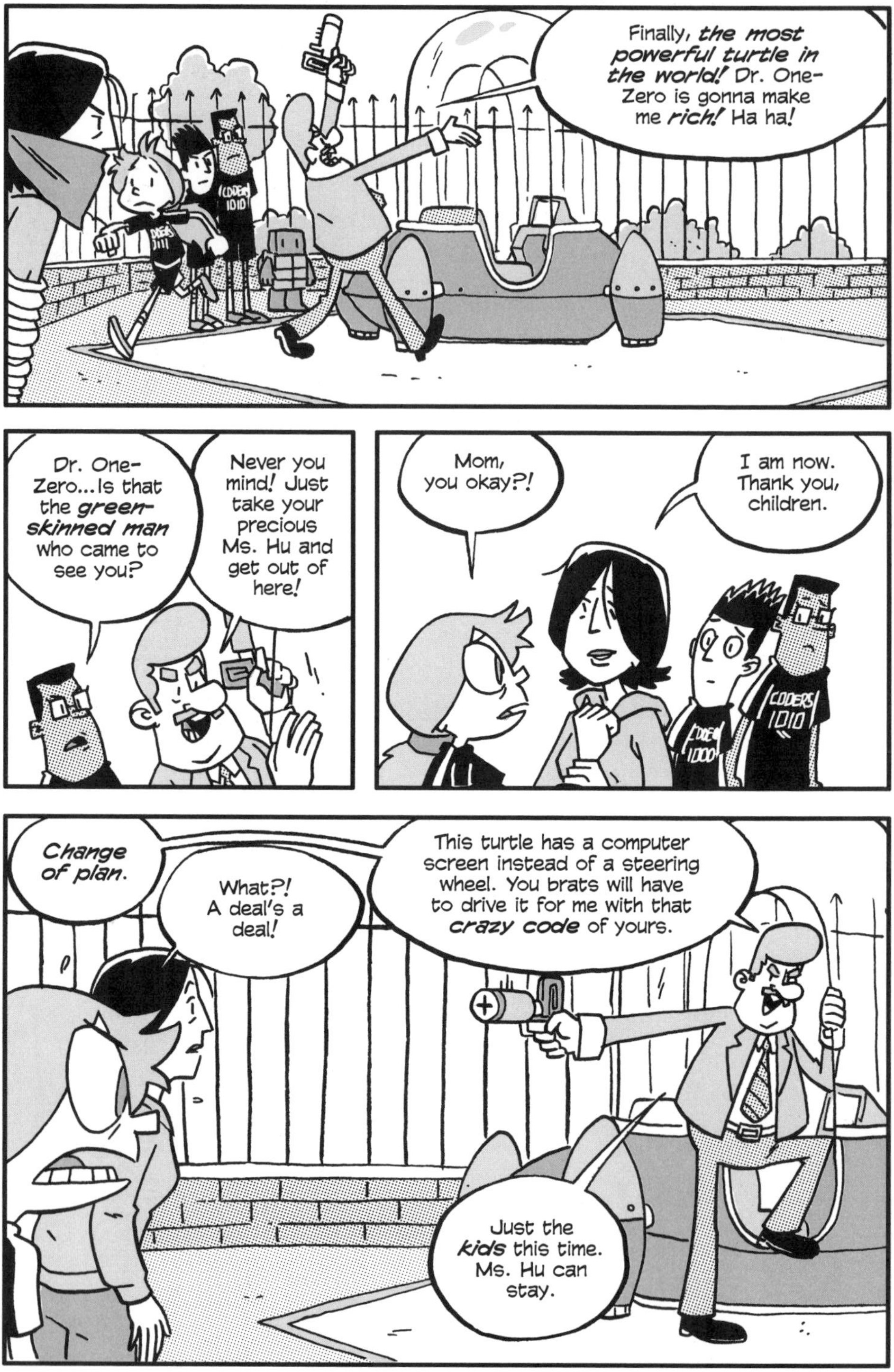
Finally, ***the most powerful turtle in the world!*** Dr. One-Zero is gonna make me ***rich!*** Ha ha!
CODERS 1010
Dr. One-Zero...Is that the ***green-skinned man*** who came to see you?
Never you mind! Just take your precious Ms. Hu and get out of here!
Mom, you okay?!
I am now. Thank you, children.
CODERS 1010
Change of plan.
What?! A deal's a deal!
This turtle has a computer screen instead of a steering wheel. You brats will have to drive it for me with that ***crazy code*** of yours.
Just the ***kids*** this time. Ms. Hu can stay.

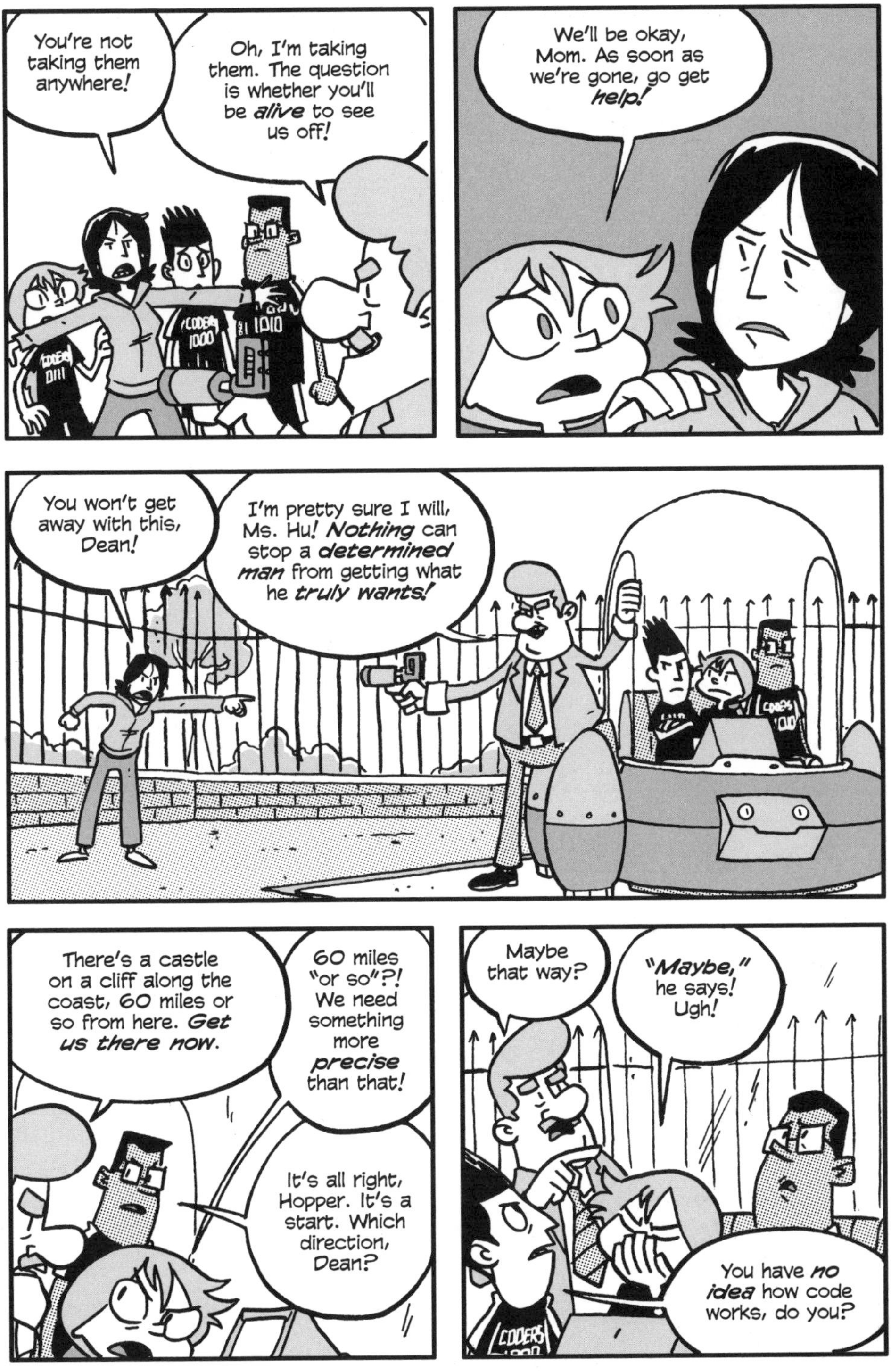
You're not taking them anywhere!
Oh, I'm taking them. The question is whether you'll be *alive* to see us off!
We'll be okay, Mom. As soon as we're gone, go get *help!*
You won't get away with this, Dean!
I'm pretty sure I will, Ms. Hu! *Nothing* can stop a *determined man* from getting what he *truly wants!*
There's a castle on a cliff along the coast, 60 miles or so from here. *Get us there now*.
60 miles "or so"?! We need something more *precise* than that!
It's all right, Hopper. It's a start. Which direction, Dean?
Maybe that way?
"*Maybe,*" he says! Ugh!
You have *no idea* how code works, do you?

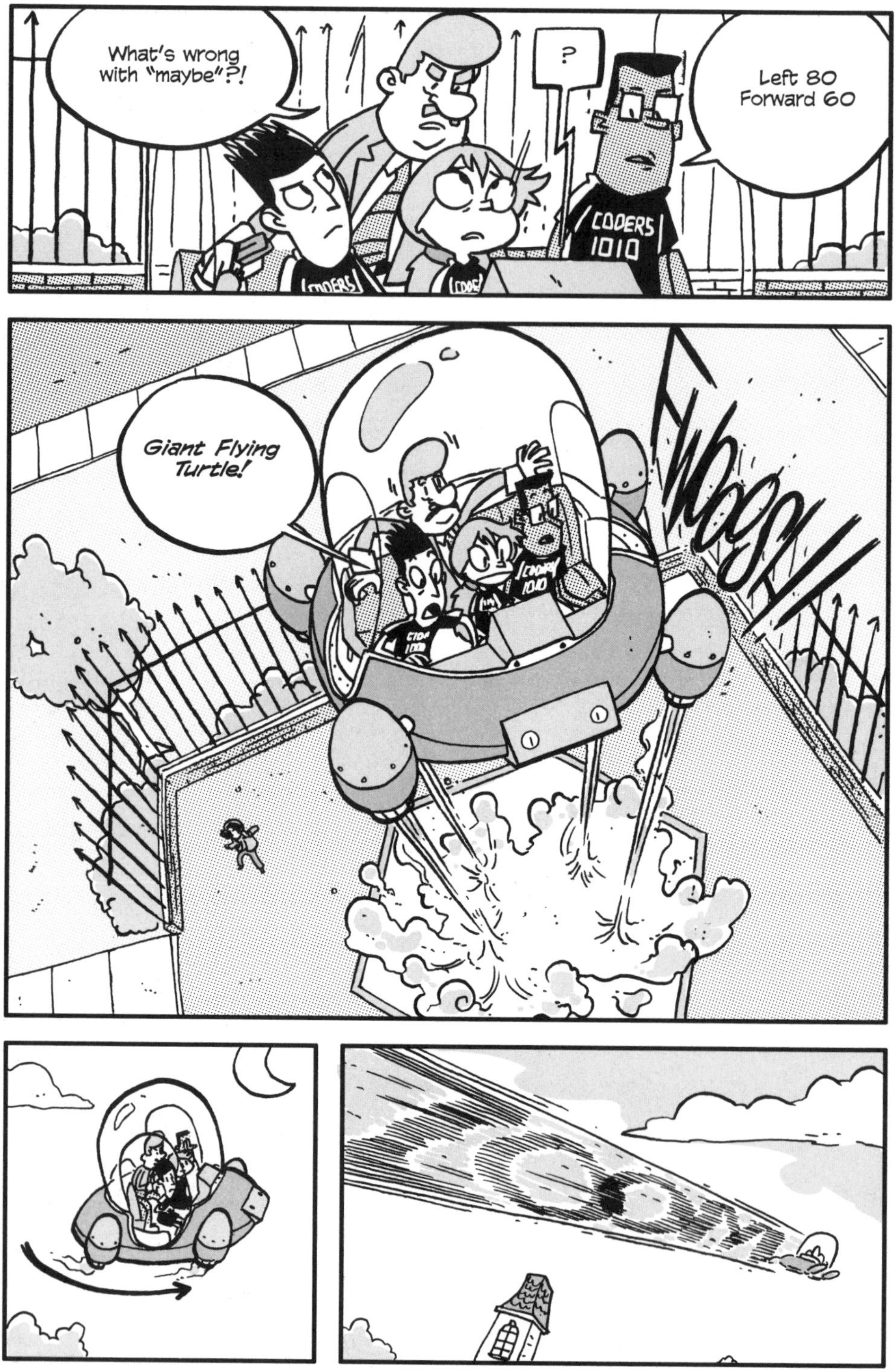
What's wrong with "maybe"?!
?
Left 80 Forward 60
CODERS 1010
Giant Flying Turtle!
FWOOSH!!

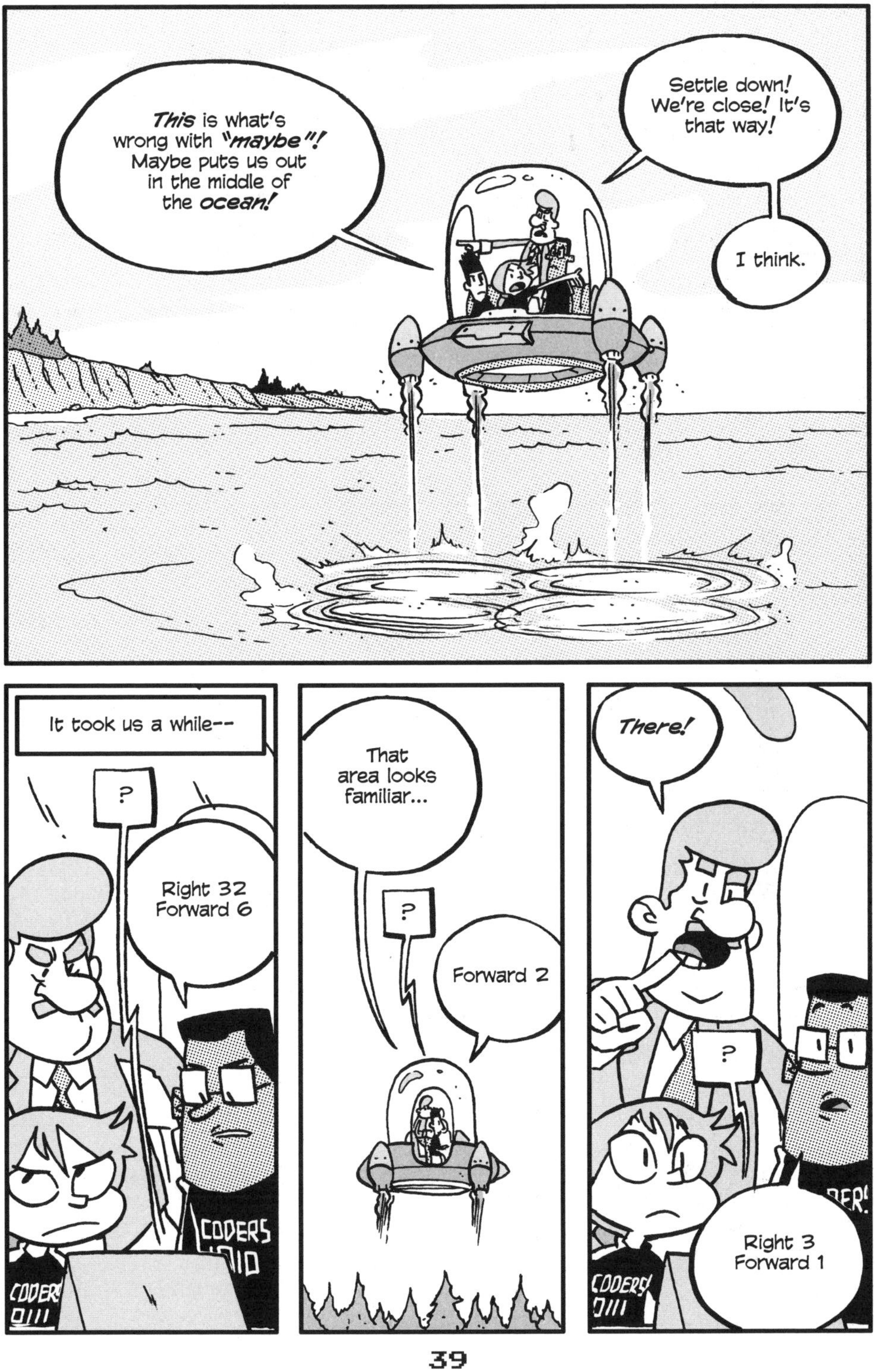
This is what's wrong with "maybe"! Maybe puts us out in the middle of the ocean!
Settle down! We're close! It's that way!
I think.
It took us a while--
?
Right 32 Forward 6
That area looks familiar...
?
Forward 2
There!
?
Right 3 Forward 1
CODERS 0111
CODERS 0111

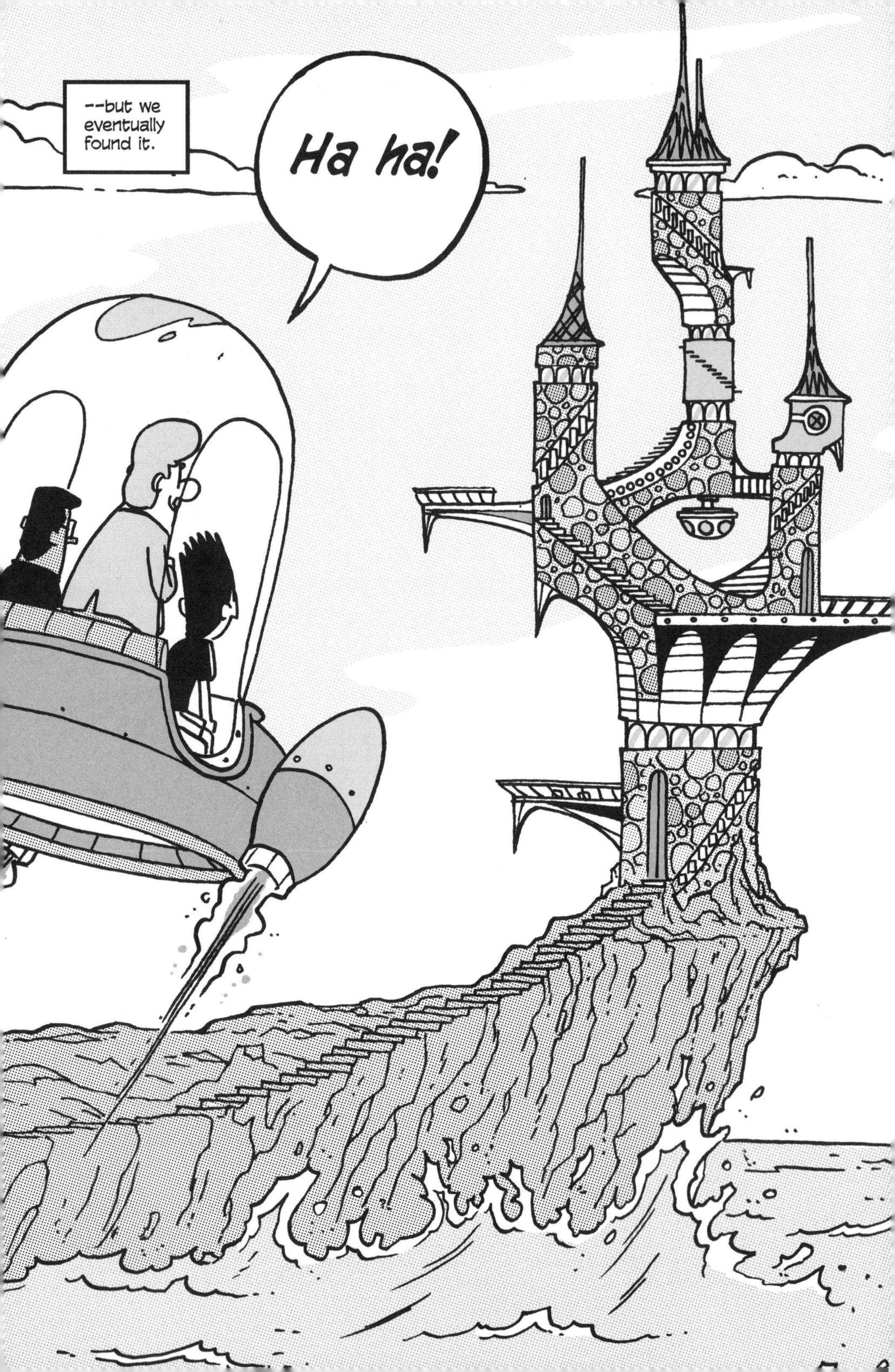
--but we eventually found it.
Ha ha!

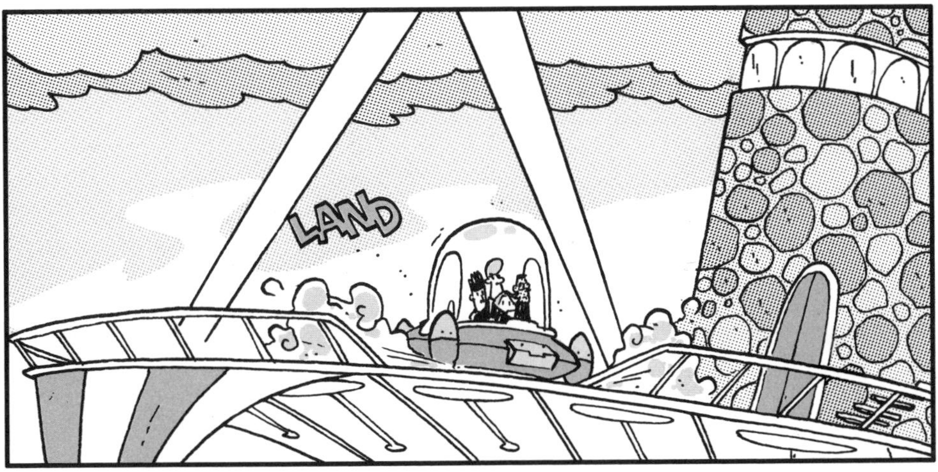
LAND

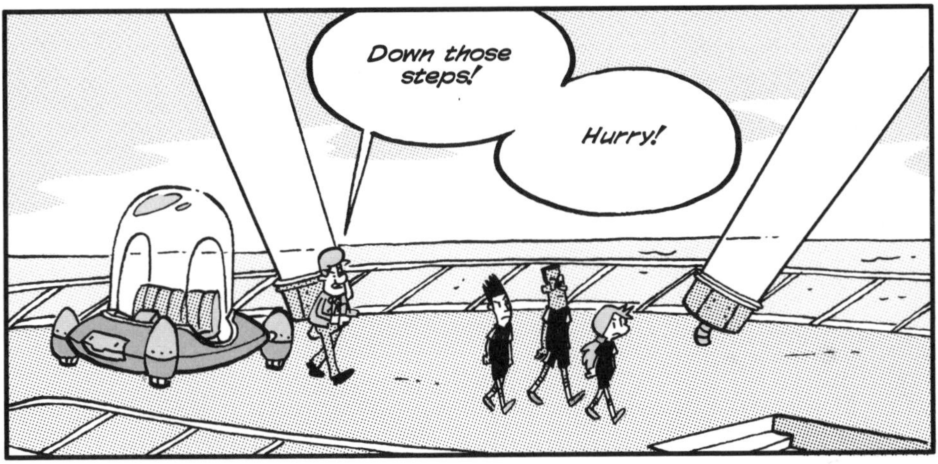
Down those steps!
Hurry!

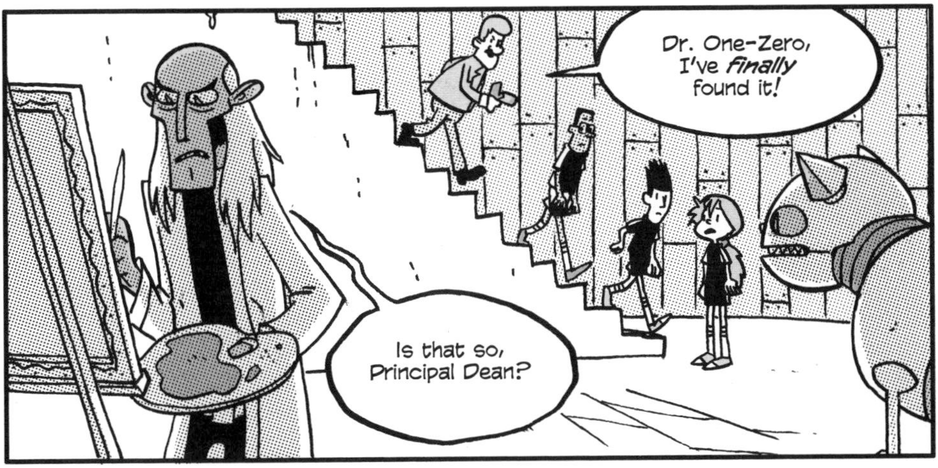
Dr. One-Zero, I've *finally* found it!
Is that so, Principal Dean?

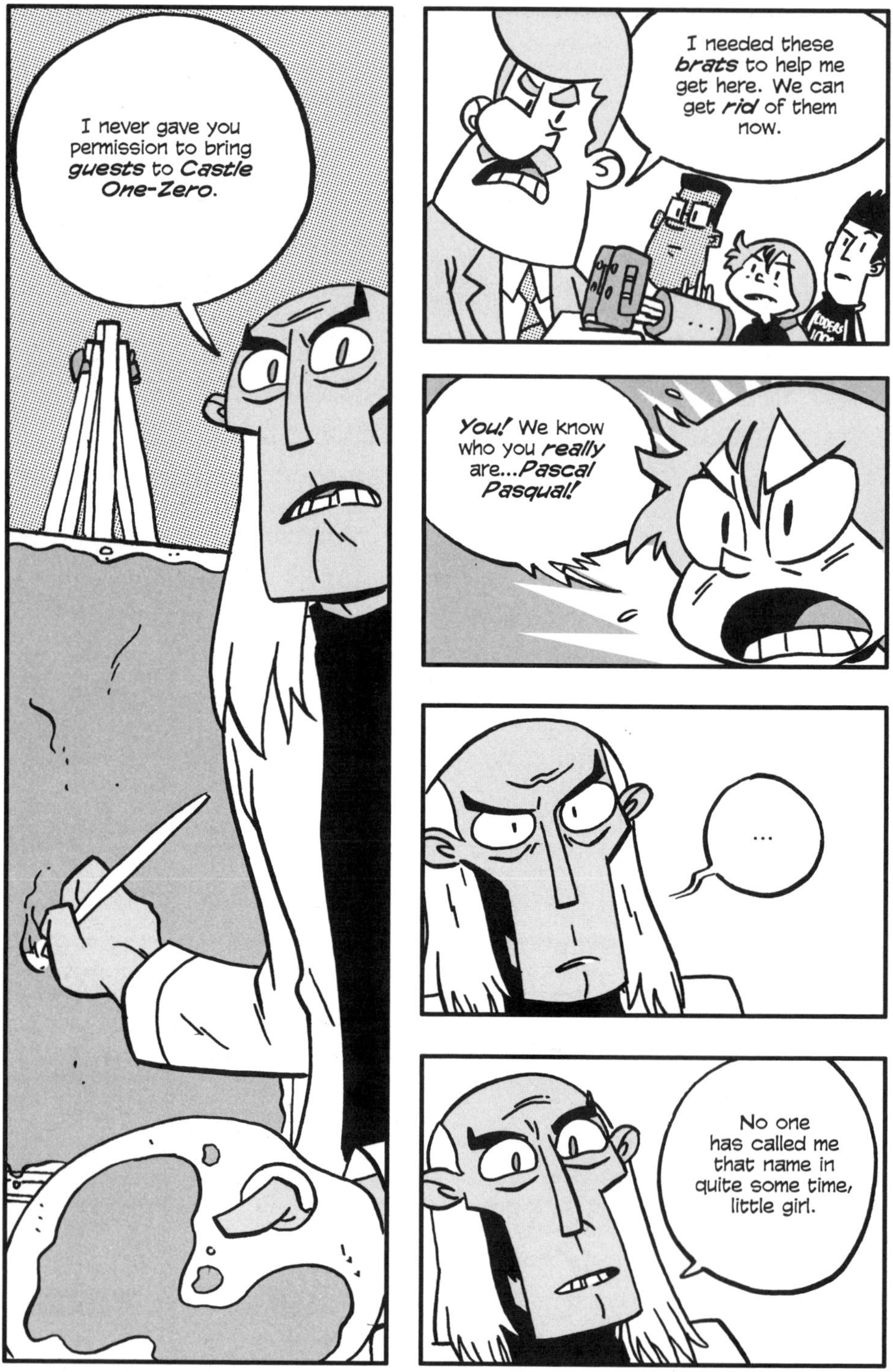
I never gave you permission to bring *guests* to *Castle One-Zero*.
I needed these *brats* to help me get here. We can get *rid* of them now.
...
You! We know who you *really* are...*Pascal Pasqual!*
...
No one has called me that name in quite some time, little girl.

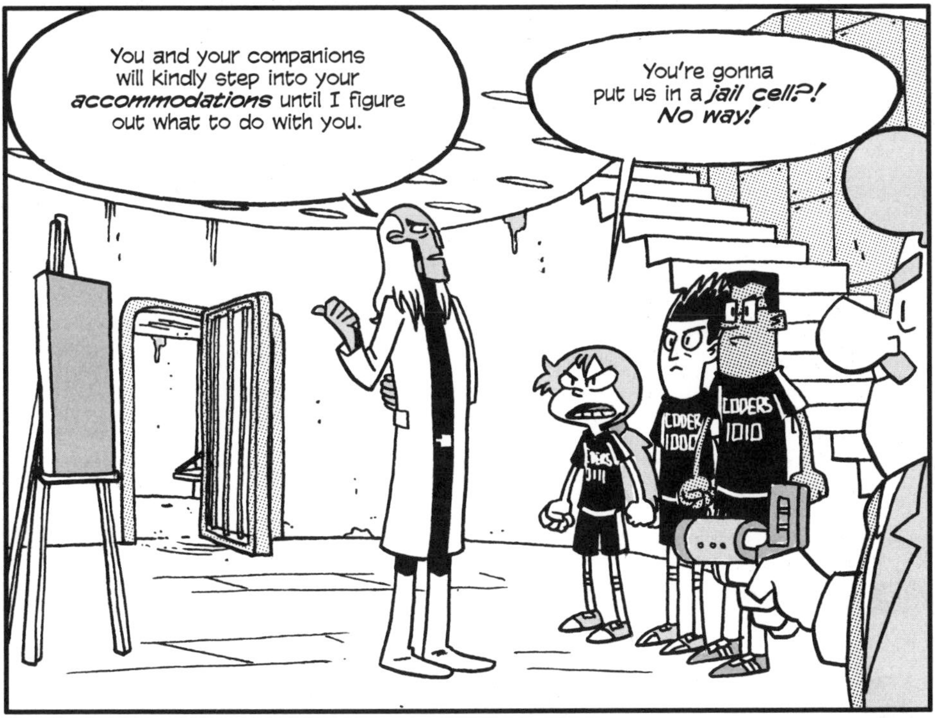
You and your companions will kindly step into your *accommodations* until I figure out what to do with you.
You're gonna put us in a *jail cell?!* *No way!*
CODERS 1010
CODERS 1010
CODERS 1010

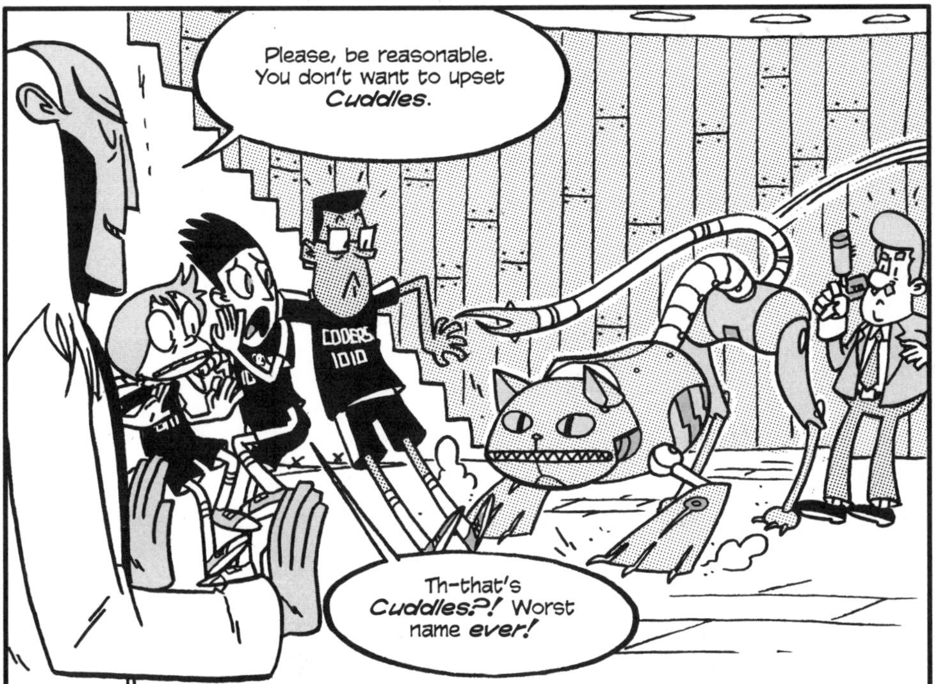
Please, be reasonable. You don't want to upset *Cuddles*.
CODERS 1010
Th-that's *Cuddles?!* Worst name *ever!*

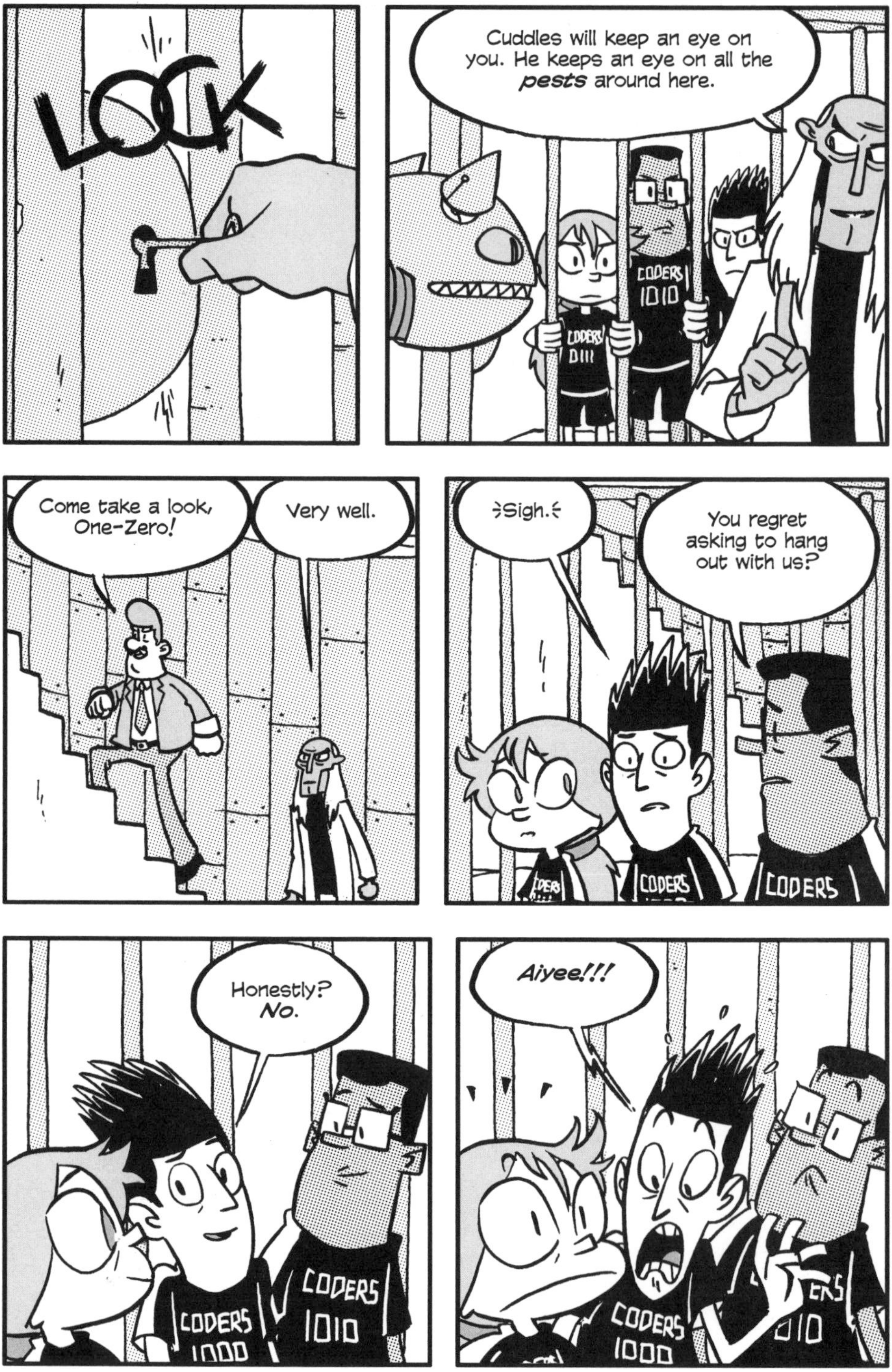
LOCK
Cuddles will keep an eye on you. He keeps an eye on all the *pests* around here.
CODERS 1011
CODERS 1010
Come take a look, One-Zero!
Very well.
Sigh.
You regret asking to hang out with us?
CODERS
CODERS
Honestly? *No.*
CODERS 1000
CODERS 1010
Aiyee!!!
CODERS 1000

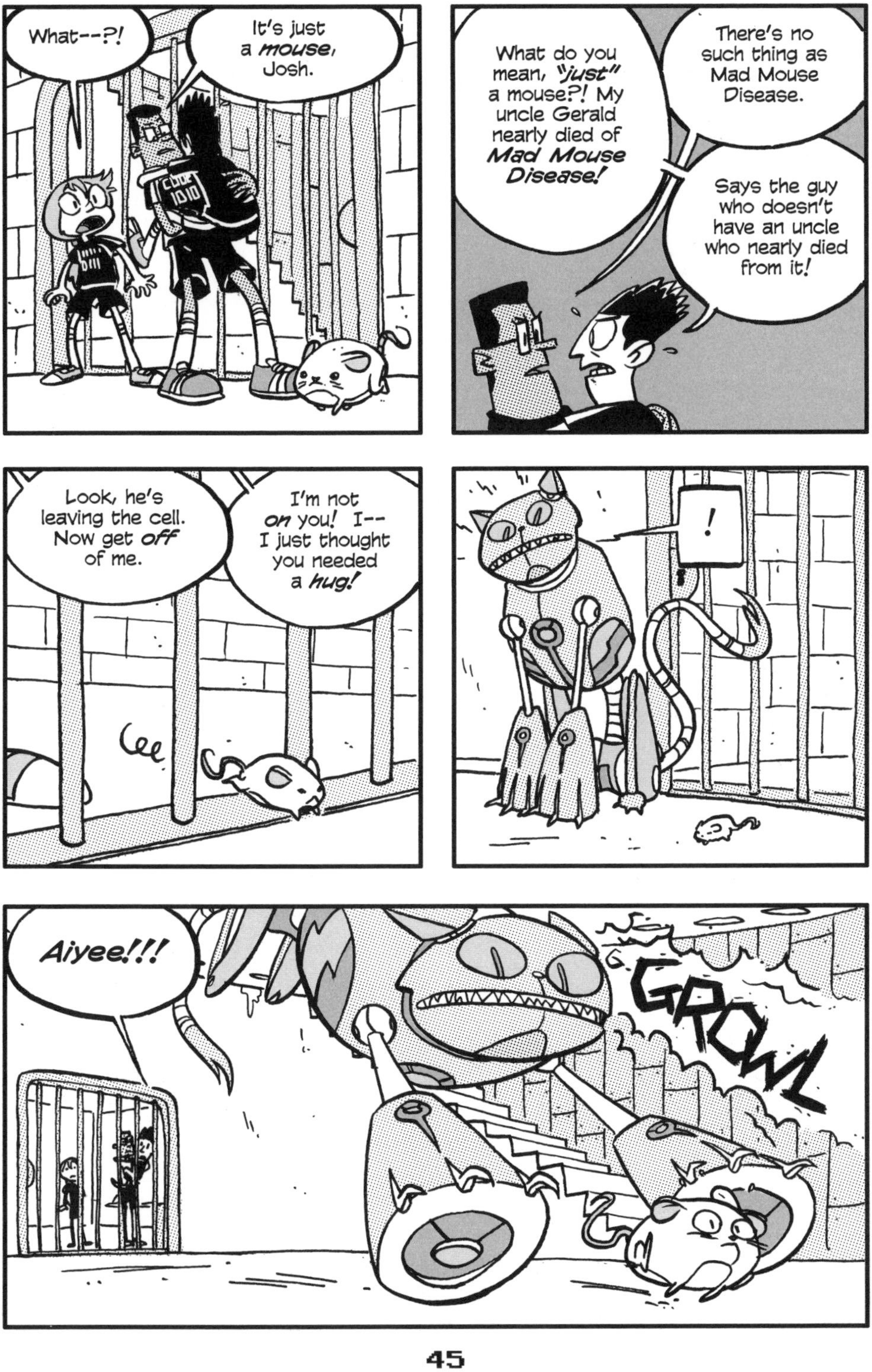
What--?!
It's just a *mouse*, Josh.
What do you mean, *"just"* a mouse?! My uncle Gerald nearly died of ***Mad Mouse Disease!***
There's no such thing as Mad Mouse Disease.
Says the guy who doesn't have an uncle who nearly died from it!
Look, he's leaving the cell. Now get *off* of me.
I'm not *on* you! I-- I just thought you needed a *hug!*
!
Aiyee!!!
GROWL

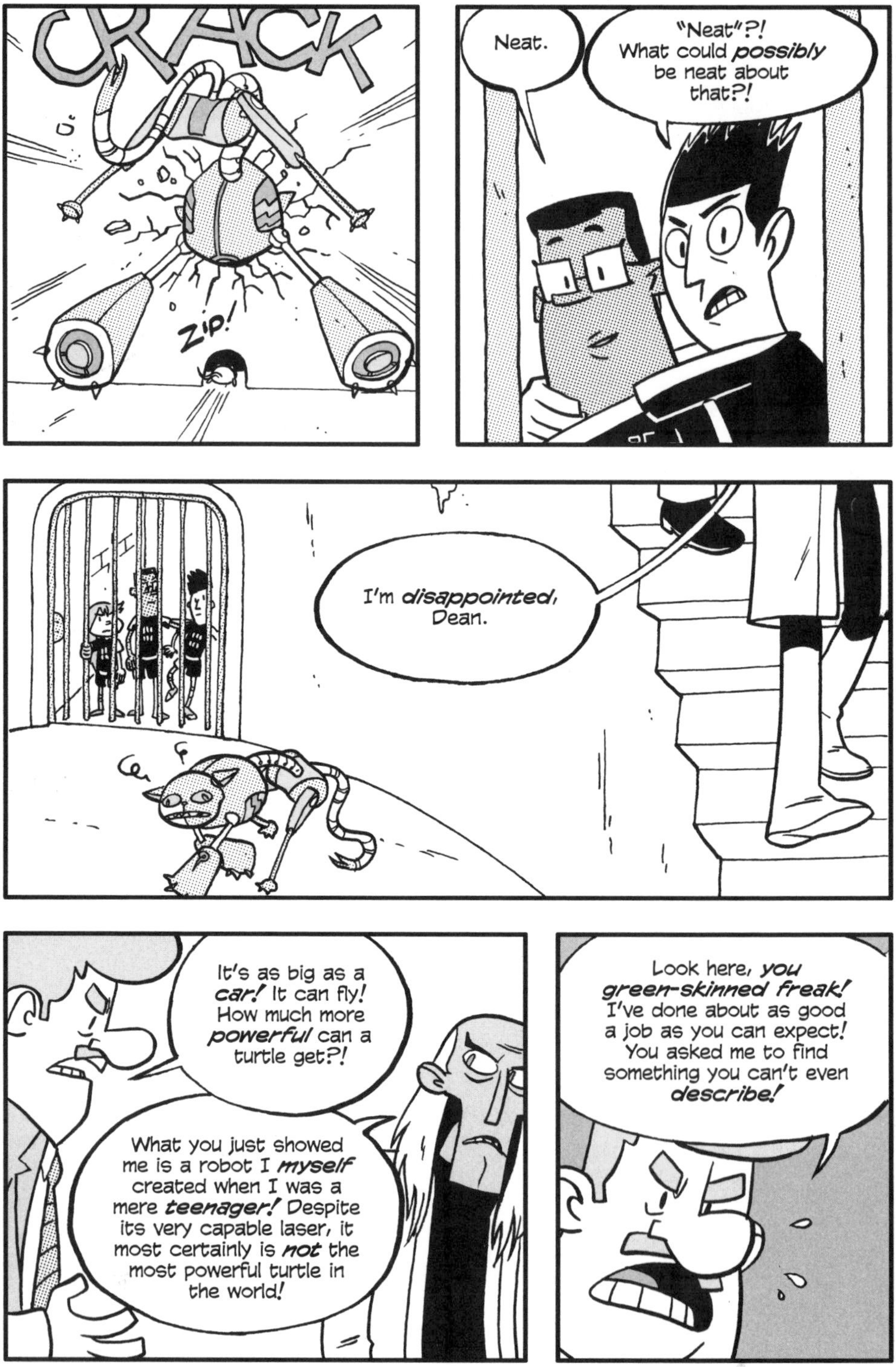
CRACK
ZIP!
Neat.
"Neat"?! What could possibly be neat about that?!
I'm disappointed, Dean.
It's as big as a car! It can fly! How much more powerful can a turtle get?!
What you just showed me is a robot I myself created when I was a mere teenager! Despite its very capable laser, it most certainly is not the most powerful turtle in the world!
Look here, you green-skinned freak! I've done about as good a job as you can expect! You asked me to find something you can't even describe!

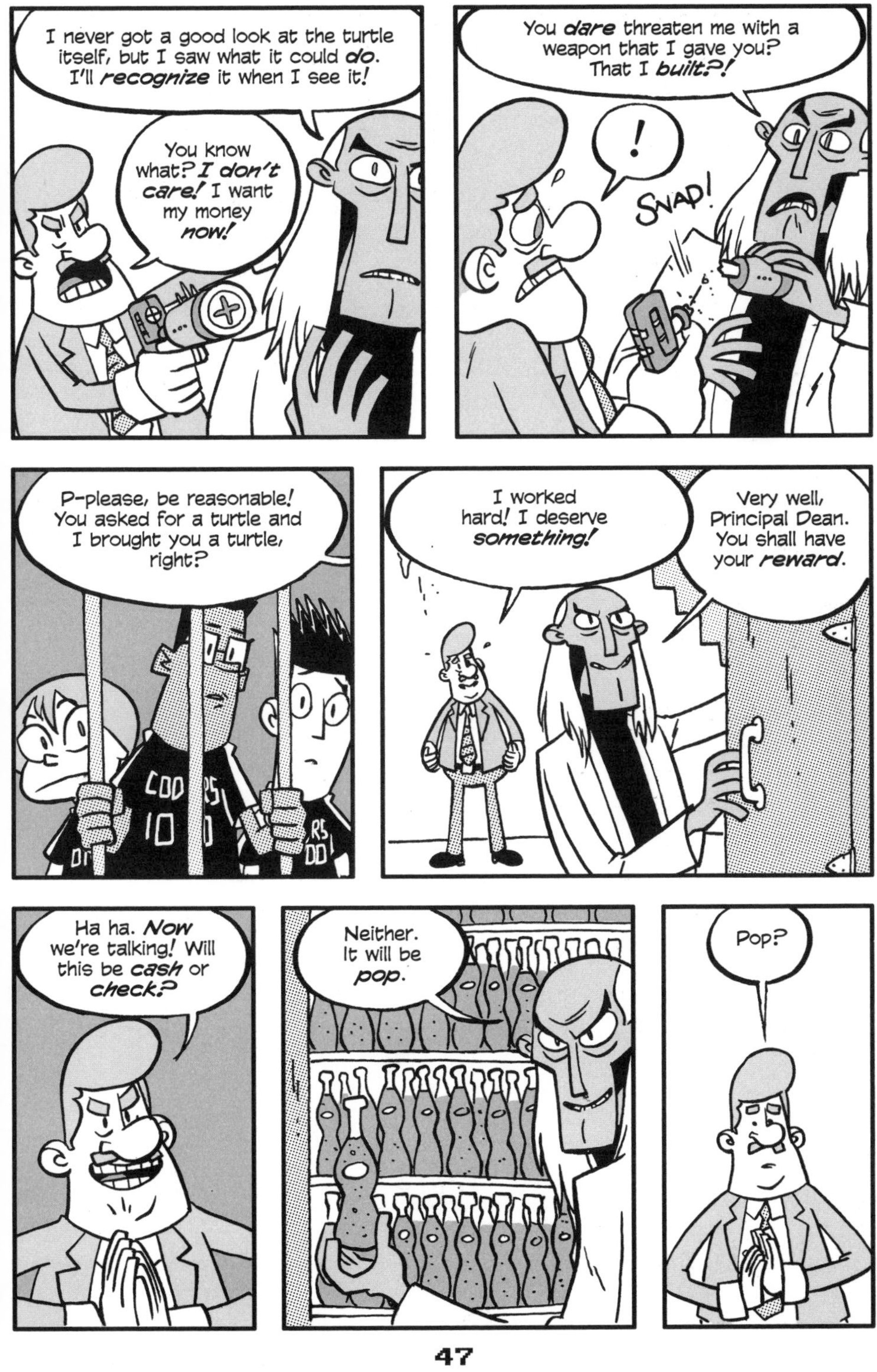
I never got a good look at the turtle itself, but I saw what it could *do*. I'll *recognize* it when I see it!
You know what? *I don't care!* I want my money *now!*
You *dare* threaten me with a weapon that I gave you? That I *built?!*
!
SNAP!
P-please, be reasonable! You asked for a turtle and I brought you a turtle, right?
I worked hard! I deserve *something!*
Very well, Principal Dean. You shall have your *reward*.
Ha ha. *Now* we're talking! Will this be *cash* or *check?*
Neither. It will be *pop*.
Pop?

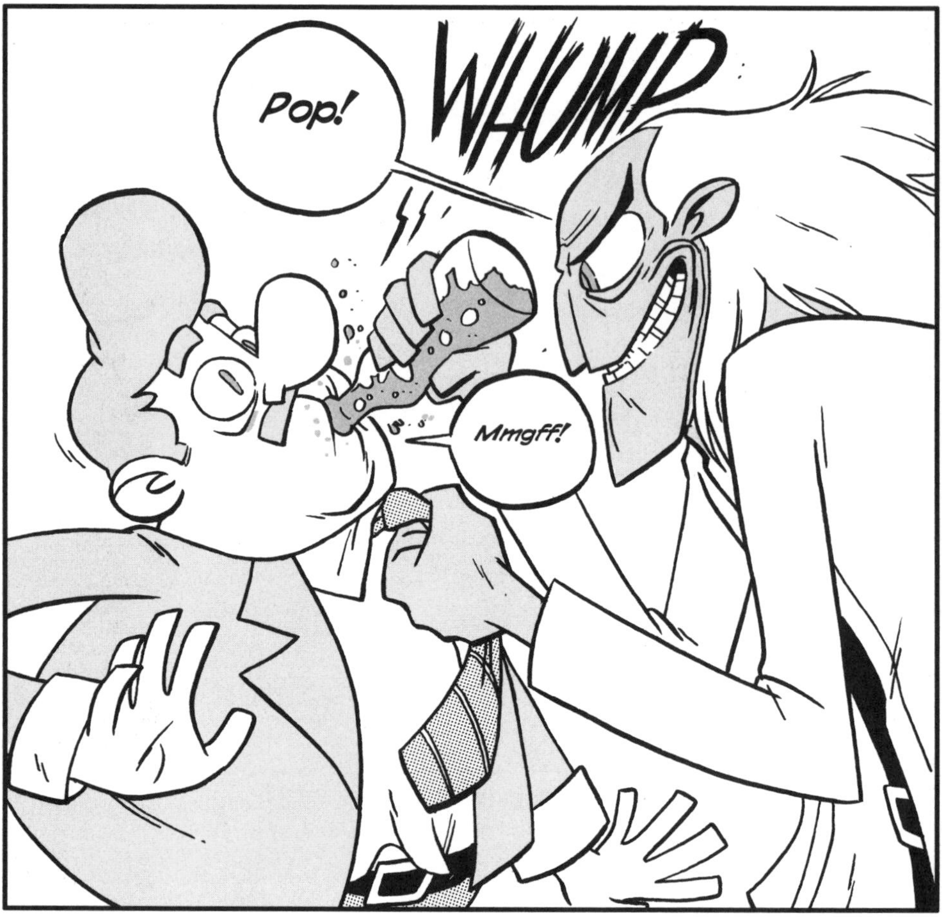
Pop!
WHUMP
Mmgff!

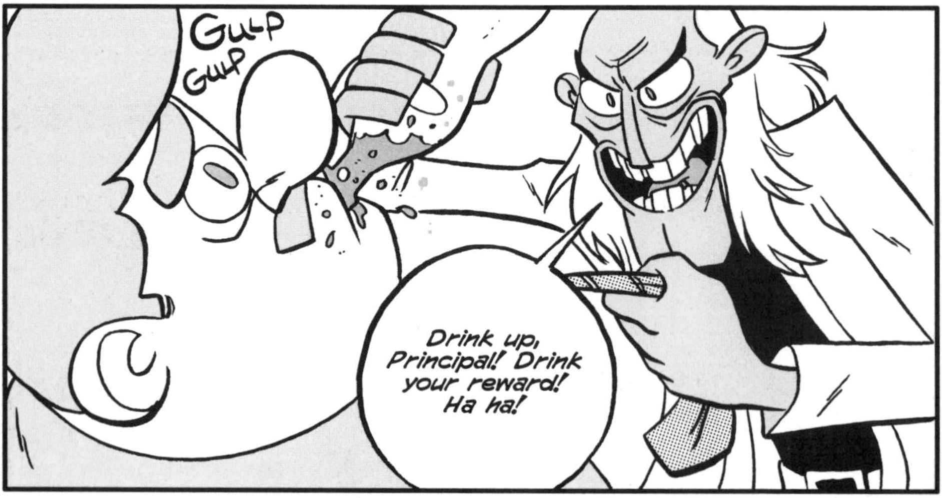
GULP
GULP
Drink up, Principal! Drink your reward! Ha ha!

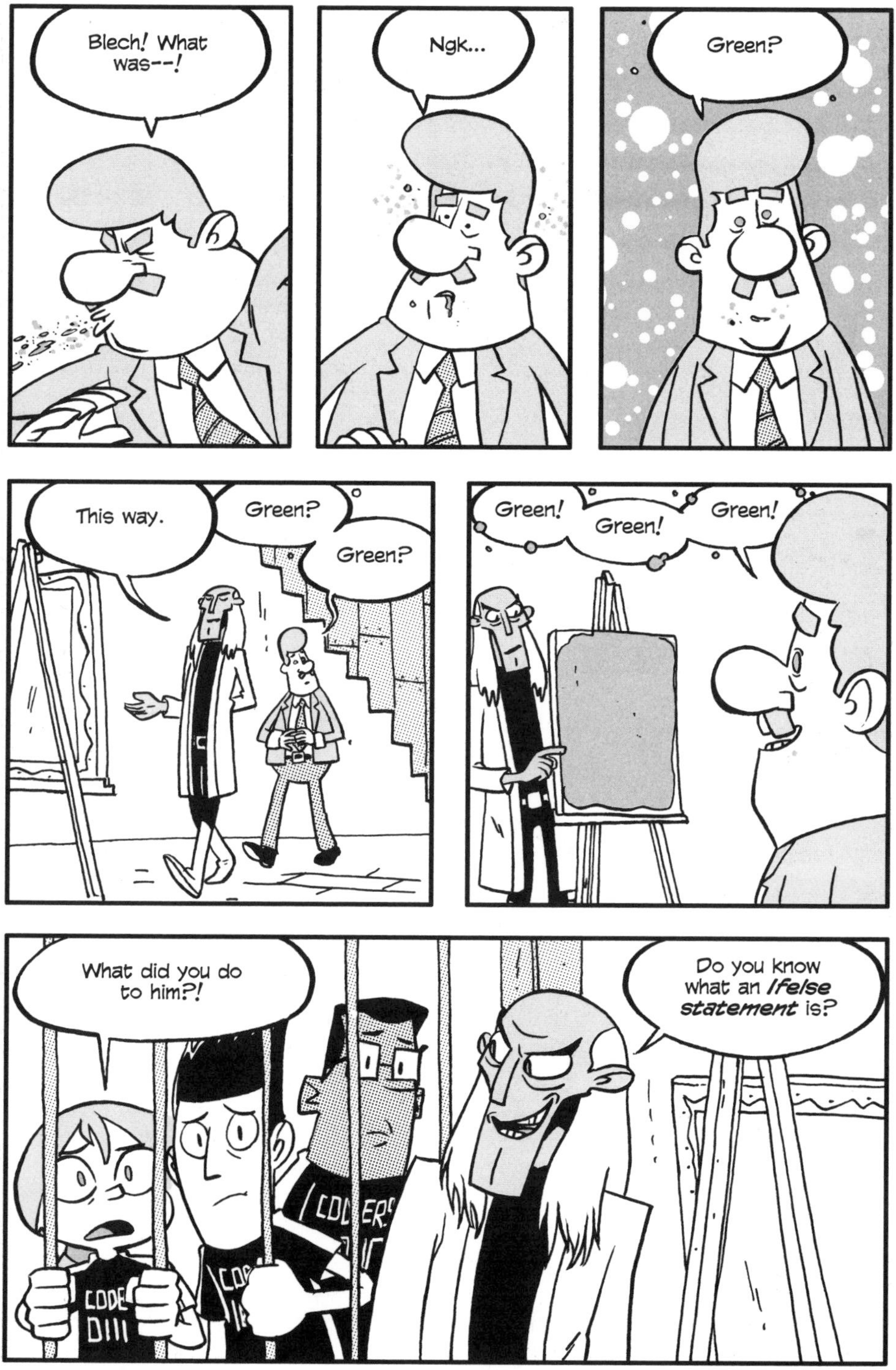
Blech! What was--!
Ngk...
Green?
This way.
Green?
Green?
Green!
Green!
Green!
What did you do to him?!
Do you know what an *If/else statement* is?
CODE
CODE
CODERS

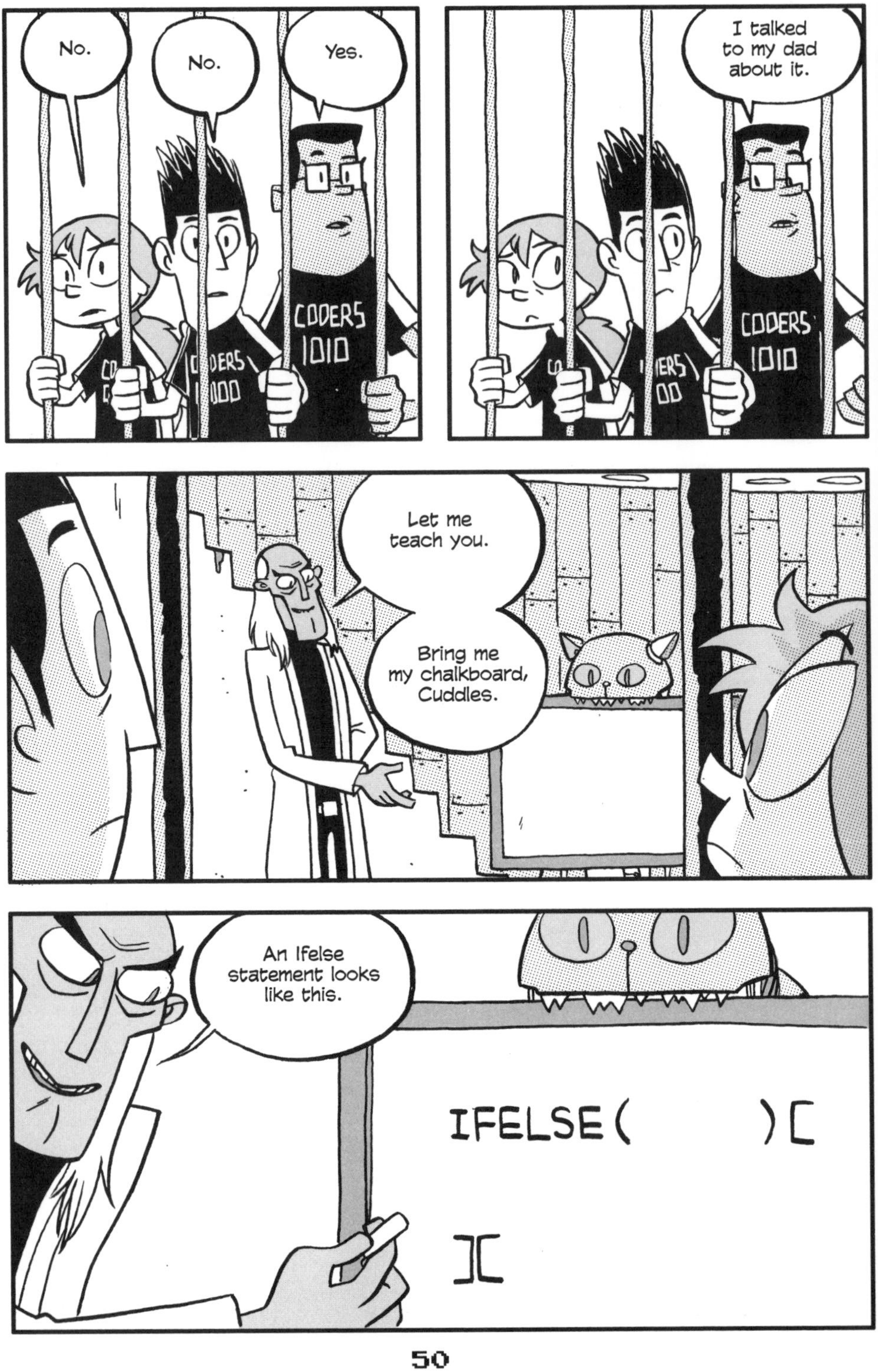

No.
No.
Yes.
CODERS 1010
I talked to my dad about it.
Let me teach you.
Bring me my chalkboard, Cuddles.
An Ifelse statement looks like this.
IFELSE( )[
]

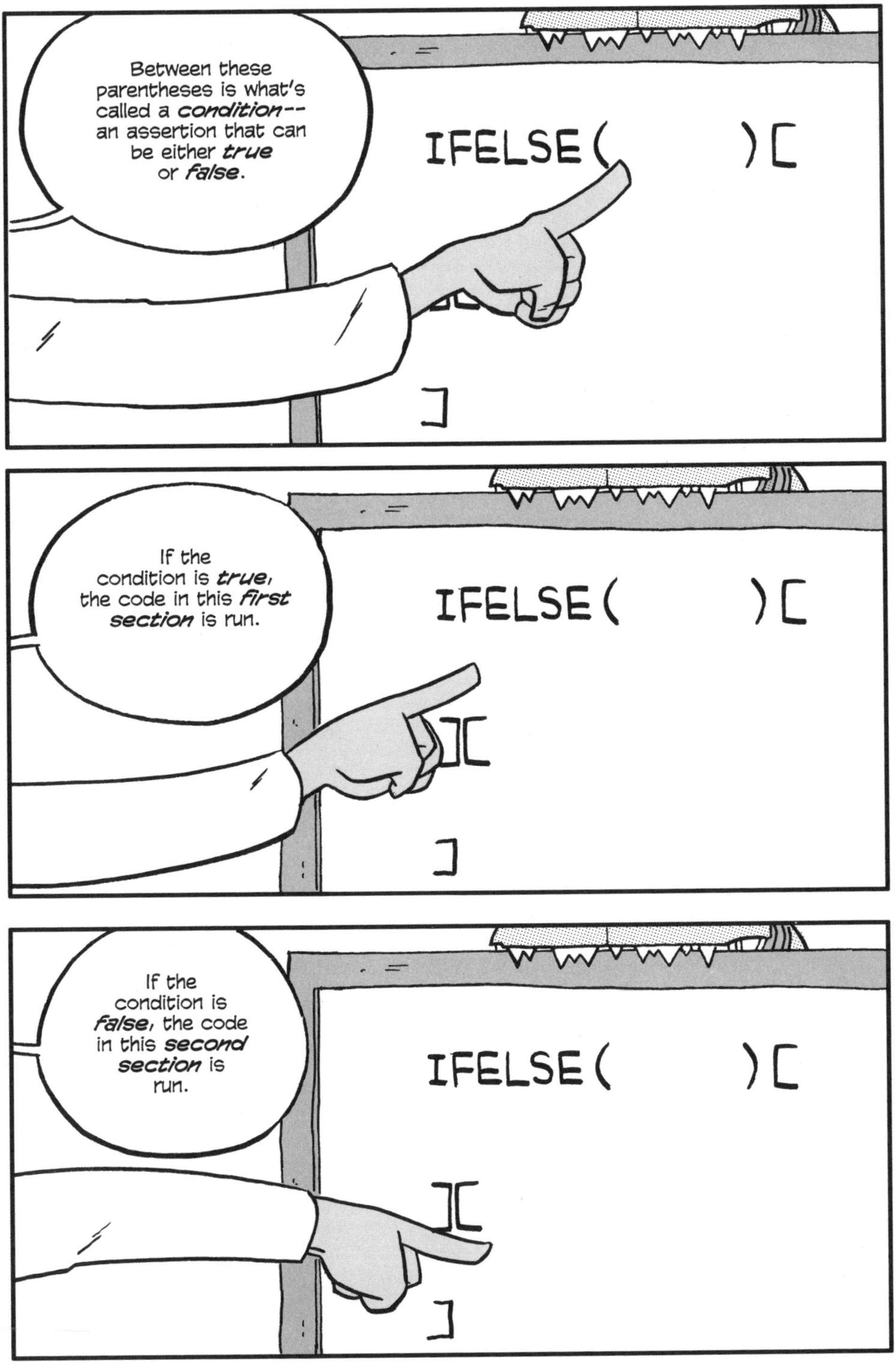
Between these parentheses is what's called a *condition*-- an assertion that can be either *true* or *false*.
IFELSE( )[
]
If the condition is *true*, the code in this *first section* is run.
IFELSE( )[
][
]
If the condition is *false*, the code in this *second section* is run.
IFELSE( )[
][
]

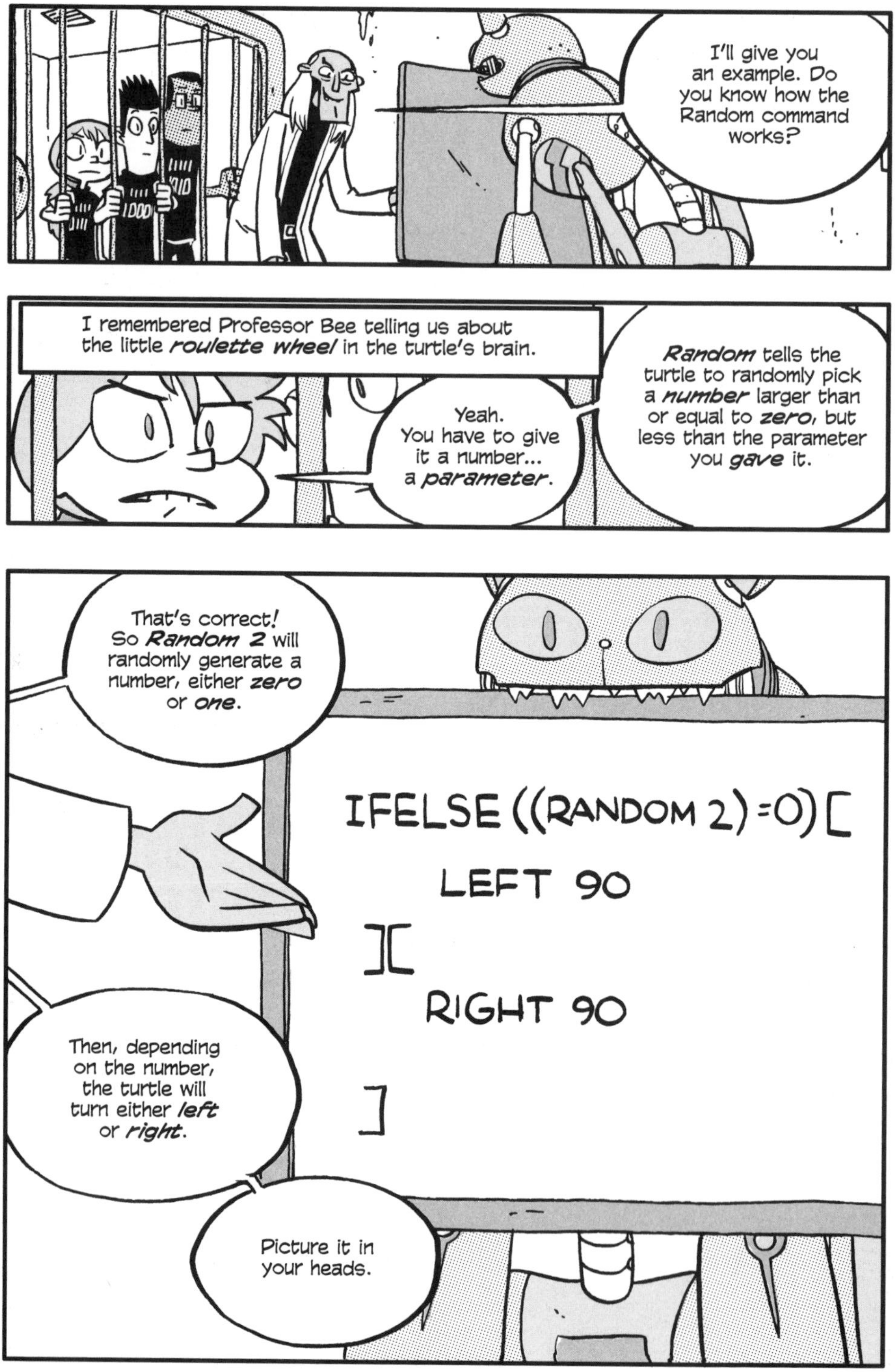
I'll give you an example. Do you know how the Random command works?
I remembered Professor Bee telling us about the little *roulette wheel* in the turtle's brain.
Yeah. You have to give it a number... a *parameter*.
Random tells the turtle to randomly pick a *number* larger than or equal to *zero*, but less than the parameter you *gave* it.
That's correct! So *Random 2* will randomly generate a number, either *zero* or *one*.
IFELSE ((RANDOM 2) =0) [
LEFT 90
] [
RIGHT 90
]
Then, depending on the number, the turtle will turn either *left* or *right*.
Picture it in your heads.

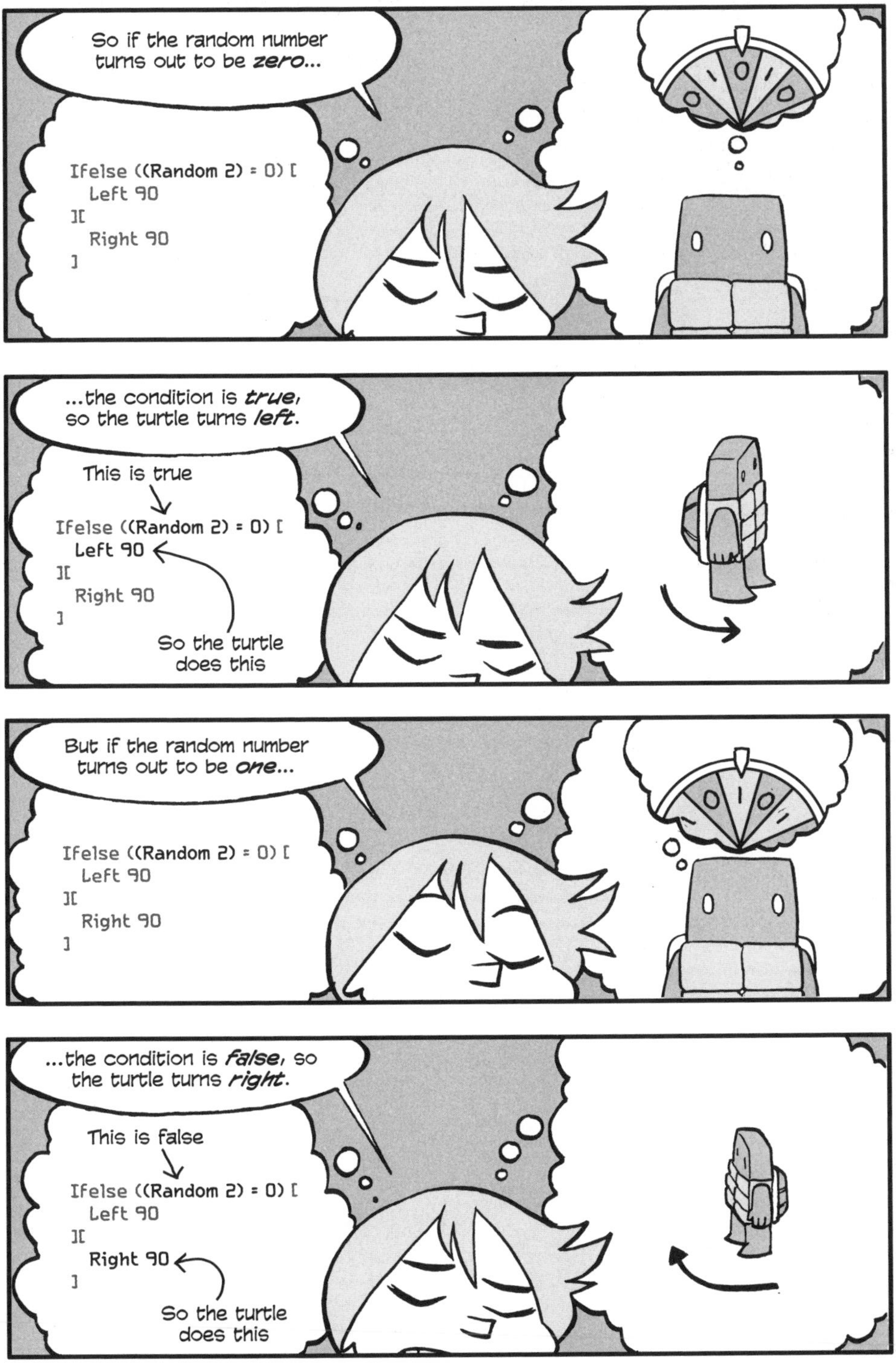

So if the random number turns out to be *zero*...
Ifelse ((Random 2) = 0) [
Left 90
][
Right 90
]
...the condition is *true*, so the turtle turns *left*.
This is true
Ifelse ((Random 2) = 0) [
Left 90
][
Right 90
]
So the turtle does this
But if the random number turns out to be *one*...
Ifelse ((Random 2) = 0) [
Left 90
][
Right 90
]
...the condition is *false*, so the turtle turns *right*.
This is false
Ifelse ((Random 2) = 0) [
Left 90
][
Right 90
]
So the turtle does this

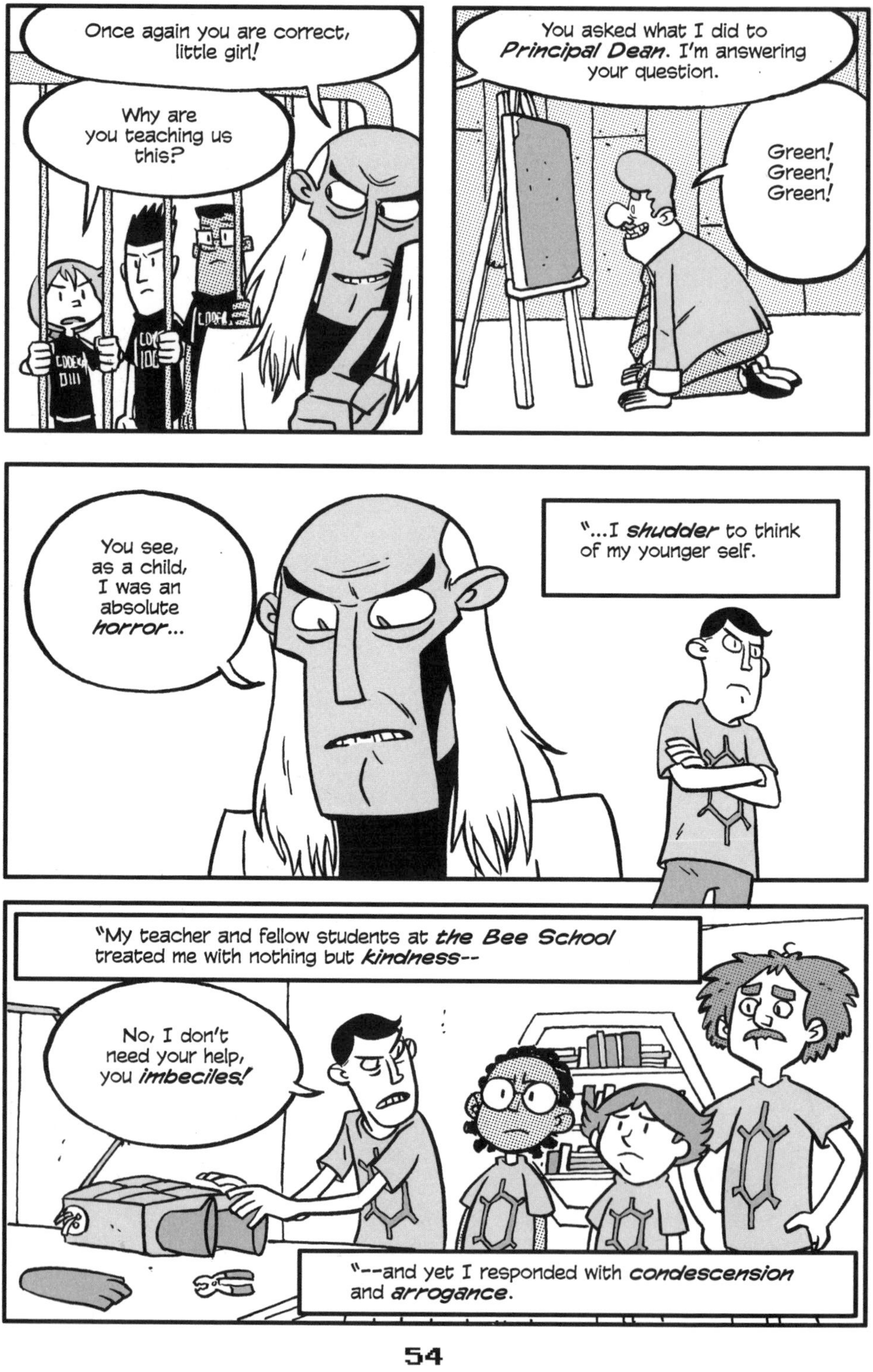

Once again you are correct, little girl!
Why are you teaching us this?
You asked what I did to Principal Dean. I'm answering your question.
Green! Green! Green!
You see, as a child, I was an absolute horror...
"...I shudder to think of my younger self.
"My teacher and fellow students at the Bee School treated me with nothing but kindness--
No, I don't need your help, you imbeciles!
"--and yet I responded with condescension and arrogance.

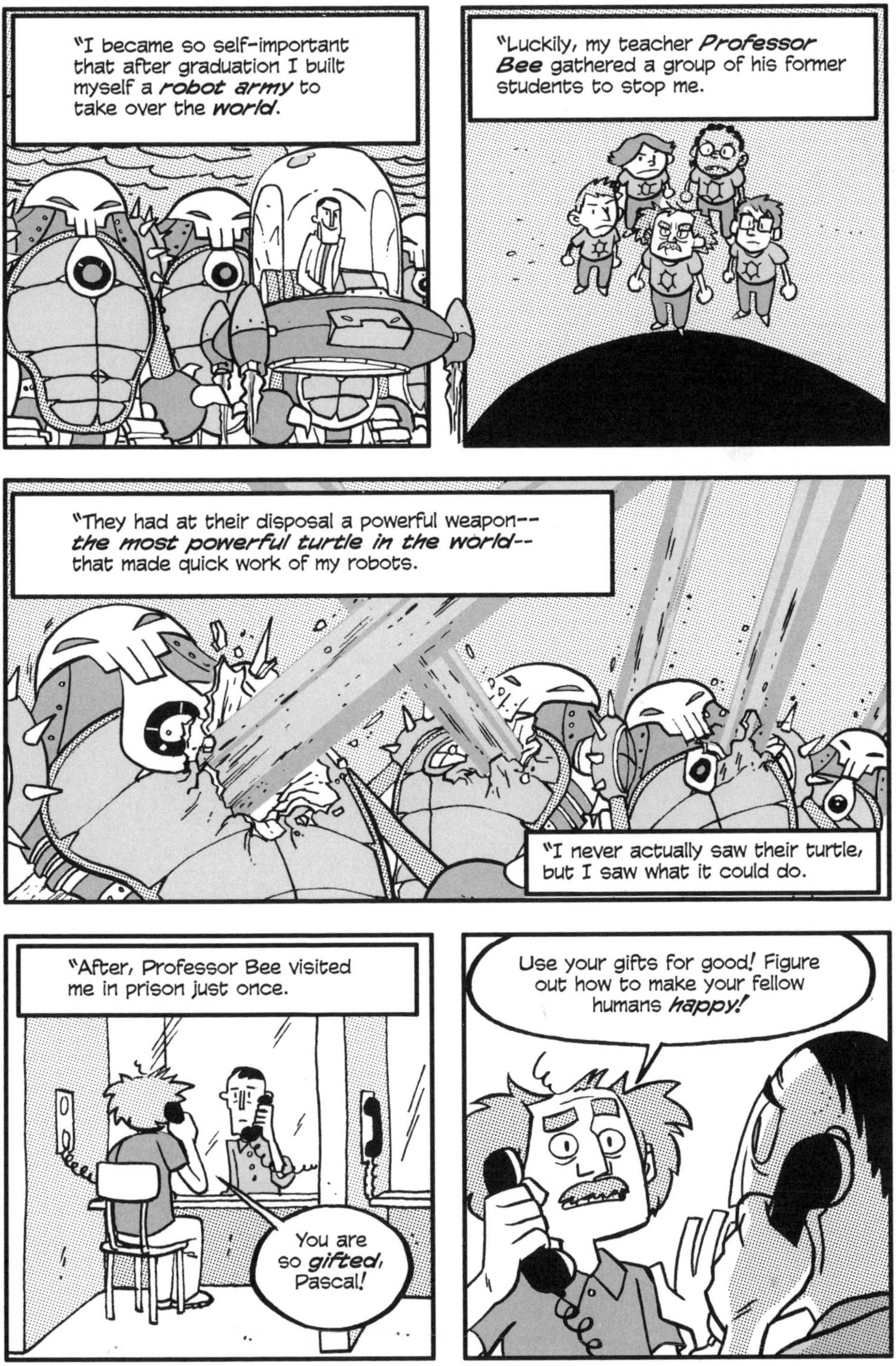
"I became so self-important that after graduation I built myself a *robot army* to take over the *world*.
"Luckily, my teacher *Professor Bee* gathered a group of his former students to stop me.
"They had at their disposal a powerful weapon-- *the most powerful turtle in the world*-- that made quick work of my robots.
"I never actually saw their turtle, but I saw what it could do.
"After, Professor Bee visited me in prison just once.
You are so *gifted*, Pascal!
Use your gifts for good! Figure out how to make your fellow humans *happy!*

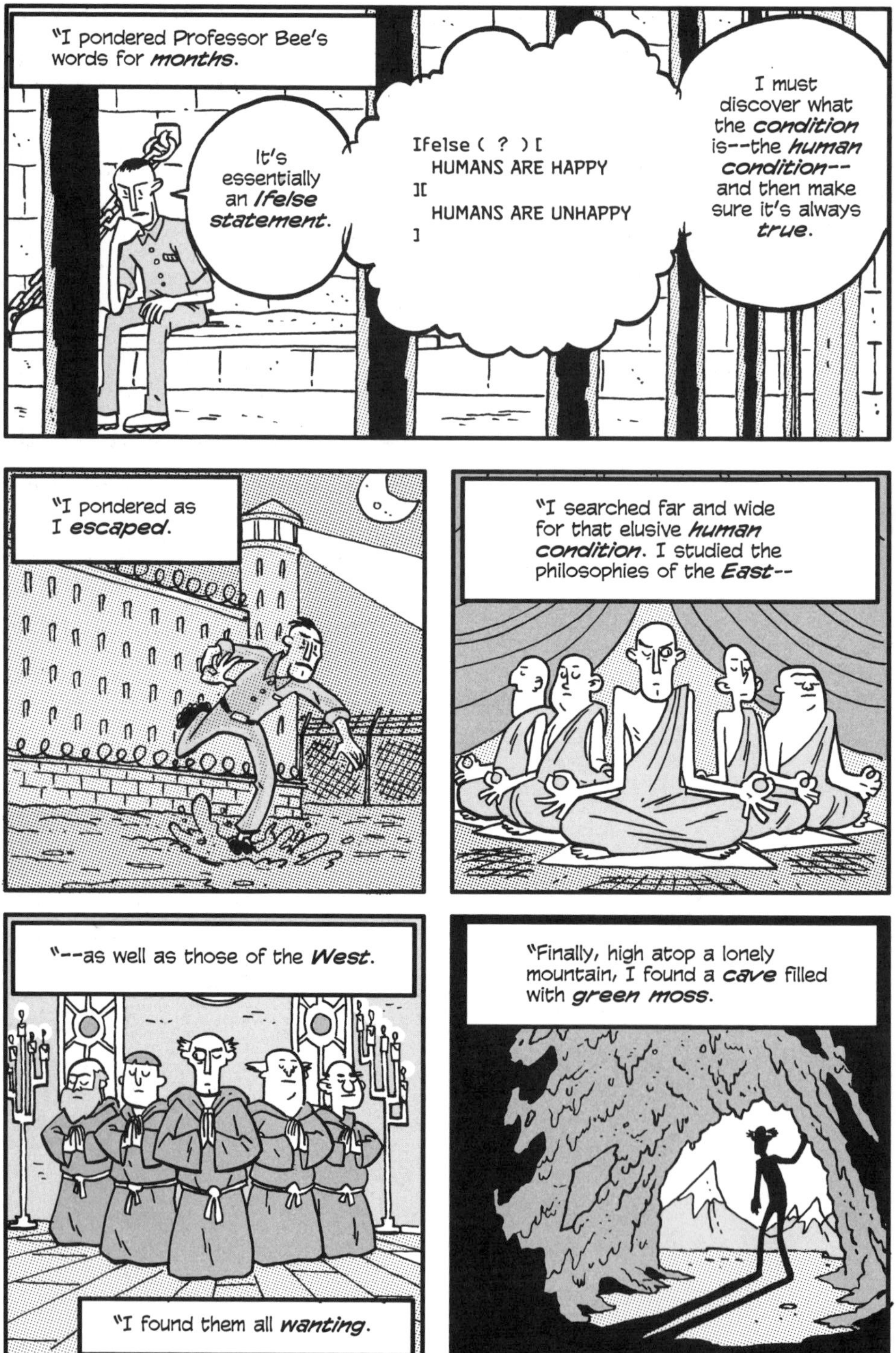
"I pondered Professor Bee's words for *months*.
It's essentially an *Ifelse statement*.
Ifelse (?) [
HUMANS ARE HAPPY
][
HUMANS ARE UNHAPPY
]
I must discover what the *condition* is--the *human condition*-- and then make sure it's always *true*.
"I pondered as I *escaped*.
"I searched far and wide for that elusive *human condition*. I studied the philosophies of the *East*--
"--as well as those of the *West*.
"I found them all *wanting*.
"Finally, high atop a lonely mountain, I found a *cave* filled with *green moss*.

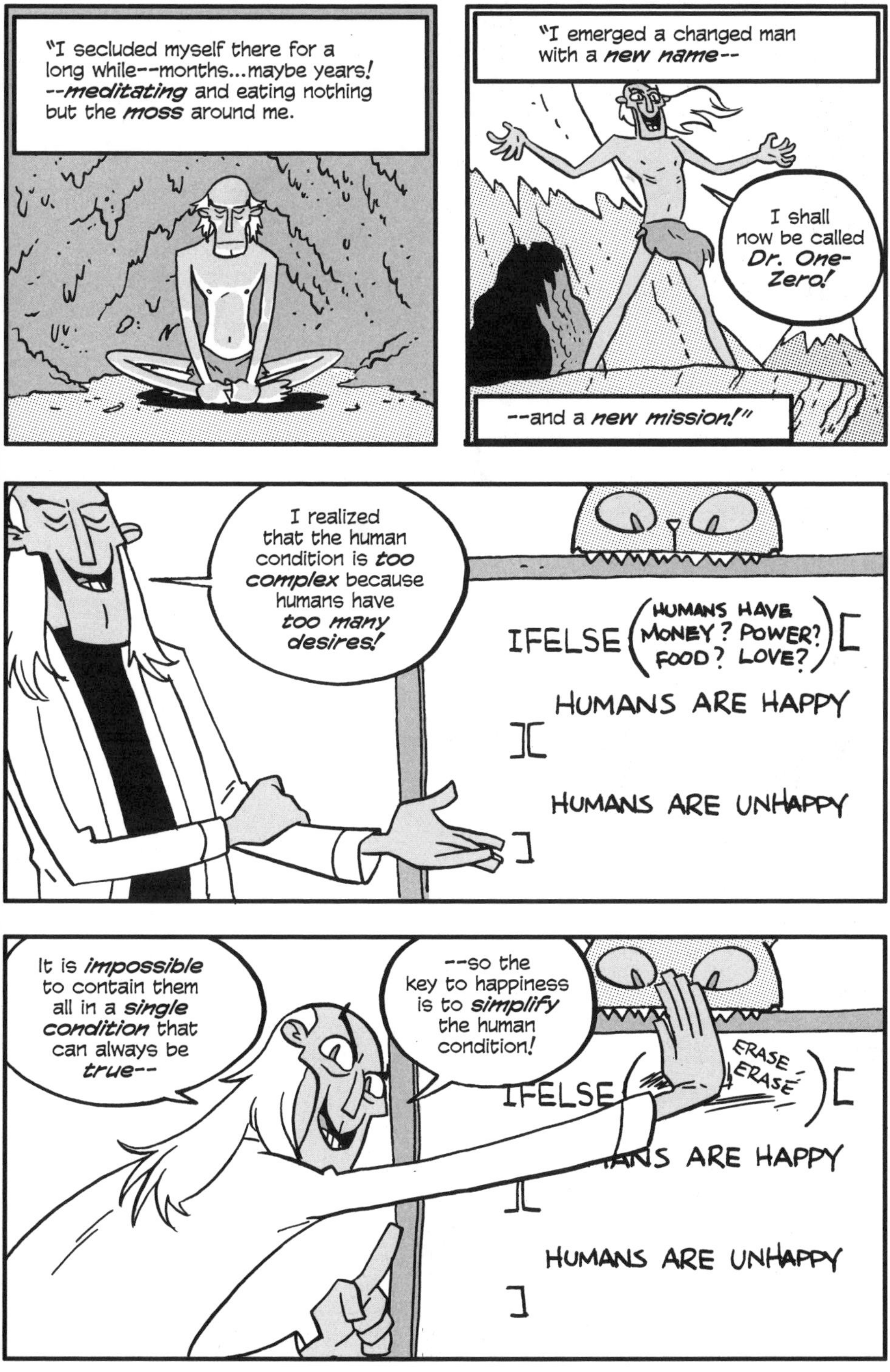
"I secluded myself there for a long while--months...maybe years! --*meditating* and eating nothing but the *moss* around me.
"I emerged a changed man with a *new name*--
I shall now be called *Dr. One-Zero!*
--and a *new mission!*"
I realized that the human condition is *too complex* because humans have *too many desires!*
IFELSE (HUMANS HAVE MONEY ? POWER? FOOD ? LOVE?) [
HUMANS ARE HAPPY
] [
HUMANS ARE UNHAPPY
]
It is *impossible* to contain them all in a *single condition* that can always be *true*--
--so the key to happiness is to *simplify* the human condition!
ERASE ERASE
IFELSE ( ) [
ANS ARE HAPPY
] [
HUMANS ARE UNHAPPY
]

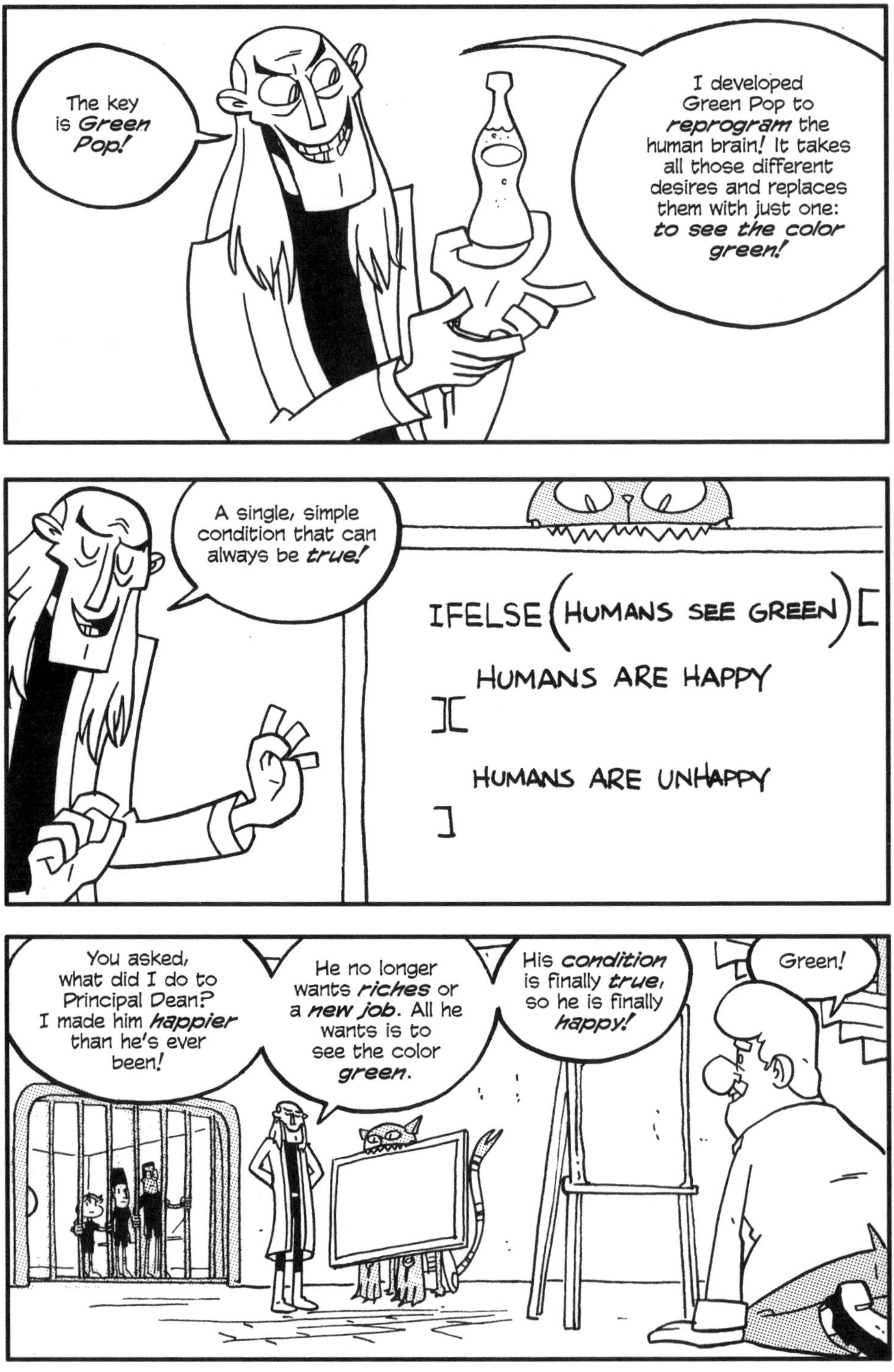
The key is *Green Pop!*
I developed Green Pop to *reprogram* the human brain! It takes all those different desires and replaces them with just one: *to see the color green!*
A single, simple condition that can always be *true!*
IFELSE (HUMANS SEE GREEN) [
HUMANS ARE HAPPY
][
HUMANS ARE UNHAPPY
]
You asked, what did I do to Principal Dean? I made him *happier* than he's ever been!
He no longer wants *riches* or a *new job*. All he wants is to see the color *green*.
His *condition* is finally *true*, so he is finally *happy!*
Green!

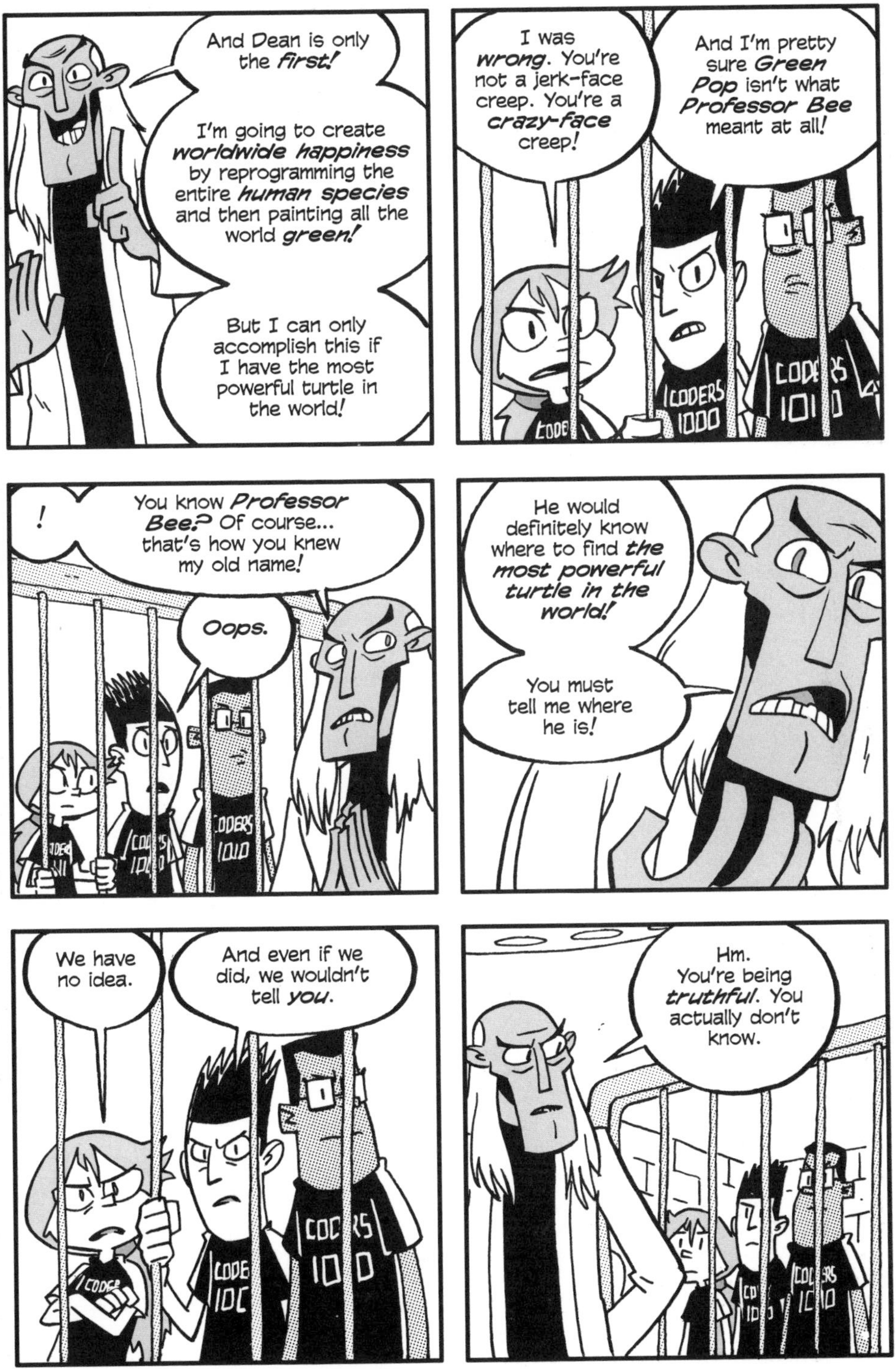
And Dean is only the *first!*
I'm going to create ***worldwide happiness*** by reprogramming the entire ***human species*** and then painting all the world ***green!***
But I can only accomplish this if I have the most powerful turtle in the world!
I was ***wrong***. You're not a jerk-face creep. You're a ***crazy-face*** creep!
And I'm pretty sure ***Green Pop*** isn't what ***Professor Bee*** meant at all!
CODERS 1010
!
You know *Professor Bee?* Of course... that's how you knew my old name!
Oops.
He would definitely know where to find ***the most powerful turtle in the world!***
You must tell me where he is!
We have no idea.
And even if we did, we wouldn't tell ***you***.
Hm. You're being ***truthful***. You actually don't know.

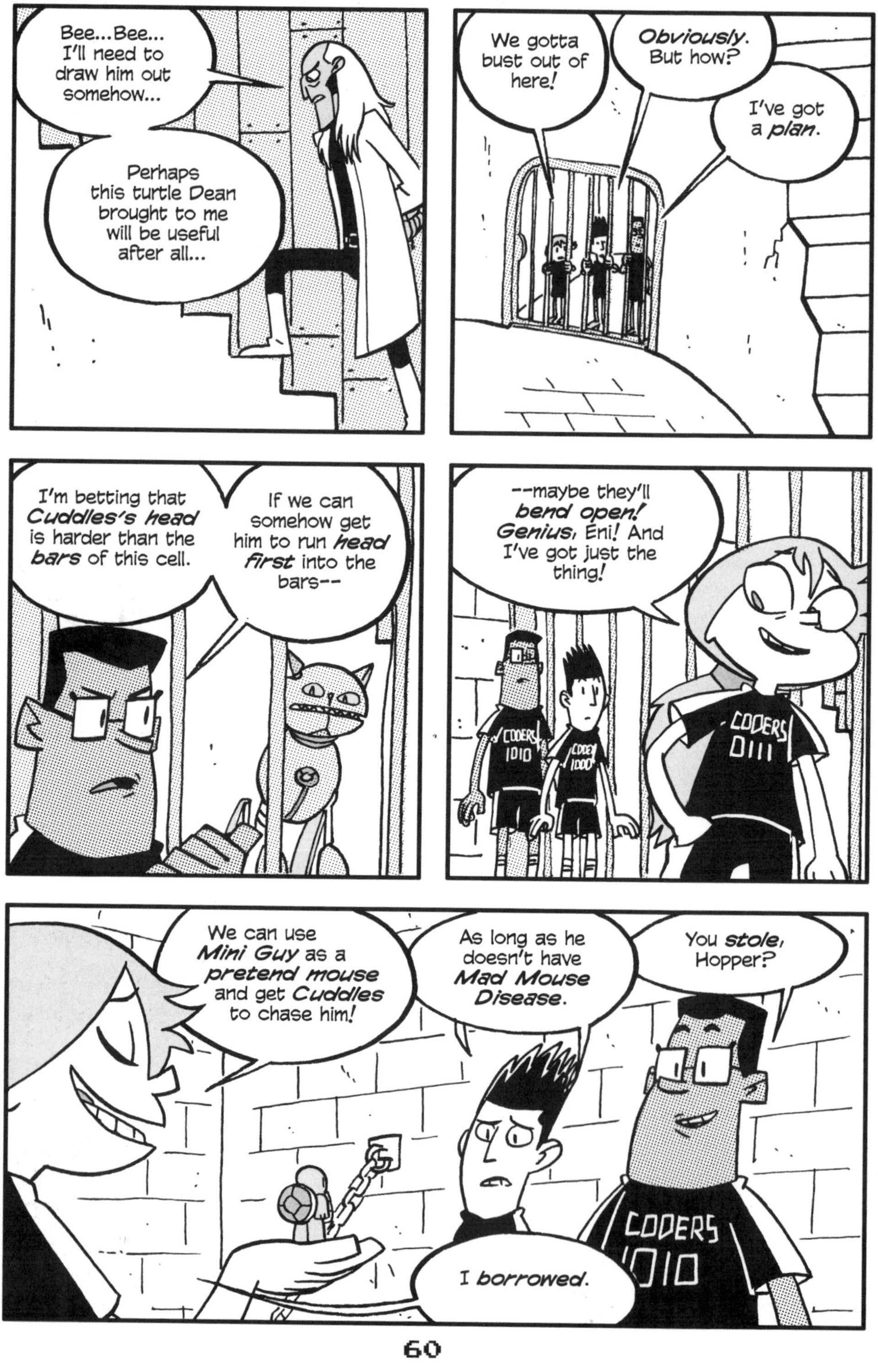
Bee...Bee... I'll need to draw him out somehow...
Perhaps this turtle Dean brought to me will be useful after all...
We gotta bust out of here!
Obviously. But how?
I've got a *plan*.
I'm betting that *Cuddles's head* is harder than the *bars* of this cell.
If we can somehow get him to run *head first* into the bars--
--maybe they'll *bend open! Genius*, Eni! And I've got just the thing!
CODERS 1010
CODERS 1000
CODERS 0111
We can use *Mini Guy* as a *pretend mouse* and get *Cuddles* to chase him!
As long as he doesn't have *Mad Mouse Disease*.
You *stole*, Hopper?
I *borrowed*.
CODERS 1010

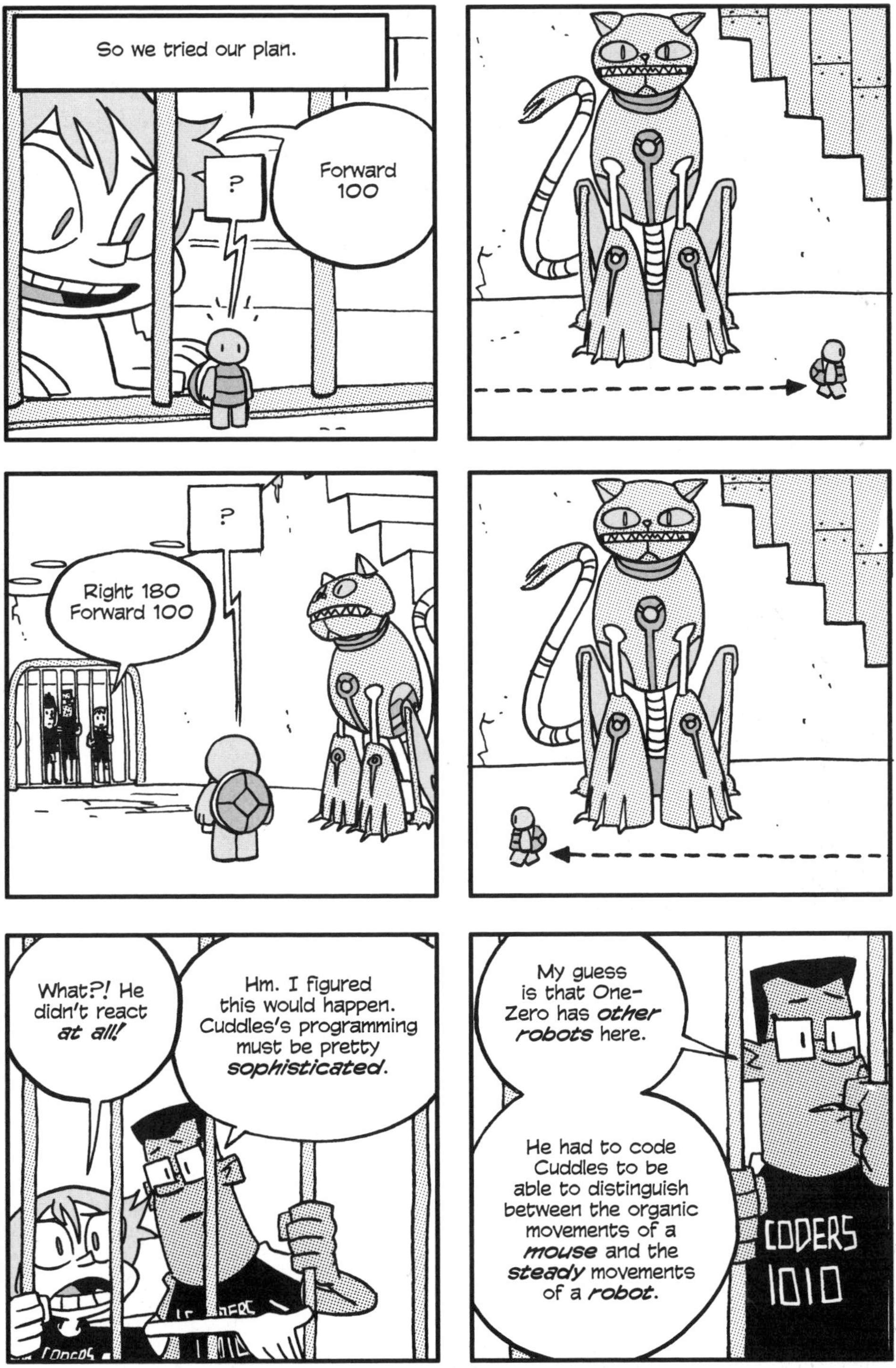
So we tried our plan.
?
Forward 100
?
Right 180 Forward 100
What?! He didn't react *at all!*
Hm. I figured this would happen. Cuddles's programming must be pretty *sophisticated*.
My guess is that One-Zero has *other robots* here.
He had to code Cuddles to be able to distinguish between the organic movements of a *mouse* and the *steady* movements of a *robot*.
CODERS
1010

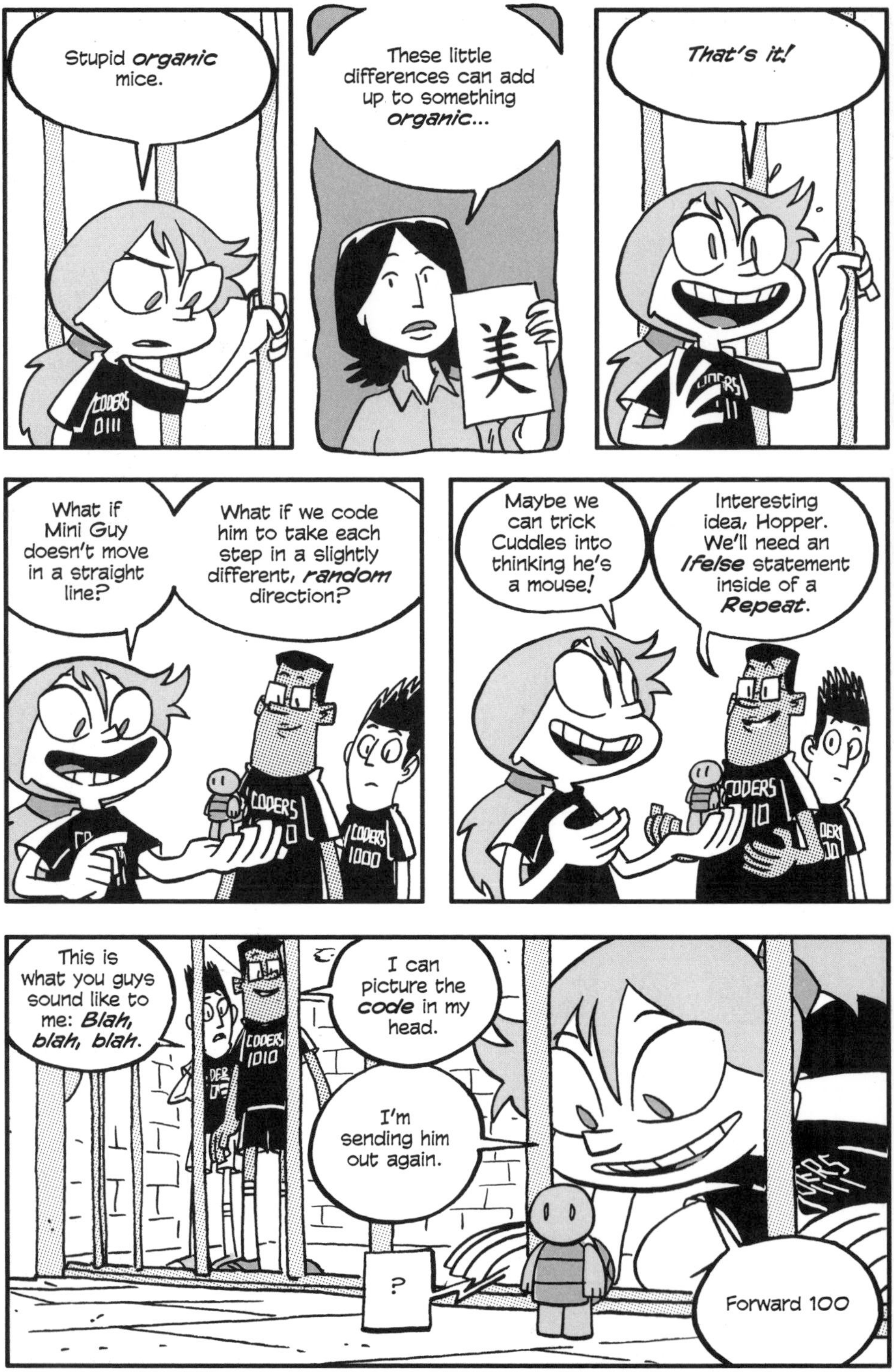
Stupid organic mice.
These little differences can add up to something organic...
美
That's it!
What if Mini Guy doesn't move in a straight line?
What if we code him to take each step in a slightly different, random direction?
Maybe we can trick Cuddles into thinking he's a mouse!
Interesting idea, Hopper. We'll need an Ifelse statement inside of a Repeat.
This is what you guys sound like to me: Blah, blah, blah.
I can picture the code in my head.
I'm sending him out again.
?
Forward 100

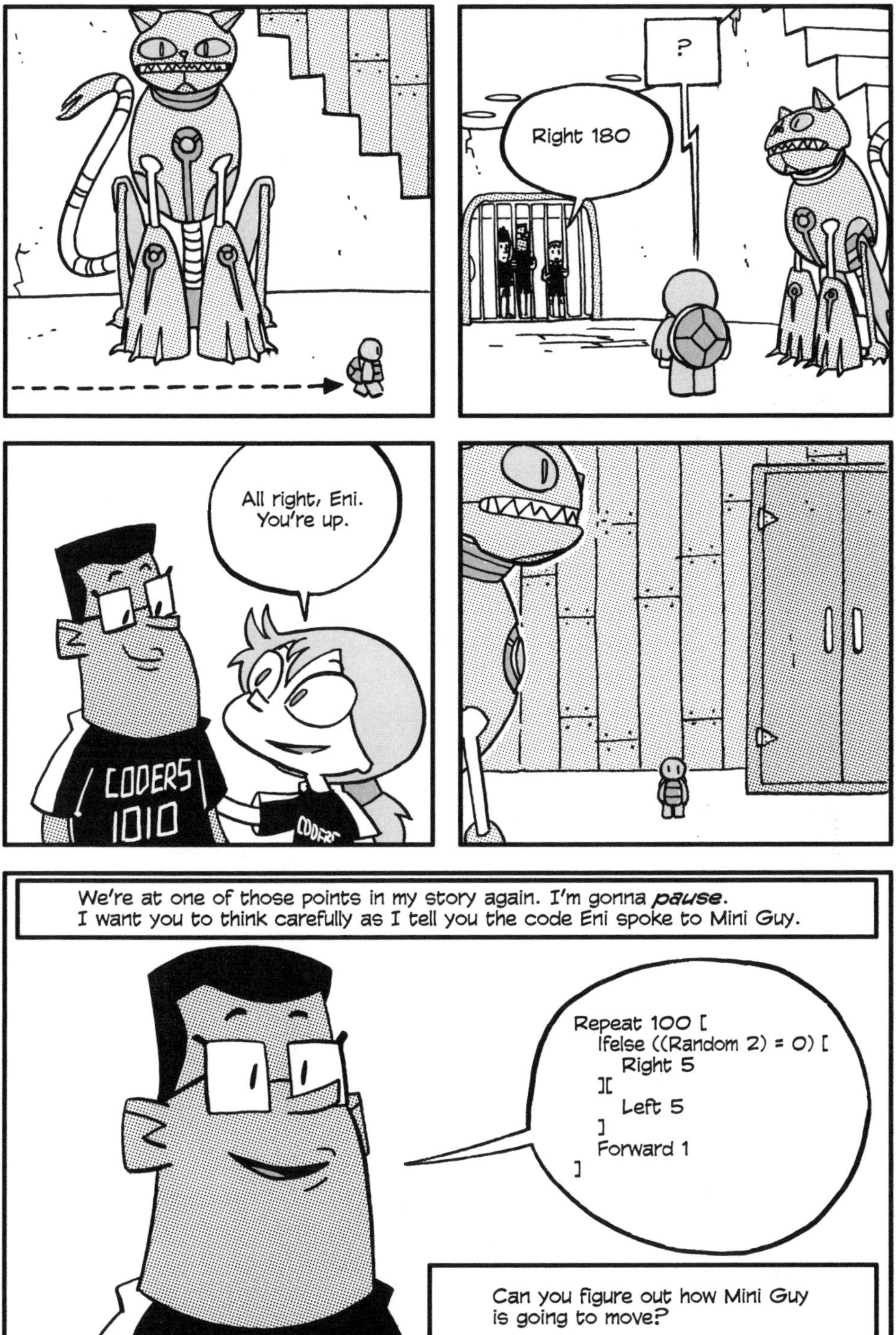
?
Right 180
All right, Eni. You're up.
CODERS 1010
We're at one of those points in my story again. I'm gonna *pause*. I want you to think carefully as I tell you the code Eni spoke to Mini Guy.
Repeat 100 [
   Ifelse ((Random 2) = 0) [
      Right 5
   ][
      Left 5
   ]
   Forward 1
]
Can you figure out how Mini Guy is going to move?

Chapter

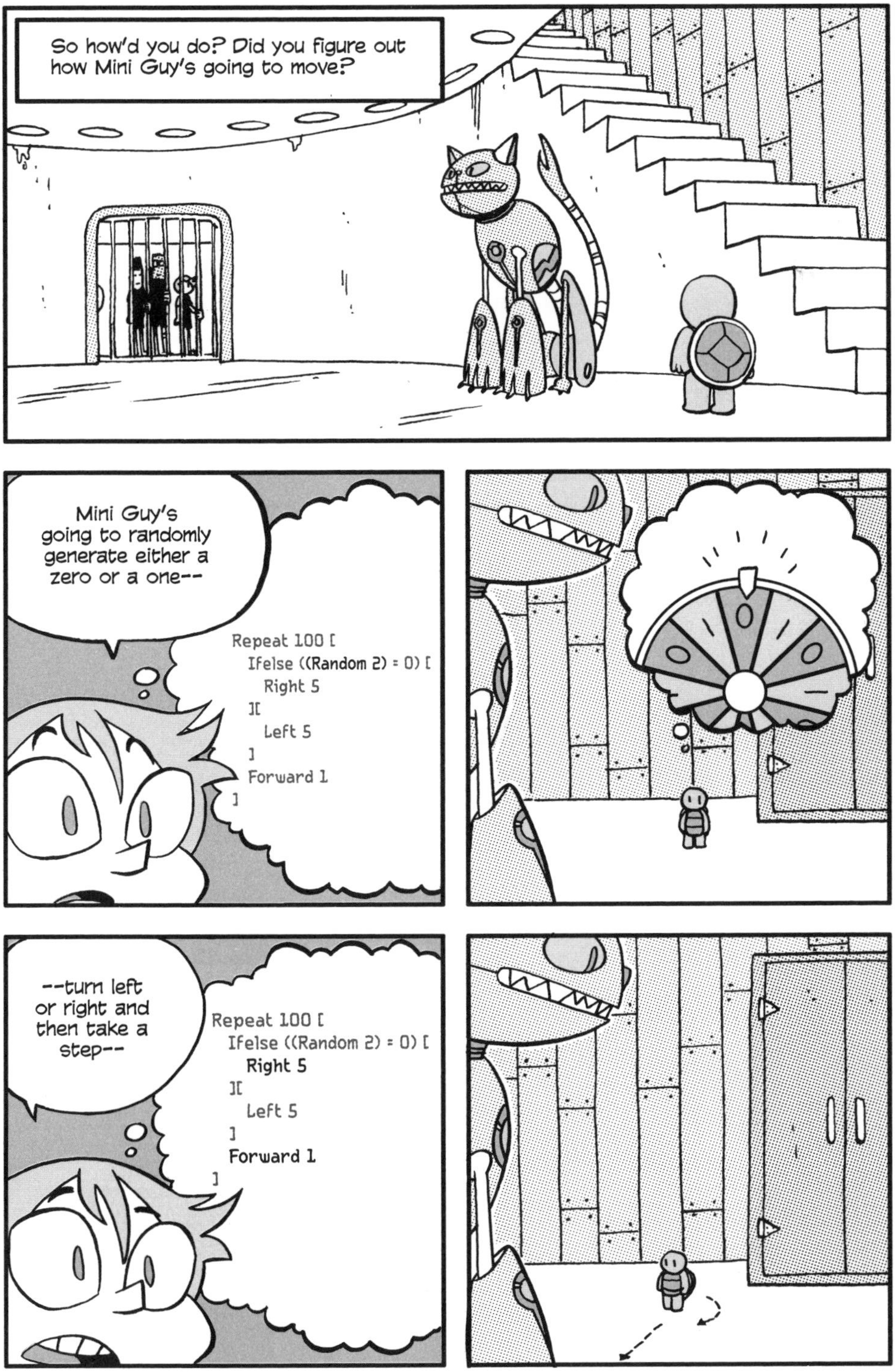
So how'd you do? Did you figure out how Mini Guy's going to move?
Mini Guy's going to randomly generate either a zero or a one--
Repeat 100 [
Ifelse ((Random 2) = 0) [
Right 5
][
Left 5
]
Forward 1
]
--turn left or right and then take a step--
Repeat 100 [
Ifelse ((Random 2) = 0) [
Right 5
][
Left 5
]
Forward 1
]

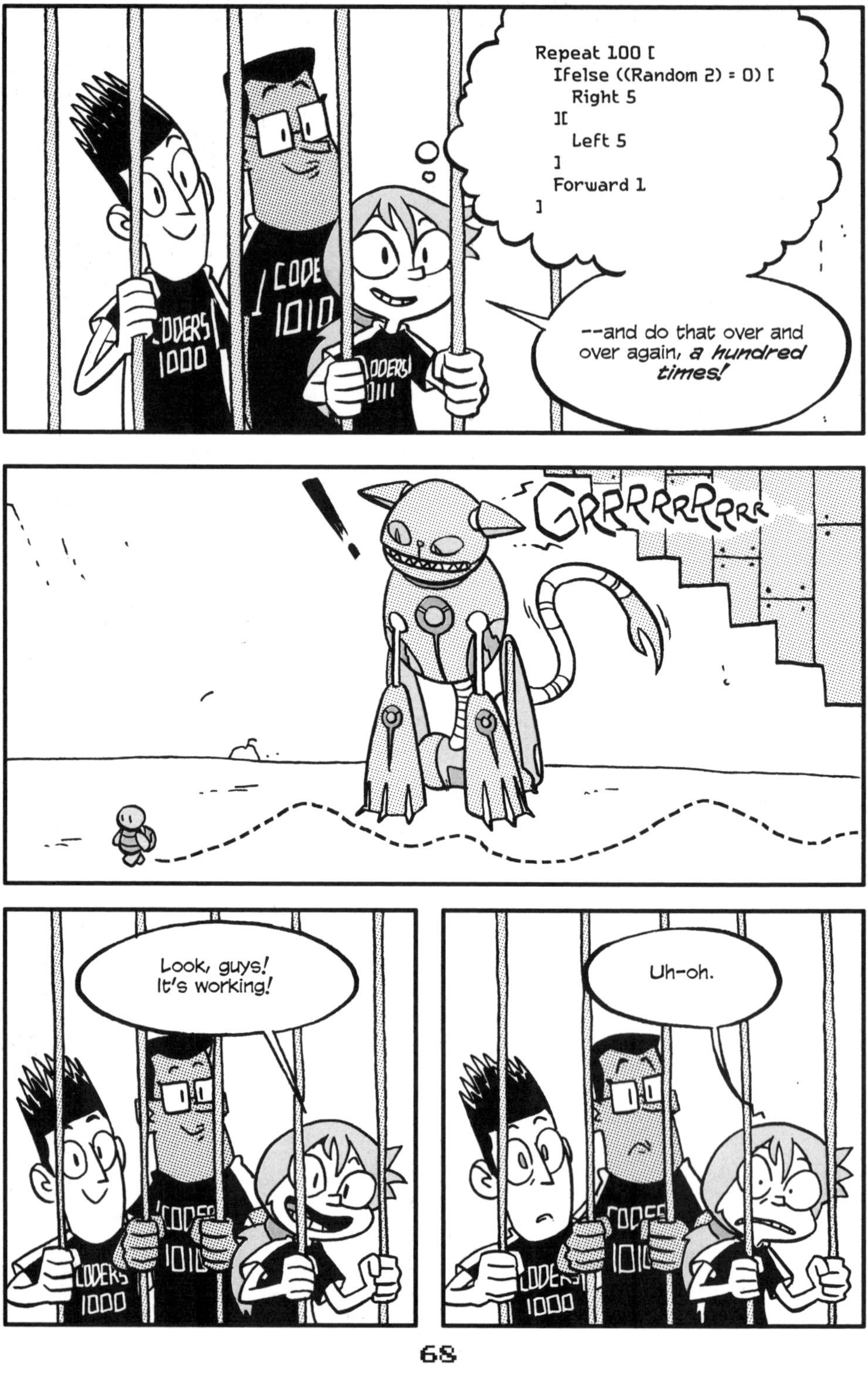
Repeat 100 [
Ifelse ((Random 2) = 0) [
Right 5
][
Left 5
]
Forward 1
]
--and do that over and over again, *a hundred times!*
!
GRRRRRRRrrr
Look, guys! It's working!
Uh-oh.

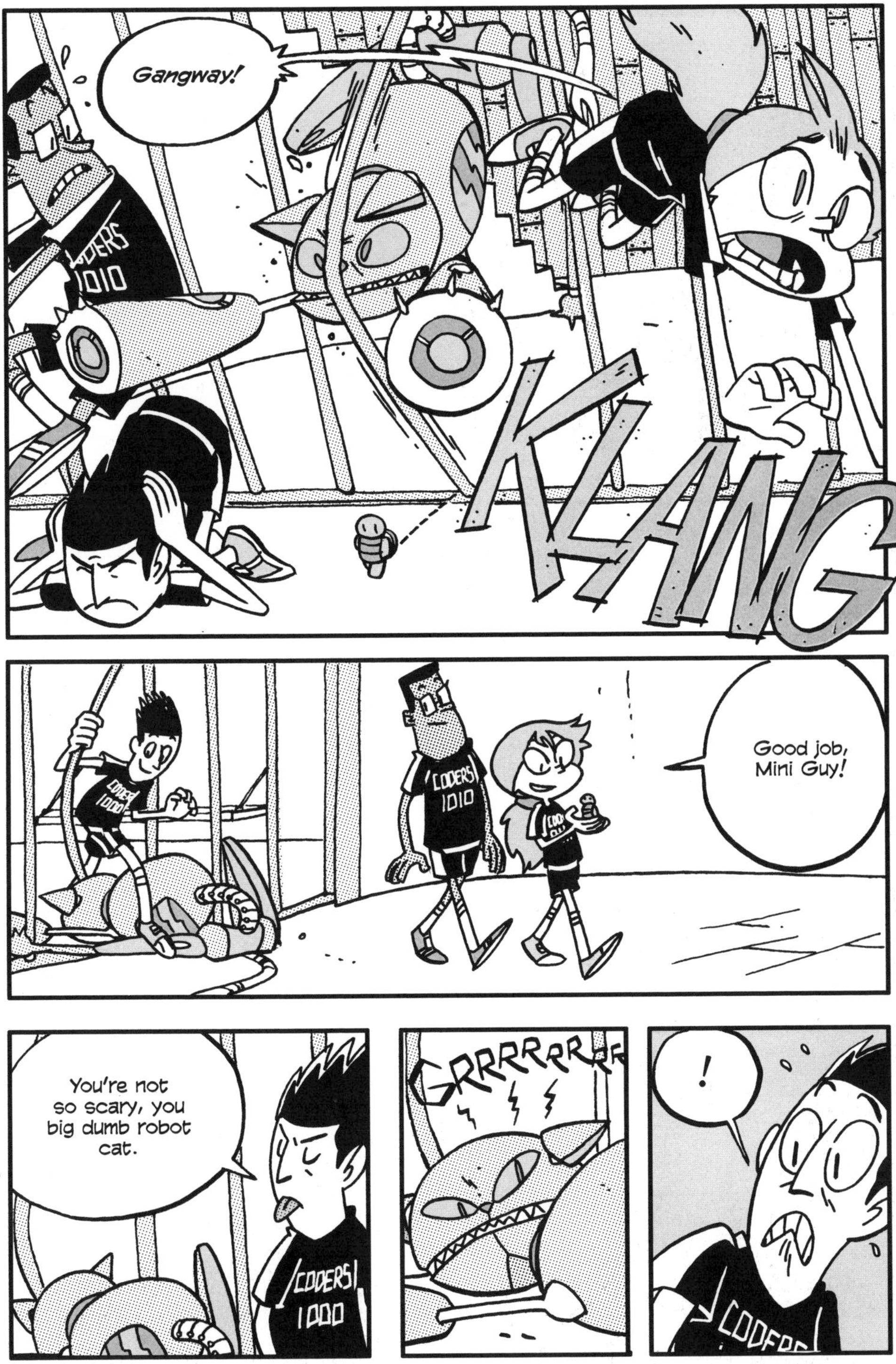
Gangway!
KLANG
CODERS 1010
Good job, Mini Guy!
CODERS 1000
CODERS 1010
You're not so scary, you big dumb robot cat.
CODERS 1000
GRRRRRRR
!

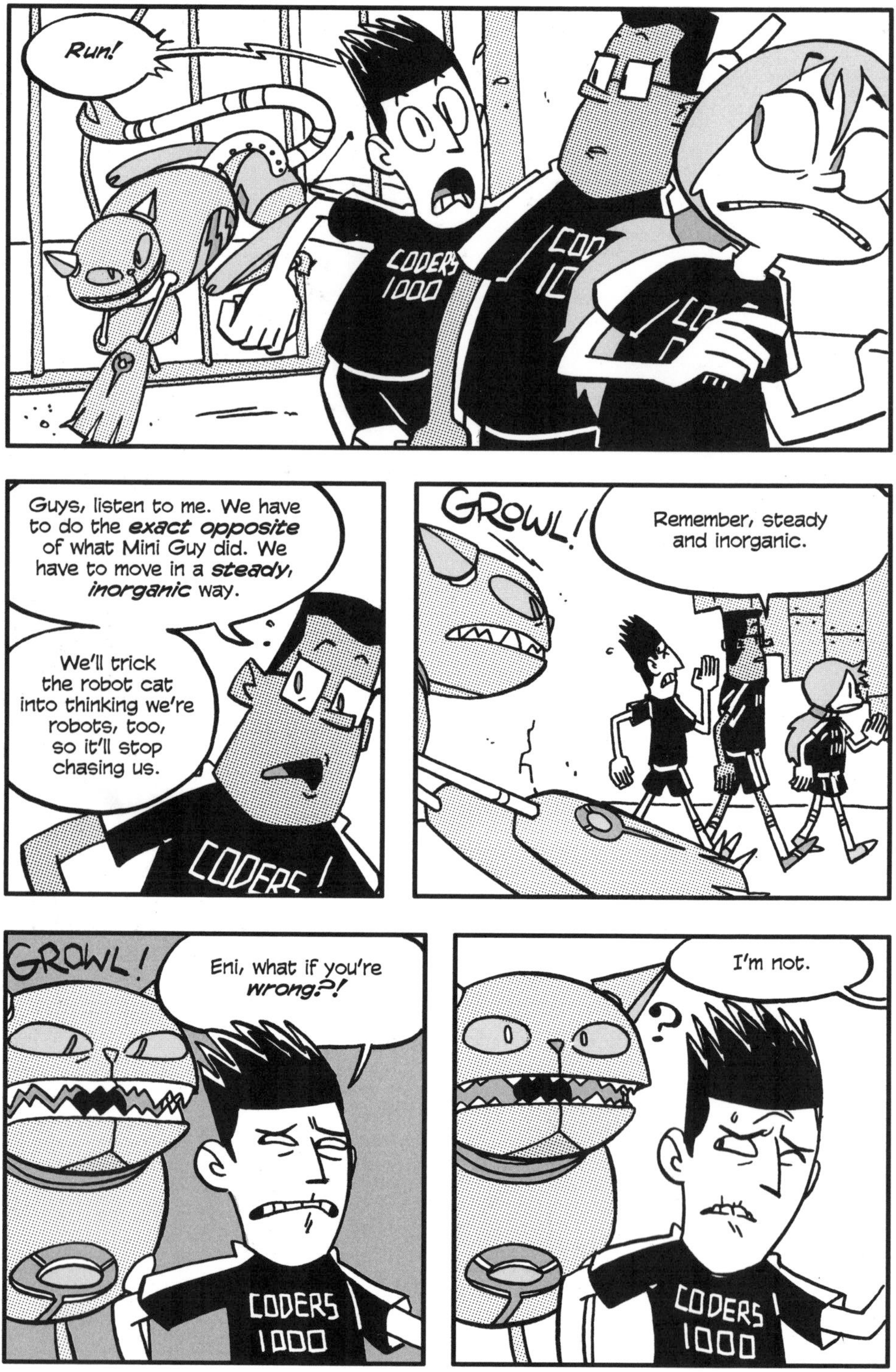
Run!
CODERS 1000
Guys, listen to me. We have to do the exact opposite of what Mini Guy did. We have to move in a steady, inorganic way.
We'll trick the robot cat into thinking we're robots, too, so it'll stop chasing us.
GROWL!
Remember, steady and inorganic.
GROWL!
Eni, what if you're wrong?!
CODERS 1000
I'm not.
?
CODERS 1000

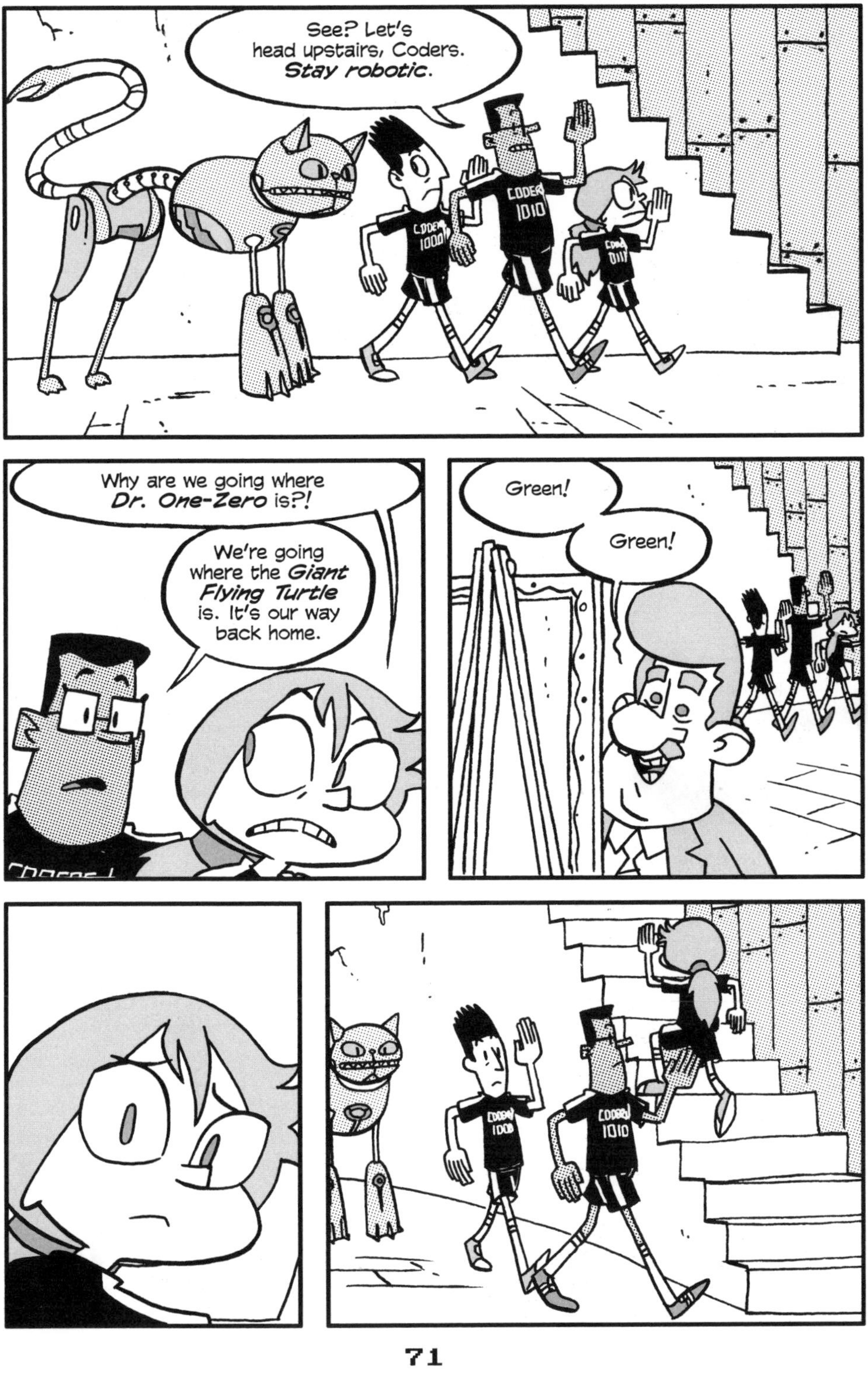
See? Let's head upstairs, Coders. *Stay robotic*.
CODER 1000
CODER 1010
Why are we going where *Dr. One-Zero* is?!
We're going where the *Giant Flying Turtle* is. It's our way back home.
Green!
Green!
CODER 1000
CODER 1010

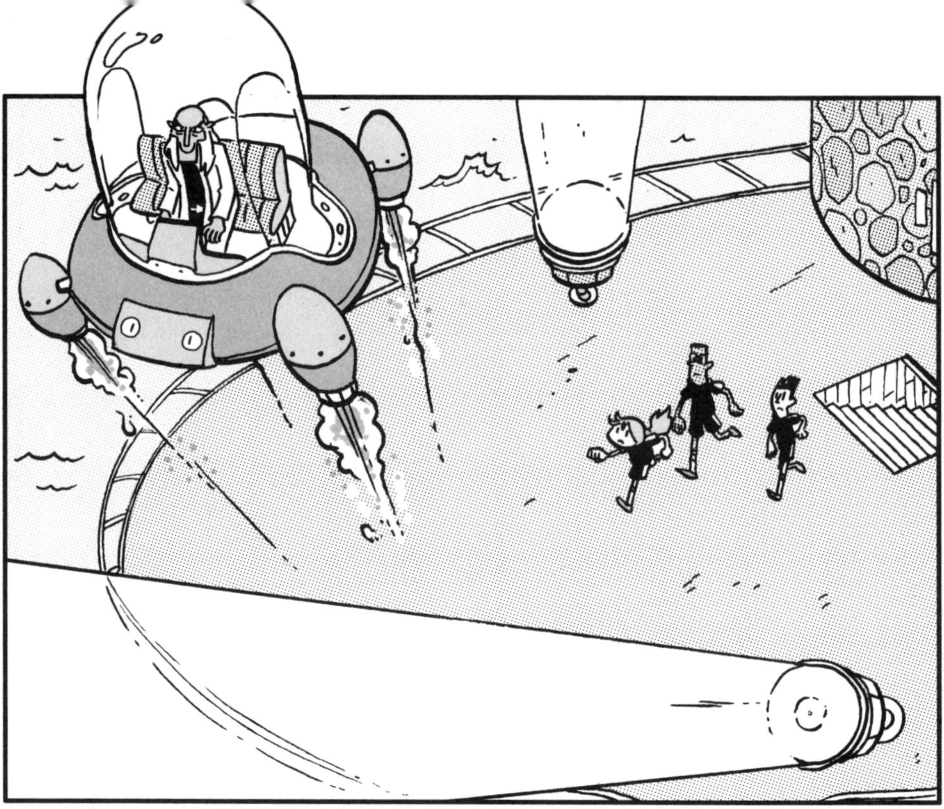

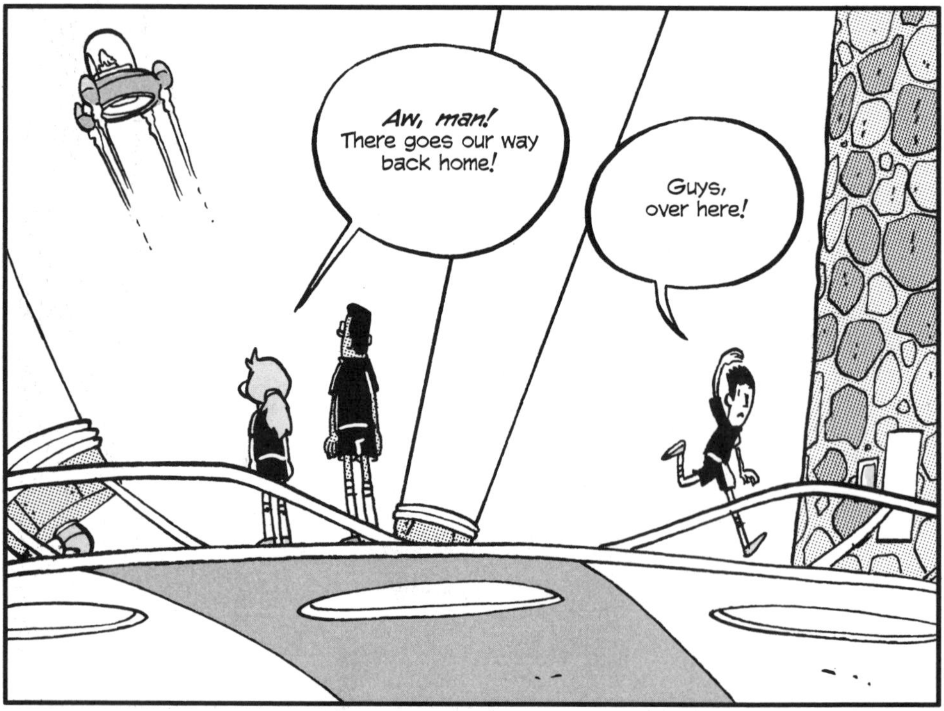
Aw, man!
There goes our way back home!
Guys, over here!

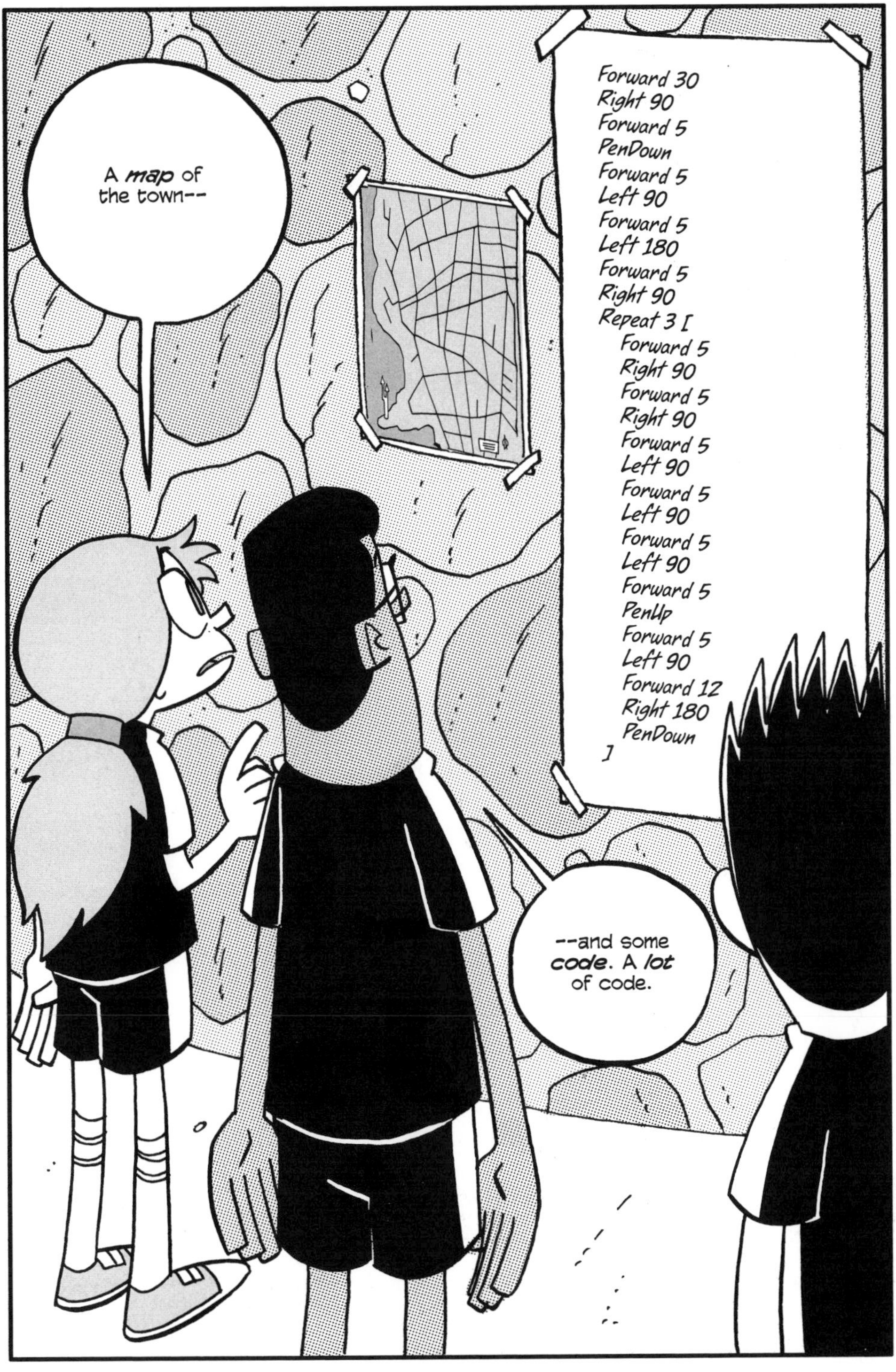
A *map* of the town--
Forward 30
Right 90
Forward 5
PenDown
Forward 5
Left 90
Forward 5
Left 180
Forward 5
Right 90
Repeat 3 [
Forward 5
Right 90
Forward 5
Right 90
Forward 5
Left 90
Forward 5
Left 90
Forward 5
Left 90
Forward 5
PenUp
Forward 5
Left 90
Forward 12
Right 180
PenDown
]
--and some *code*. A *lot* of code.

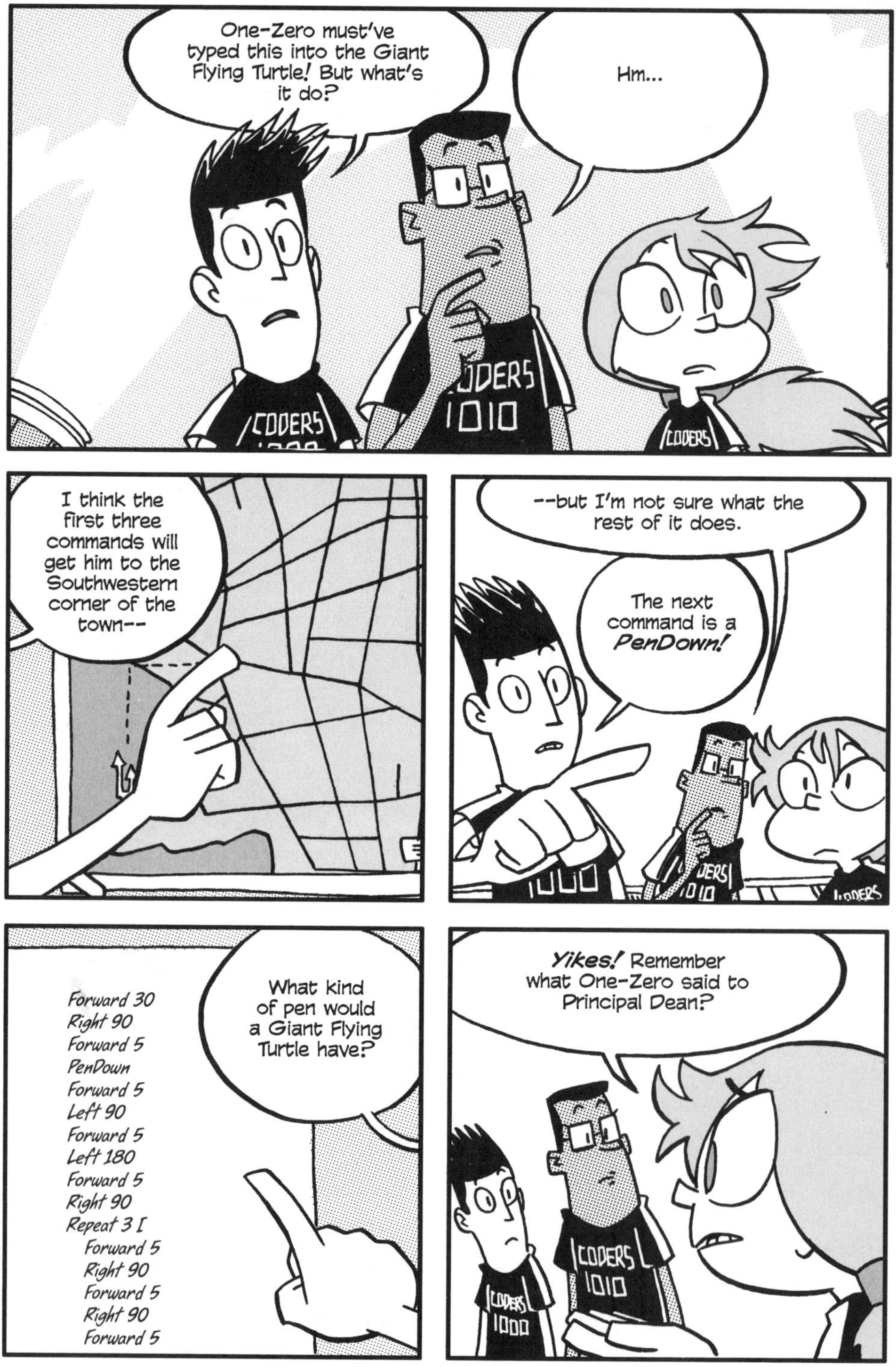
One-Zero must've typed this into the Giant Flying Turtle! But what's it do?
Hm...
CODERS 1010
I think the first three commands will get him to the Southwestern corner of the town--
--but I'm not sure what the rest of it does.
The next command is a *PenDown!*
Forward 30
Right 90
Forward 5
PenDown
Forward 5
Left 90
Forward 5
Left 180
Forward 5
Right 90
Repeat 3 [
Forward 5
Right 90
Forward 5
Right 90
Forward 5
What kind of pen would a Giant Flying Turtle have?
Yikes! Remember what One-Zero said to Principal Dean?
CODERS 1000
CODERS 1010

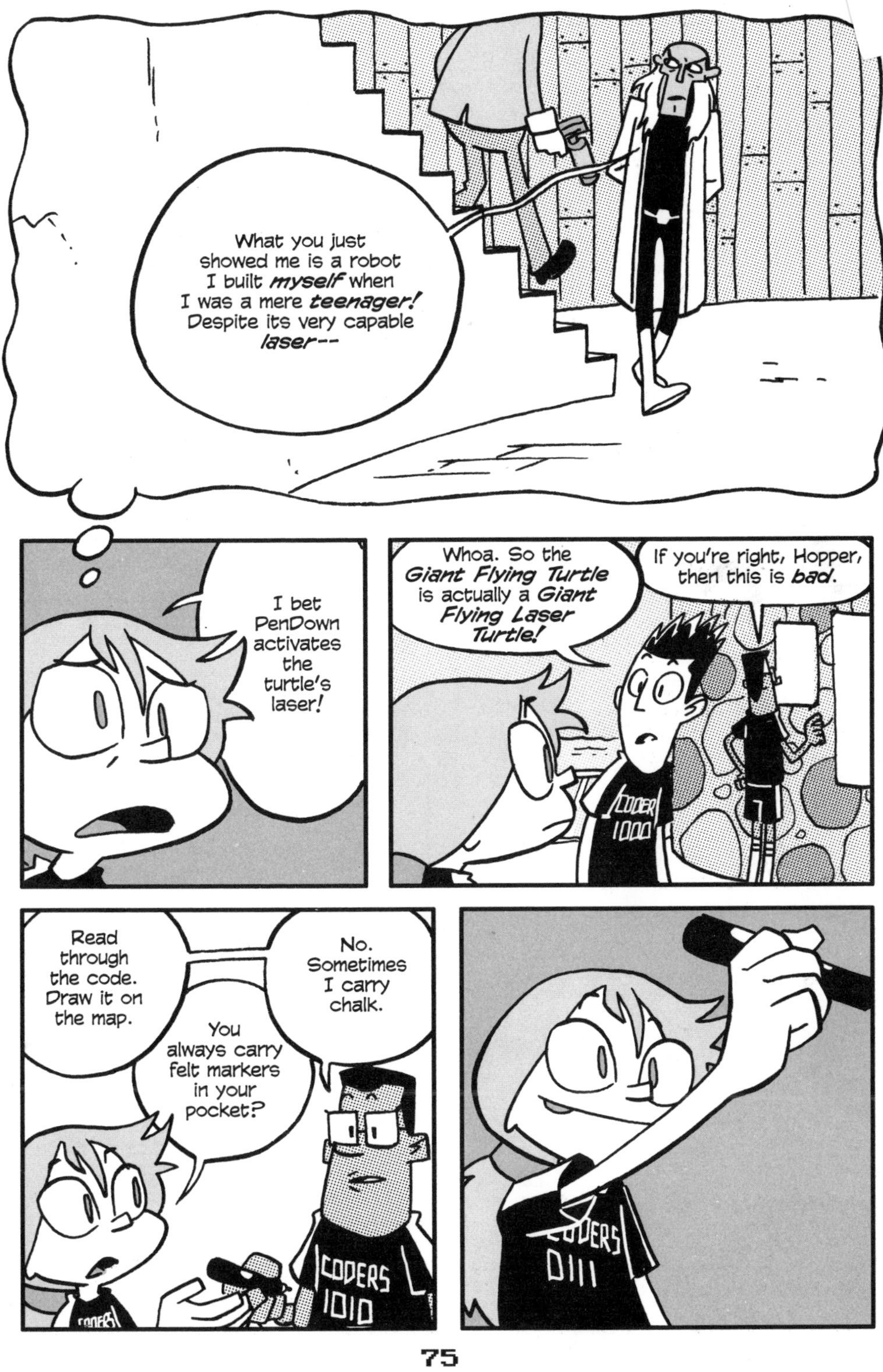
What you just showed me is a robot I built *myself* when I was a mere *teenager!* Despite its very capable *laser--*
I bet PenDown activates the turtle's laser!
Whoa. So the *Giant Flying Turtle* is actually a *Giant Flying Laser Turtle!*
If you're right, Hopper, then this is *bad*.
CODER 1000
Read through the code. Draw it on the map.
You always carry felt markers in your pocket?
No. Sometimes I carry chalk.
CODERS 1010
CODERS 0111

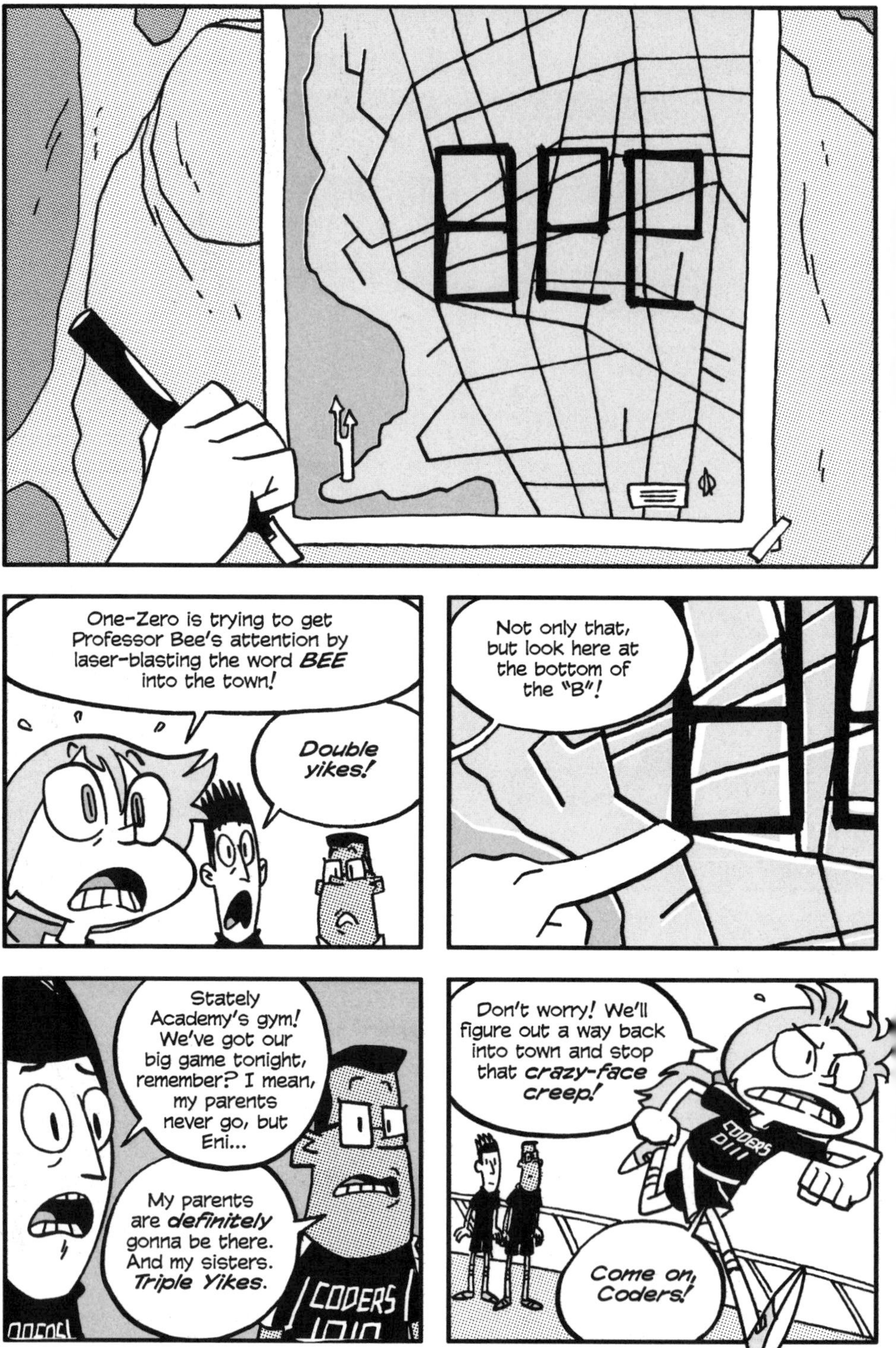
BEE
One-Zero is trying to get Professor Bee's attention by laser-blasting the word BEE into the town!
Double yikes!
Not only that, but look here at the bottom of the "B"!
Stately Academy's gym! We've got our big game tonight, remember? I mean, my parents never go, but Eni...
My parents are definitely gonna be there. And my sisters. Triple Yikes.
CODERS
Don't worry! We'll figure out a way back into town and stop that crazy-face creep!
CODERS
Come on, Coders!

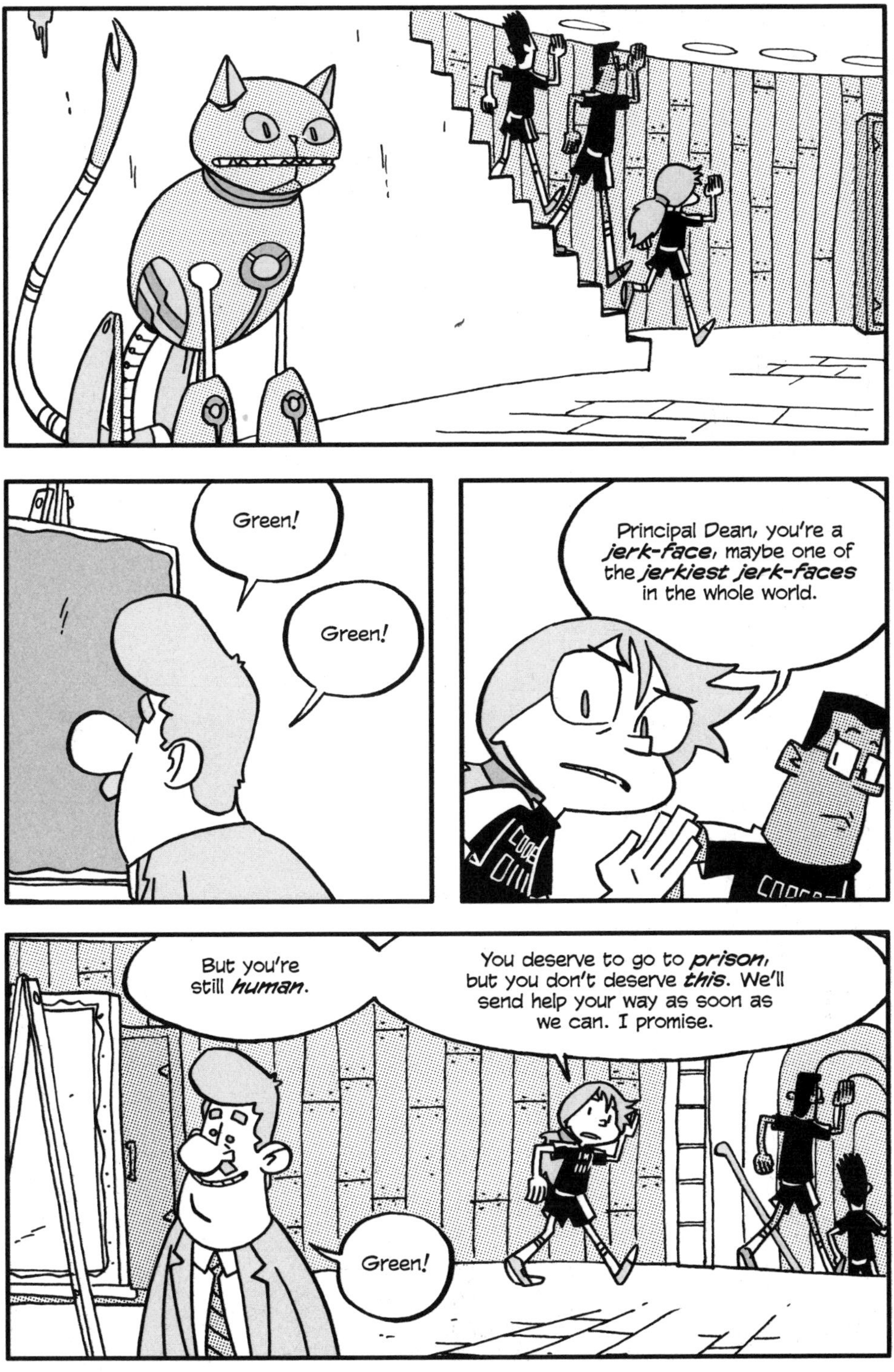

Green!
Green!
Principal Dean, you're a *jerk-face*, maybe one of the *jerkiest jerk-faces* in the whole world.
But you're still *human*.
You deserve to go to *prison*, but you don't deserve *this*. We'll send help your way as soon as we can. I promise.
Green!

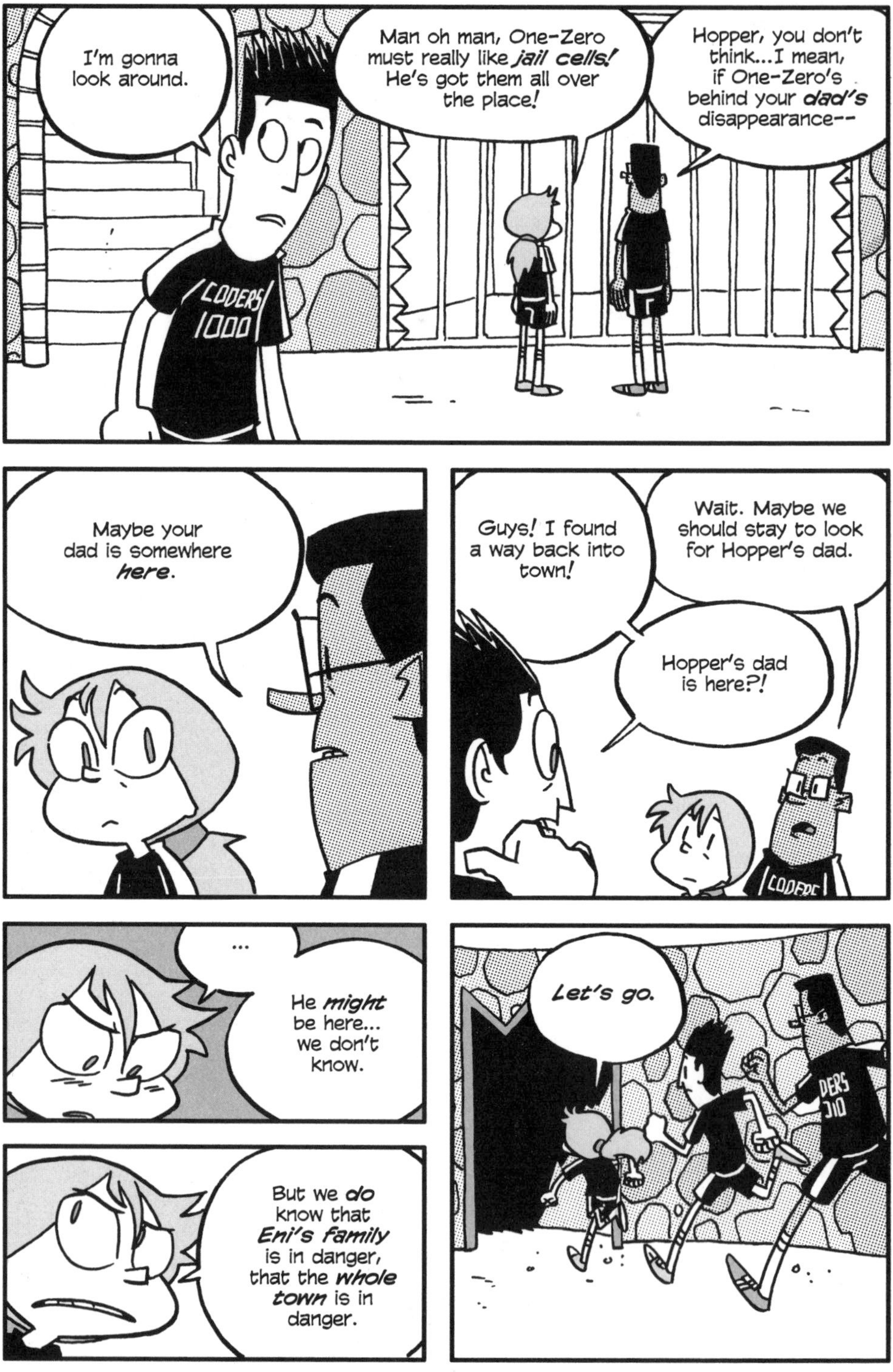
I'm gonna look around.
Man oh man, One-Zero must really like *jail cells!* He's got them all over the place!
Hopper, you don't think...I mean, if One-Zero's behind your *dad's* disappearance--
CODERS 1000
Maybe your dad is somewhere *here*.
Guys! I found a way back into town!
Wait. Maybe we should stay to look for Hopper's dad.
Hopper's dad is here?!
...
He *might* be here... we don't know.
But we *do* know that *Eni's family* is in danger, that the *whole town* is in danger.
Let's go.

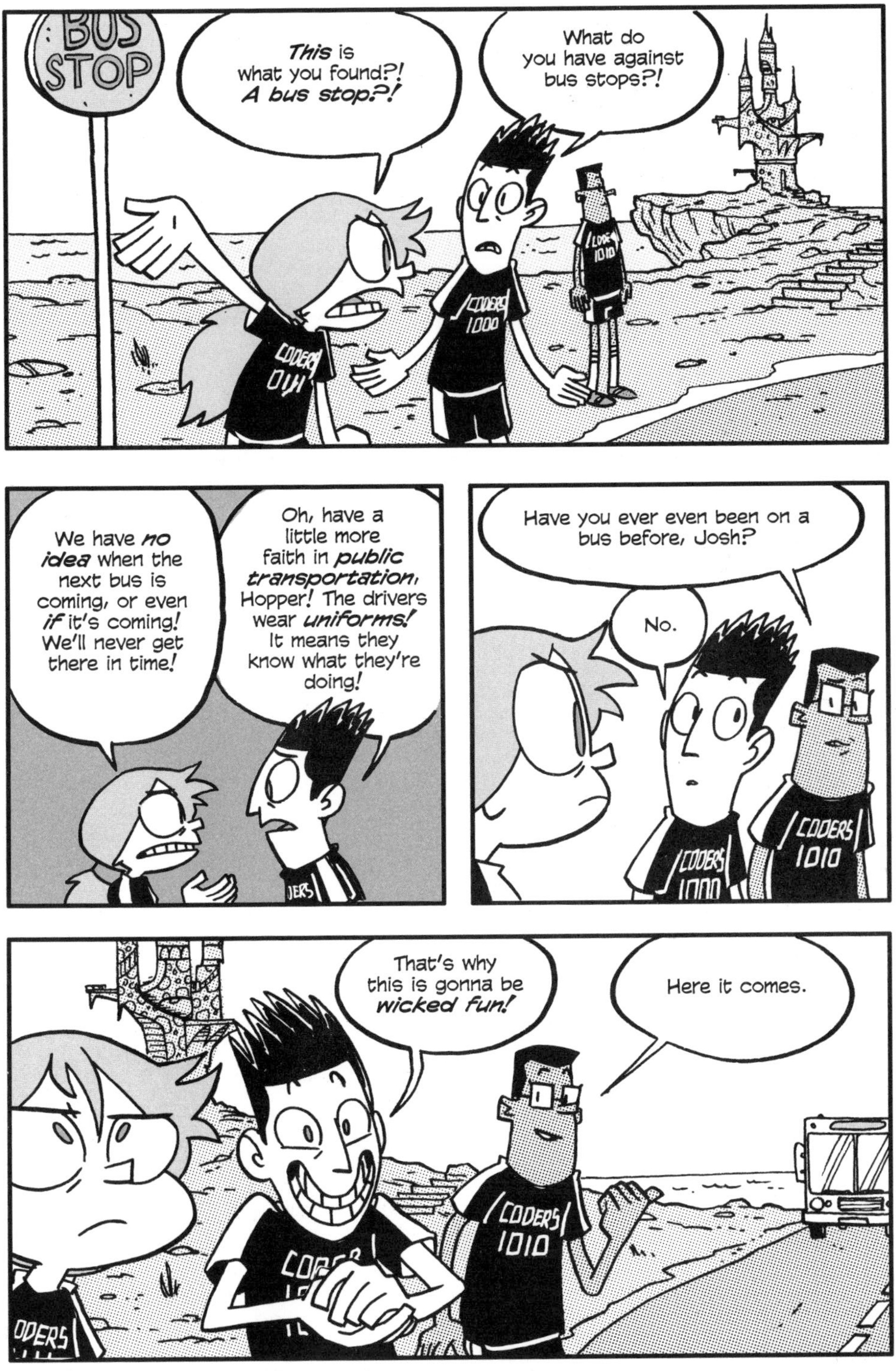
BUS STOP
This is what you found?! *A bus stop?!*
What do you have against bus stops?!
CODERS 1010
We have *no idea* when the next bus is coming, or even *if* it's coming! We'll never get there in time!
Oh, have a little more faith in *public transportation*, Hopper! The drivers wear *uniforms!* It means they know what they're doing!
Have you ever even been on a bus before, Josh?
No.
CODERS 1000
CODERS 1010
That's why this is gonna be *wicked fun!*
Here it comes.
CODERS 1010

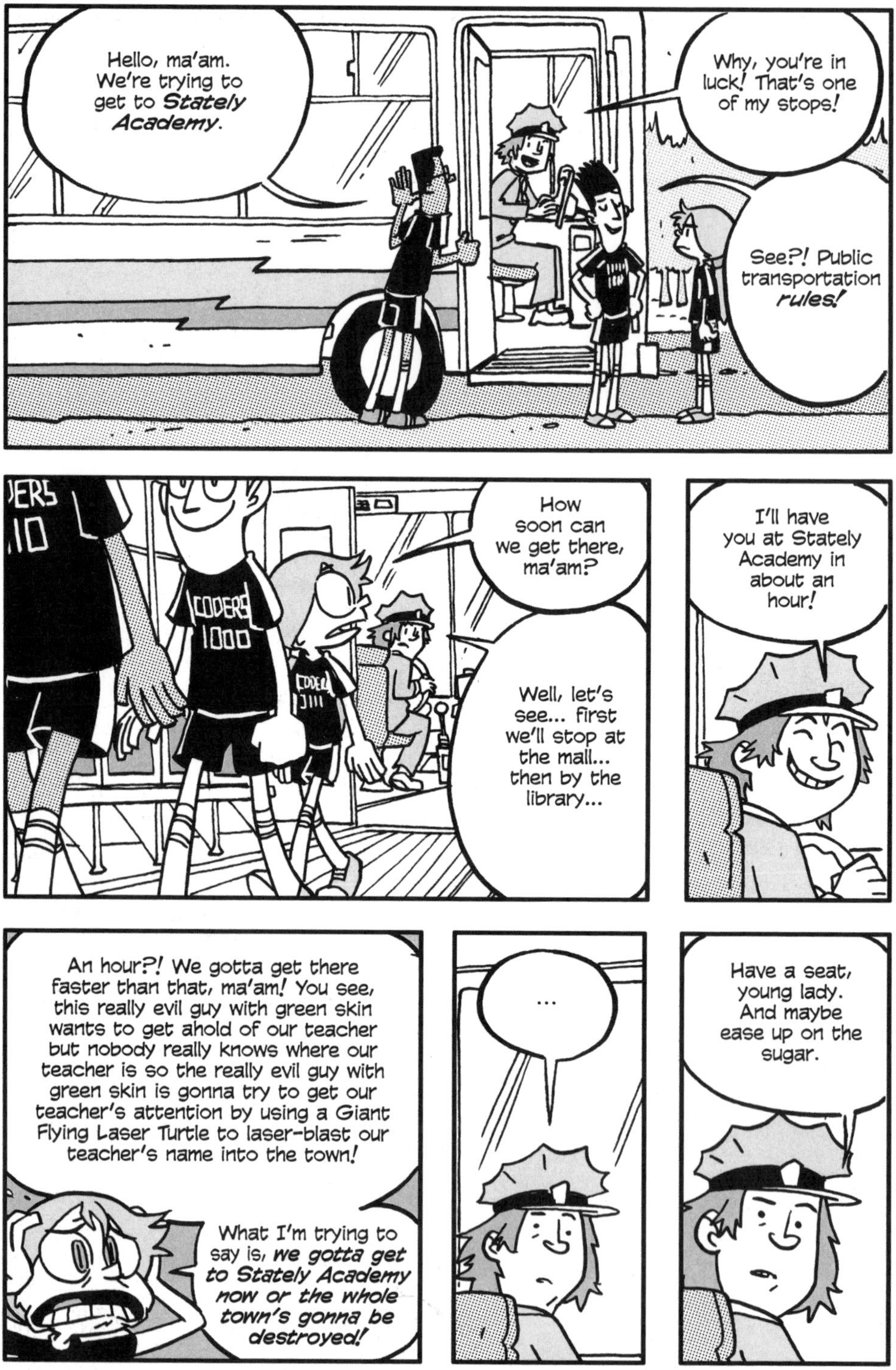
Hello, ma'am. We're trying to get to *Stately Academy*.
Why, you're in luck! That's one of my stops!
See?! Public transportation *rules!*
How soon can we get there, ma'am?
Well, let's see... first we'll stop at the mall... then by the library...
CODERS 1000
I'll have you at Stately Academy in about an hour!
An hour?! We gotta get there faster than that, ma'am! You see, this really evil guy with green skin wants to get ahold of our teacher but nobody really knows where our teacher is so the really evil guy with green skin is gonna try to get our teacher's attention by using a Giant Flying Laser Turtle to laser-blast our teacher's name into the town!
What I'm trying to say is, ***we gotta get to Stately Academy now or the whole town's gonna be destroyed!***
...
Have a seat, young lady. And maybe ease up on the sugar.

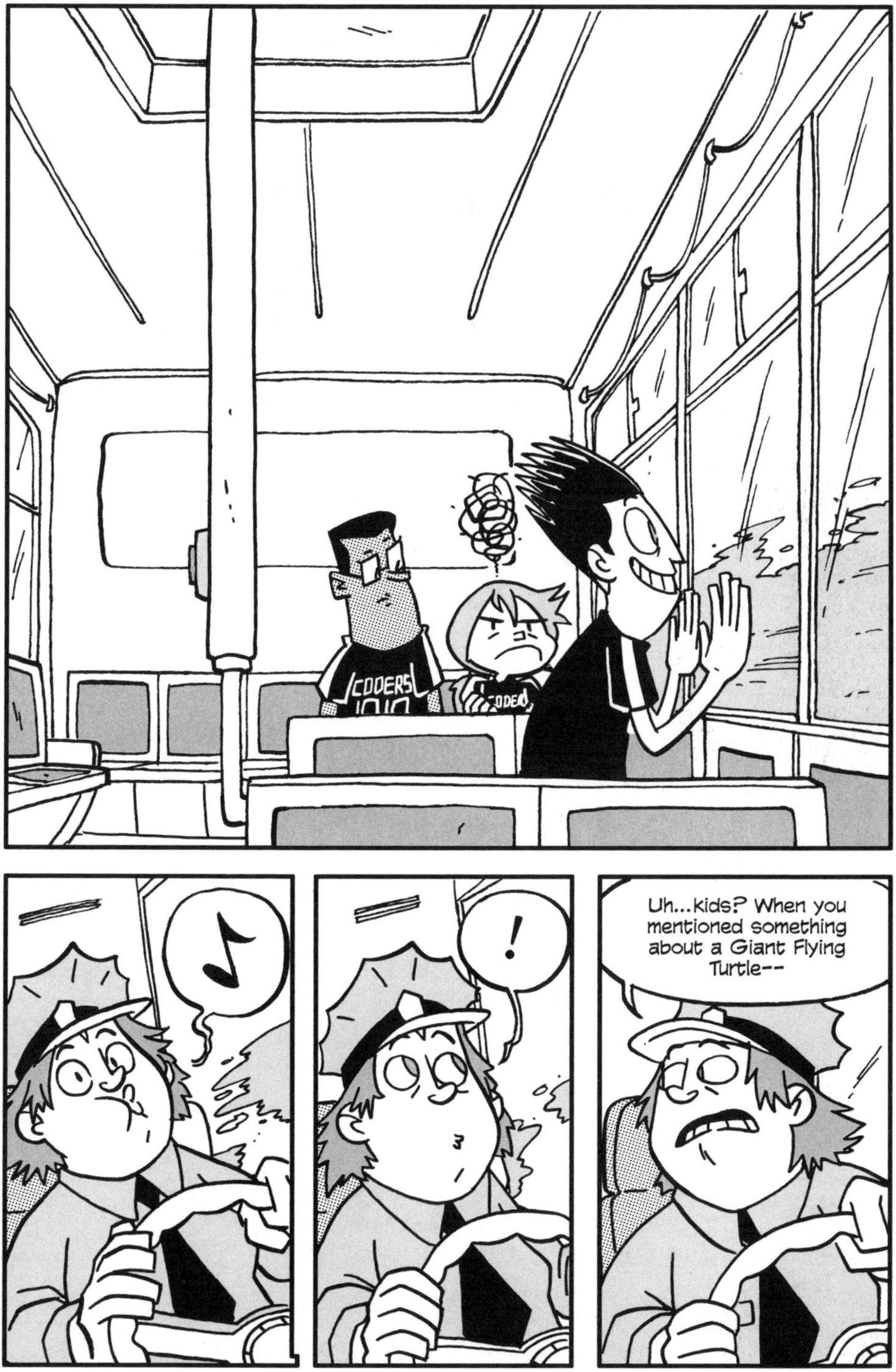
CODERS
!
Uh...kids? When you mentioned something about a Giant Flying Turtle--

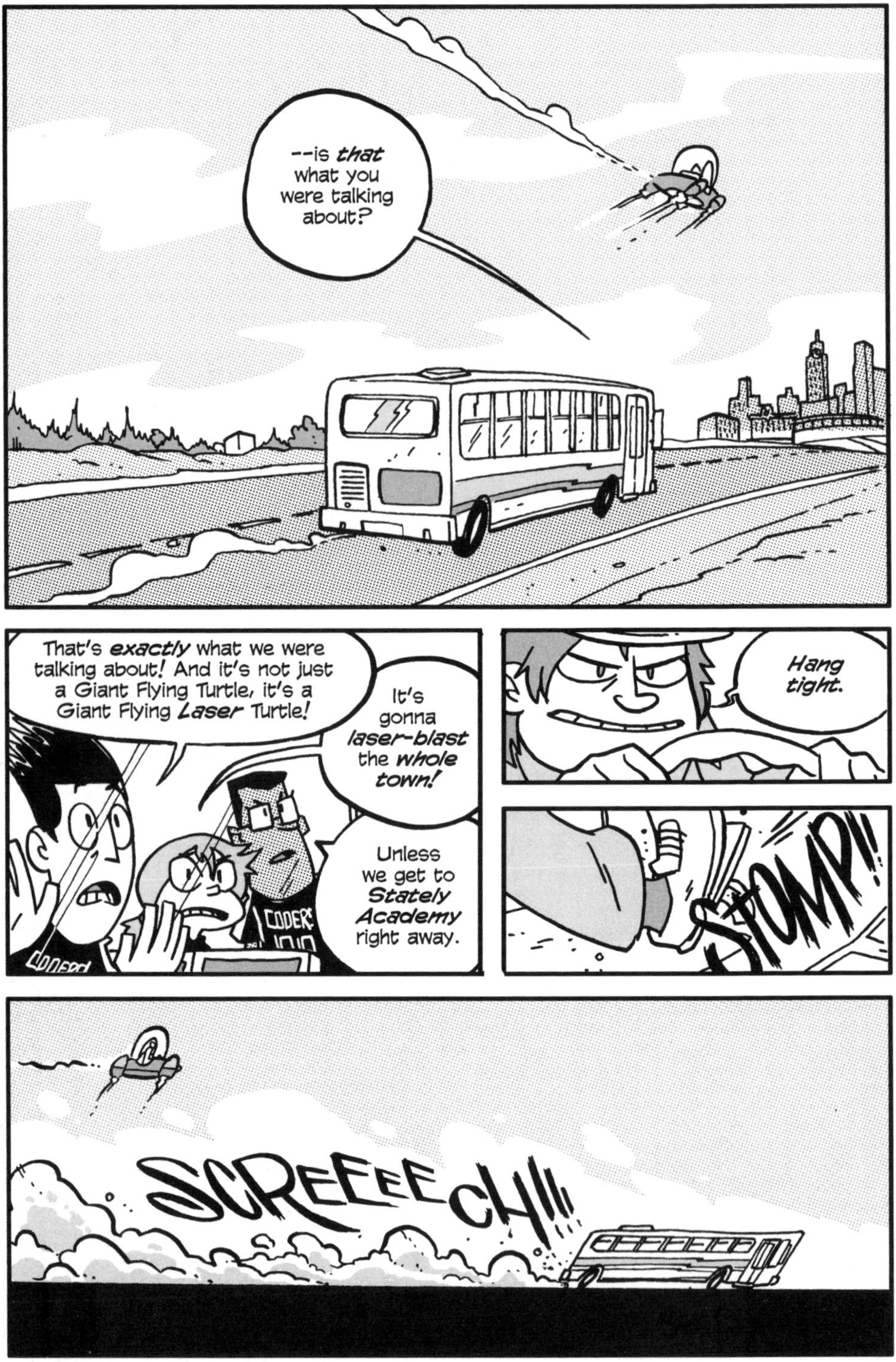

--is *that* what you were talking about?
That's *exactly* what we were talking about! And it's not just a Giant Flying Turtle, it's a Giant Flying *Laser* Turtle!
It's gonna *laser-blast* the *whole town!*
Unless we get to *Stately Academy* right away.
CODERS
Hang tight.
STOMP!!
SCREEEECH!!!

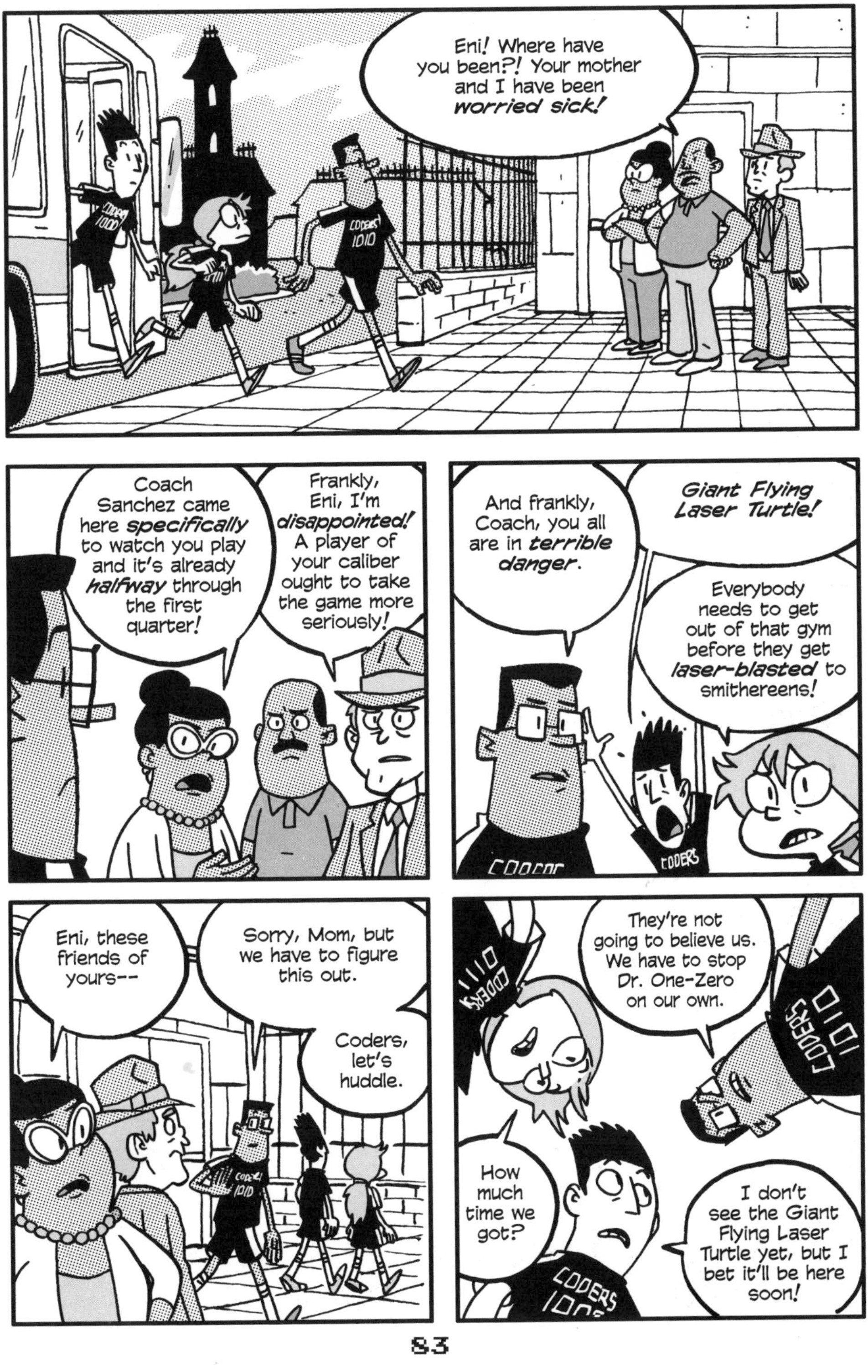
Eni! Where have you been?! Your mother and I have been *worried sick!*
Coach Sanchez came here *specifically* to watch you play and it's already *halfway* through the first quarter!
Frankly, Eni, I'm *disappointed!* A player of your caliber ought to take the game more seriously!
And frankly, Coach, you all are in *terrible danger*.
Giant Flying Laser Turtle!
Everybody needs to get out of that gym before they get *laser-blasted* to smithereens!
Eni, these friends of yours--
Sorry, Mom, but we have to figure this out.
Coders, let's huddle.
They're not going to believe us. We have to stop Dr. One-Zero on our own.
How much time we got?
I don't see the Giant Flying Laser Turtle yet, but I bet it'll be here soon!

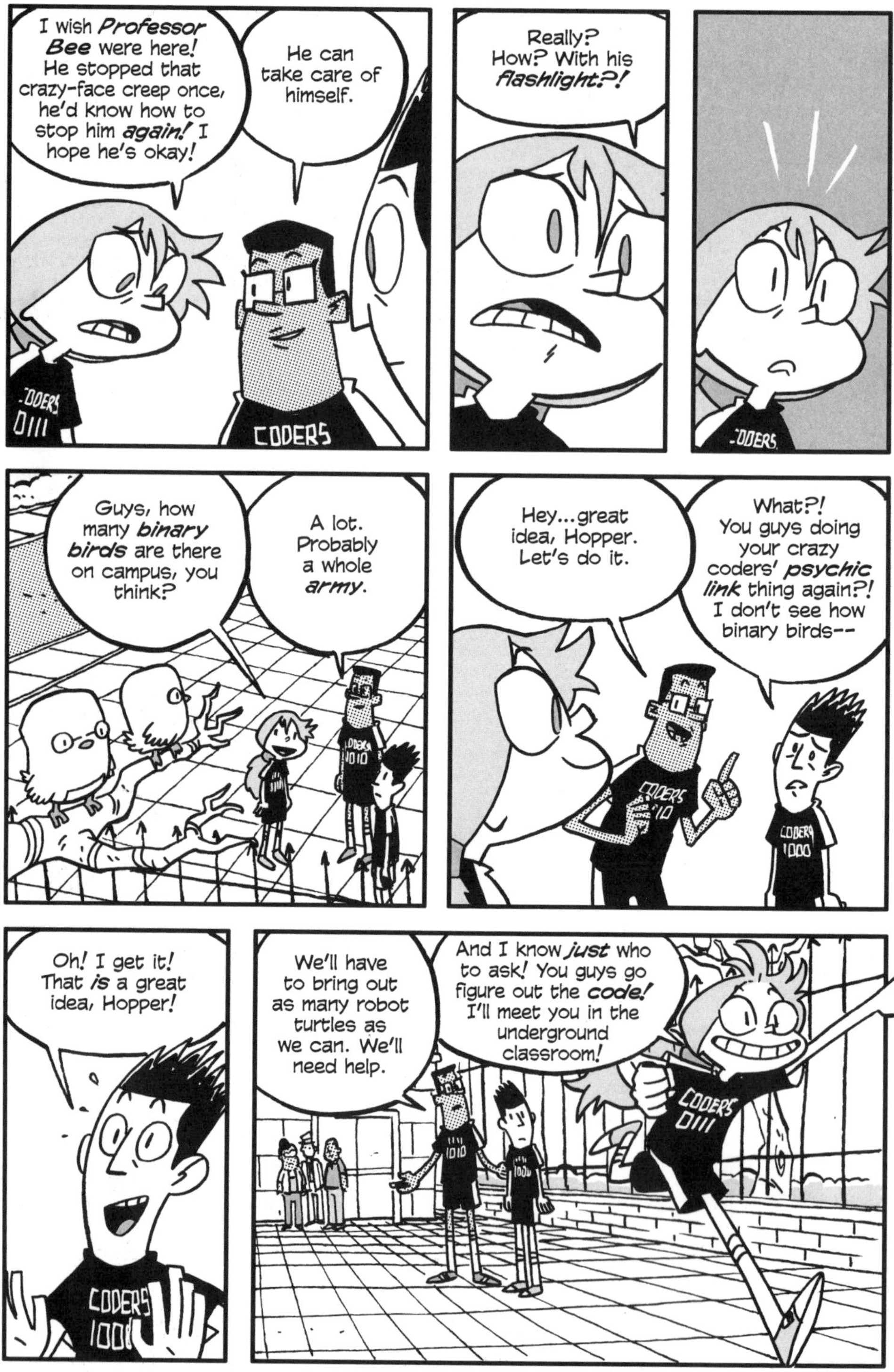
I wish *Professor Bee* were here! He stopped that crazy-face creep once, he'd know how to stop him *again!* I hope he's okay!
He can take care of himself.
CODERS 0111
CODERS
Really? How? With his *flashlight?!*
CODERS
Guys, how many *binary birds* are there on campus, you think?
A lot. Probably a whole *army*.
Hey...great idea, Hopper. Let's do it.
What?! You guys doing your crazy coders' *psychic link* thing again?! I don't see how binary birds--
CODERS
Oh! I get it! That *is* a great idea, Hopper!
We'll have to bring out as many robot turtles as we can. We'll need help.
And I know *just* who to ask! You guys go figure out the *code!* I'll meet you in the underground classroom!
CODERS 0111
1010

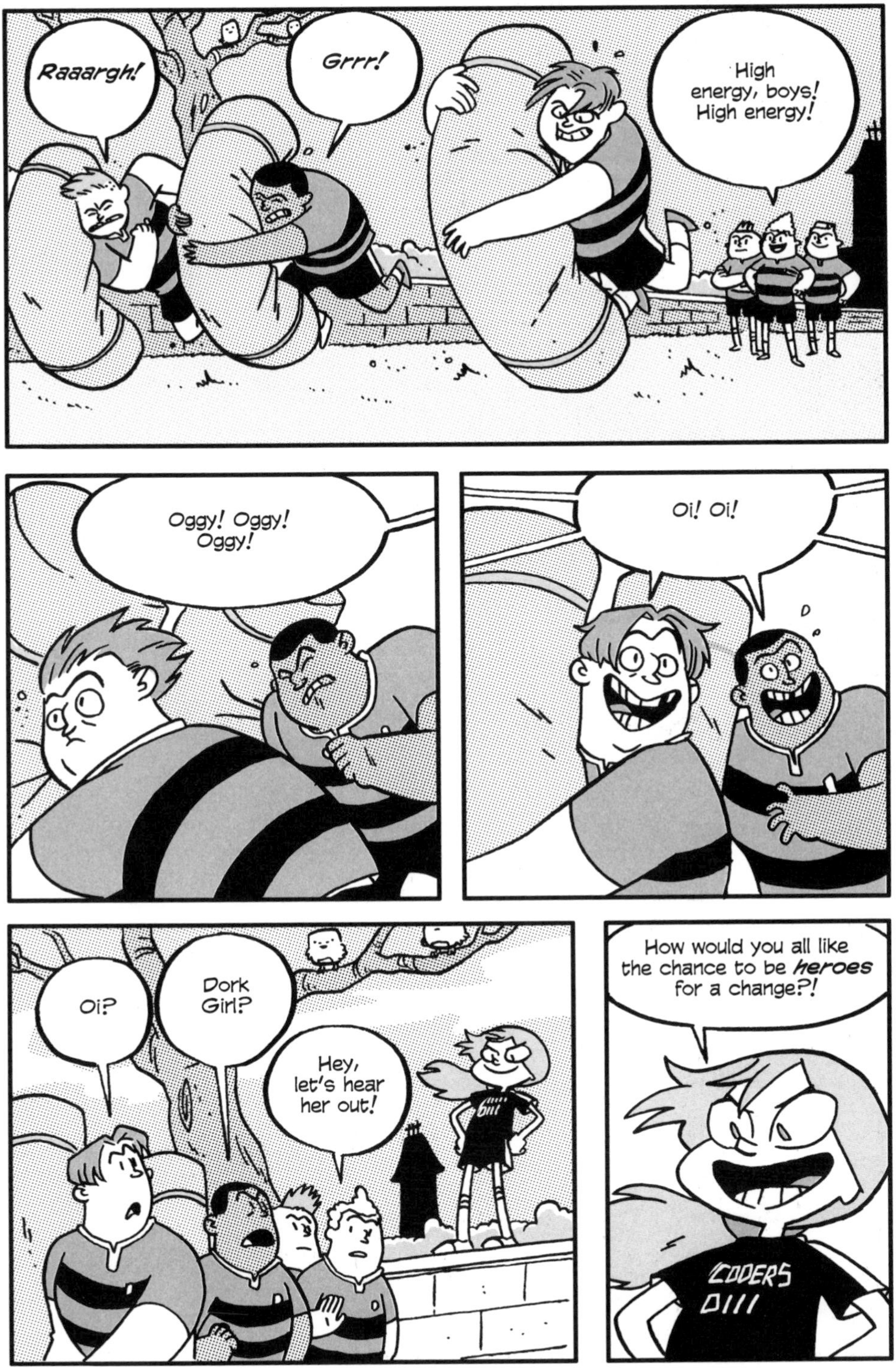
Raaargh!
Grrr!
High energy, boys! High energy!
Oggy! Oggy! Oggy!
Oi! Oi!
Oi?
Dork Girl?
Hey, let's hear her out!
How would you all like the chance to be *heroes* for a change?!
CODERS
DIII

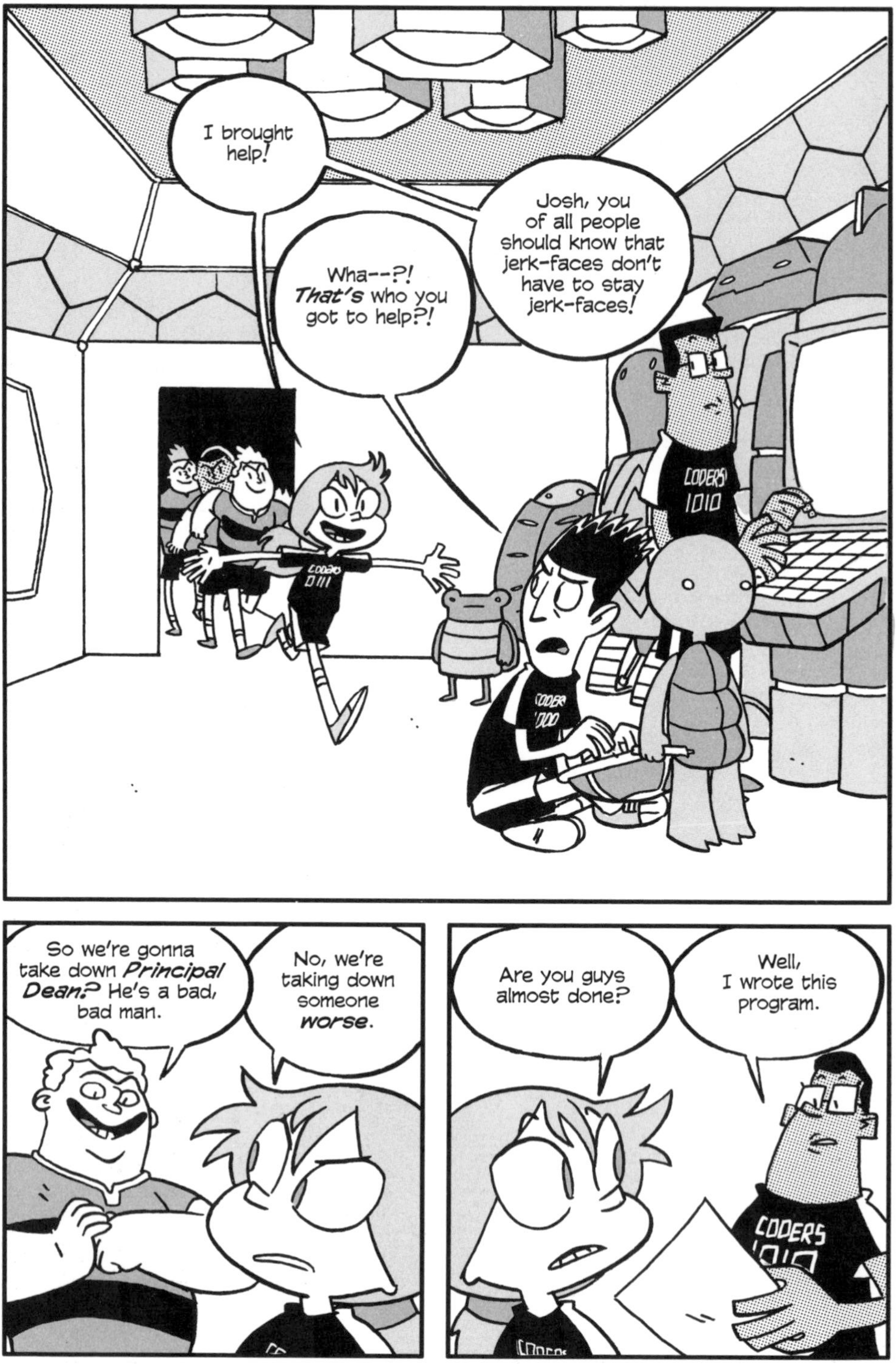

I brought help!
Wha--?! *That's* who you got to help?!
Josh, you of all people should know that jerk-faces don't have to stay jerk-faces!
CODERS 1010
So we're gonna take down *Principal Dean?* He's a bad, bad man.
No, we're taking down someone *worse*.
Are you guys almost done?
Well, I wrote this program.
CODERS 1010

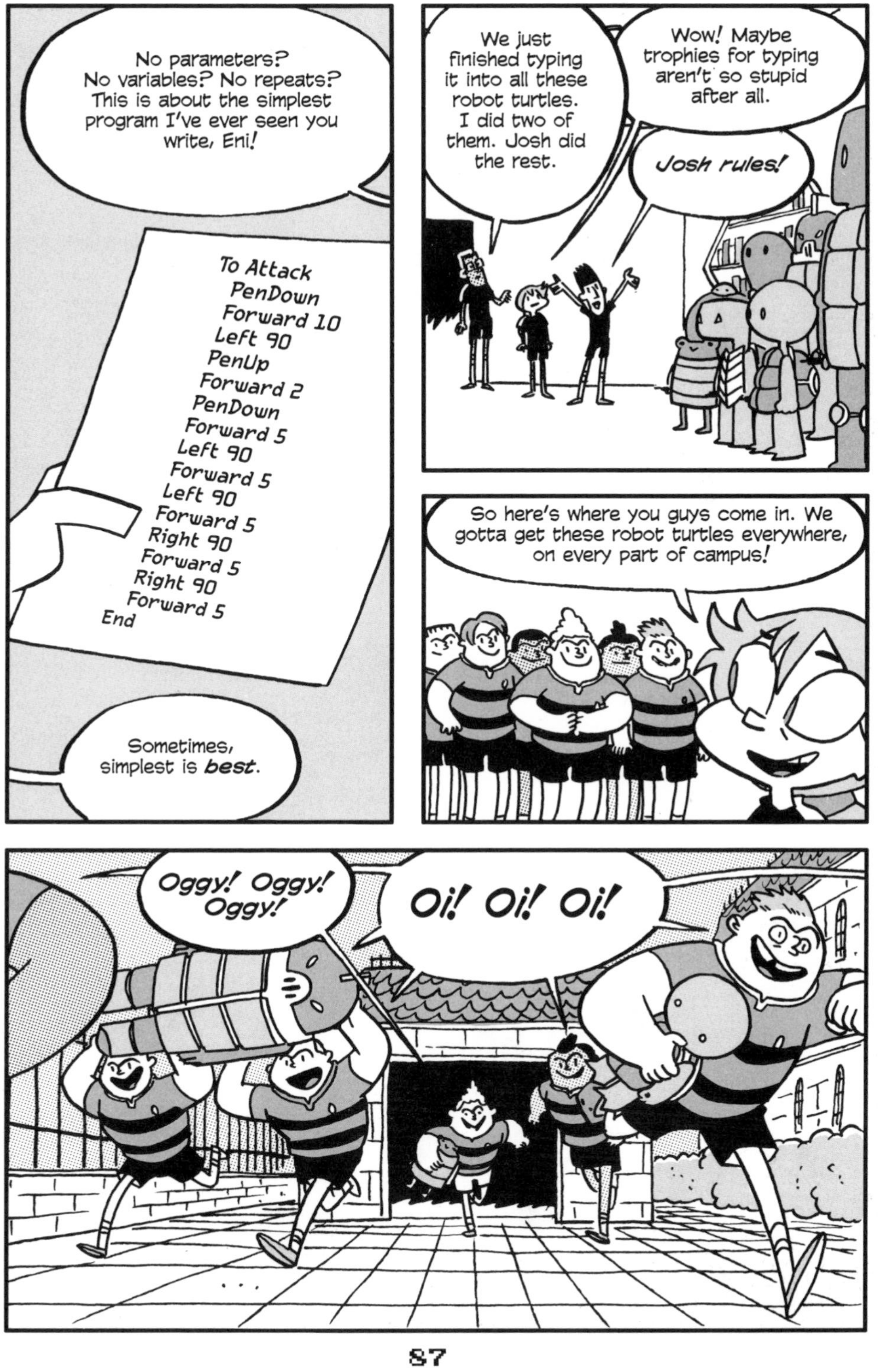
No parameters? No variables? No repeats? This is about the simplest program I've ever seen you write, Eni!
To Attack
PenDown
Forward 10
Left 90
PenUp
Forward 2
PenDown
Forward 5
Left 90
Forward 5
Left 90
Forward 5
Right 90
Forward 5
Right 90
Forward 5
End
Sometimes, simplest is *best*.
We just finished typing it into all these robot turtles. I did two of them. Josh did the rest.
Wow! Maybe trophies for typing aren't so stupid after all.
Josh rules!
So here's where you guys come in. We gotta get these robot turtles everywhere, on every part of campus!
Oggy! Oggy! Oggy!
Oi! Oi! Oi!
. . .

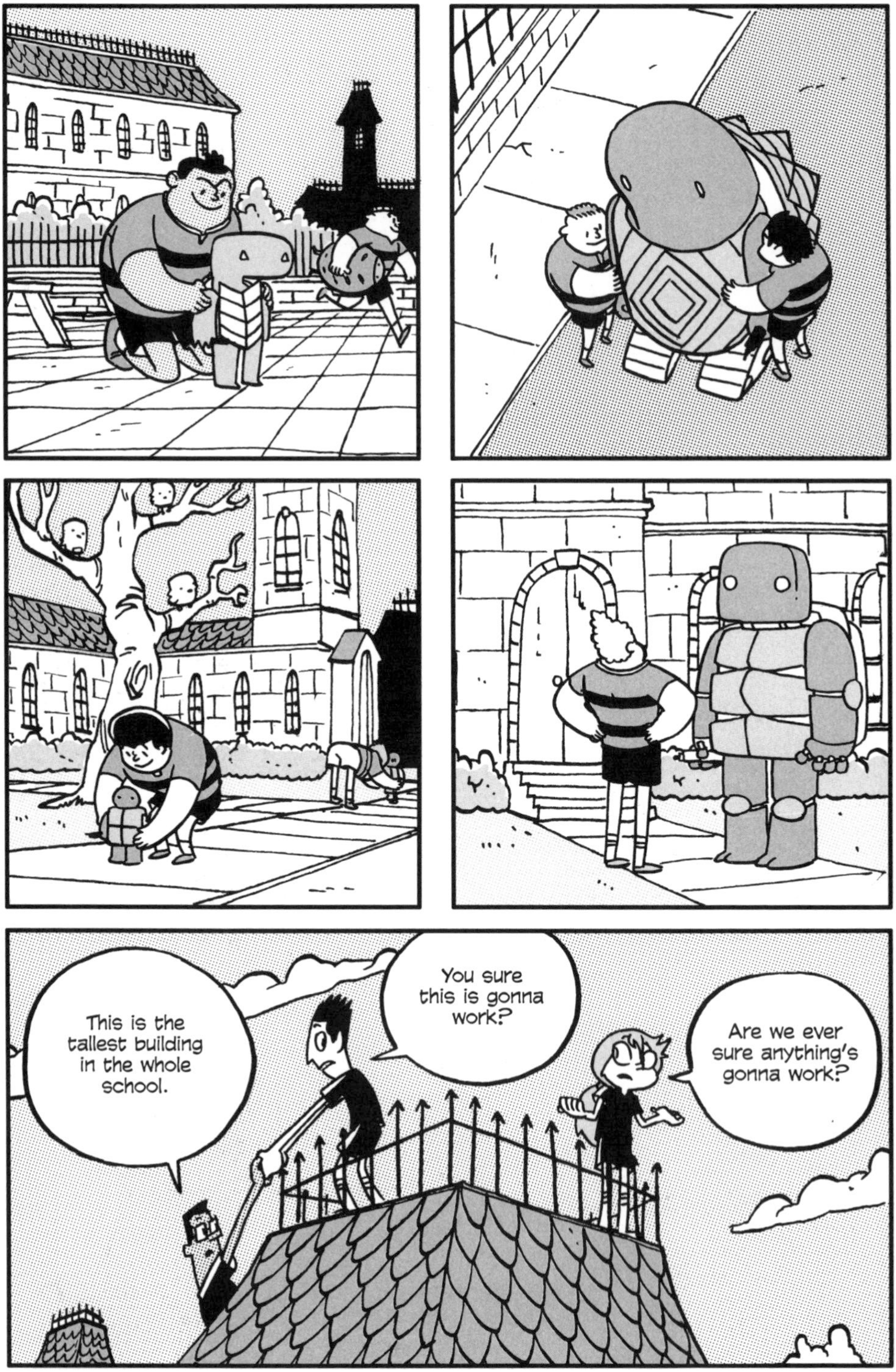
This is the tallest building in the whole school.
You sure this is gonna work?
Are we ever sure anything's gonna work?

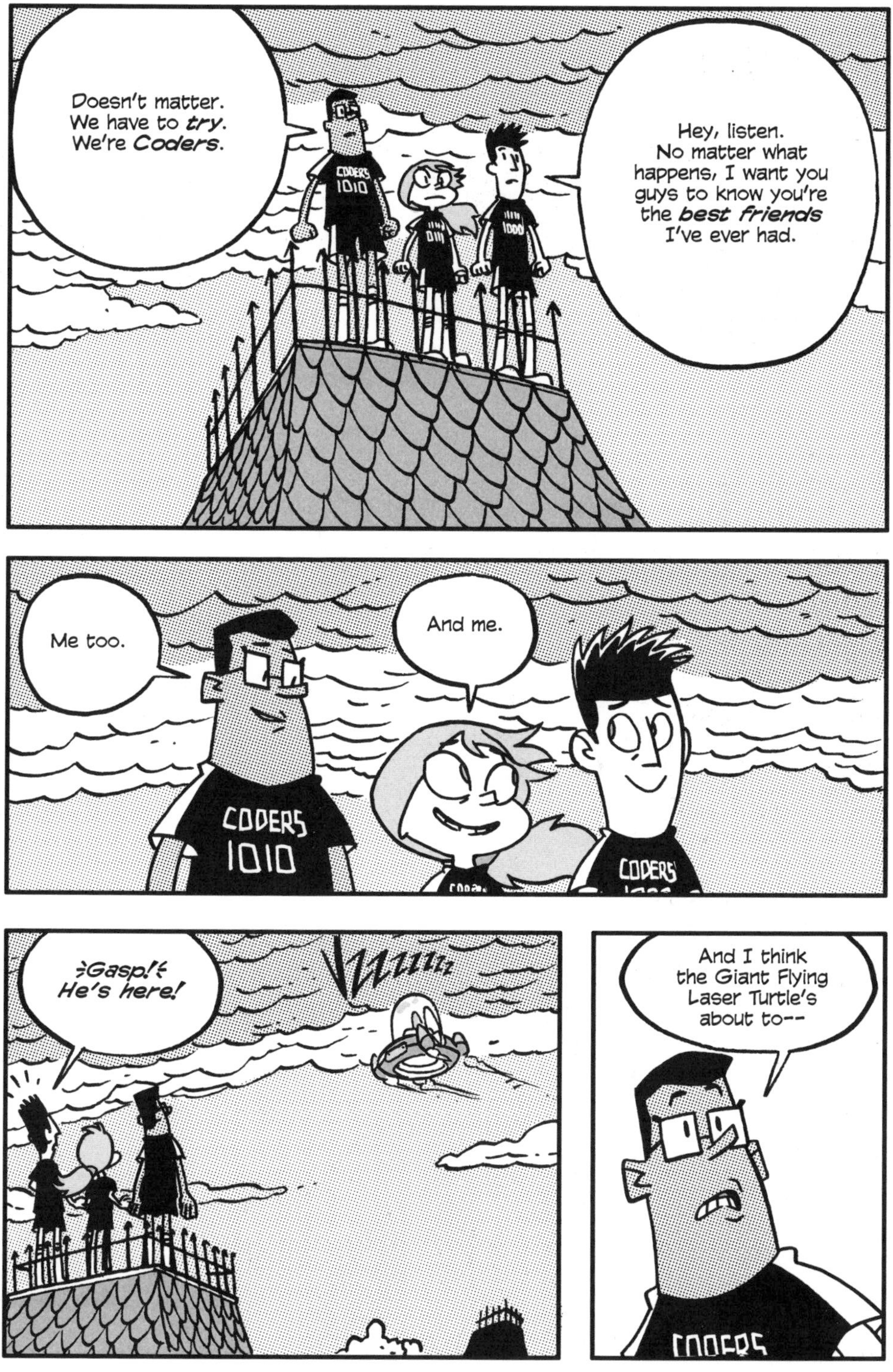
Doesn't matter. We have to *try*. We're *Coders*.
Hey, listen. No matter what happens, I want you guys to know you're the ***best friends*** I've ever had.
CODERS 1010
Me too.
And me.
CODERS 1010
CODERS
Gasp! He's here!
ZZZZZZz
And I think the Giant Flying Laser Turtle's about to--
CODERS

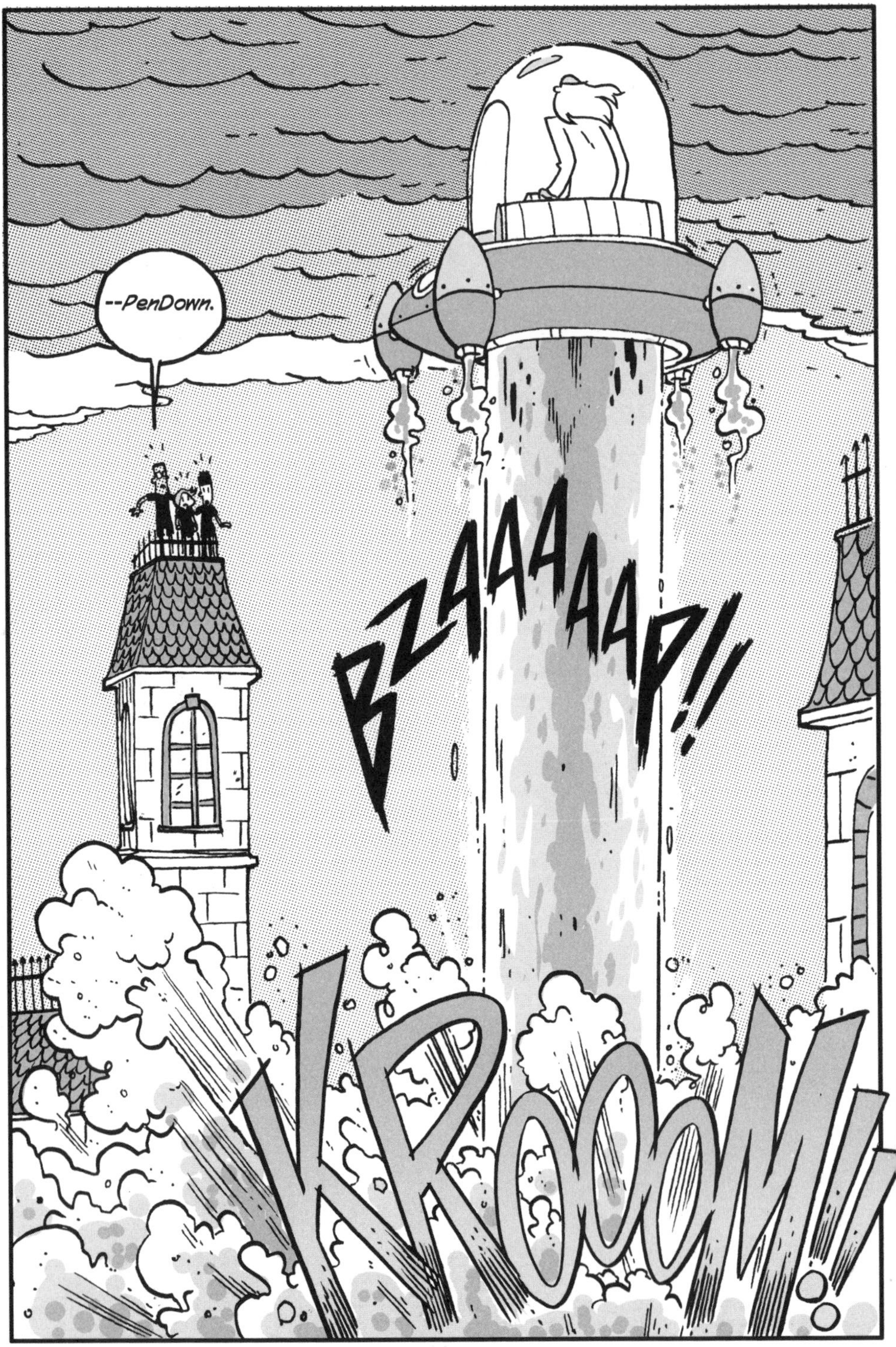
--PenDown.
BZAAAAAP!!
KROOOM!!

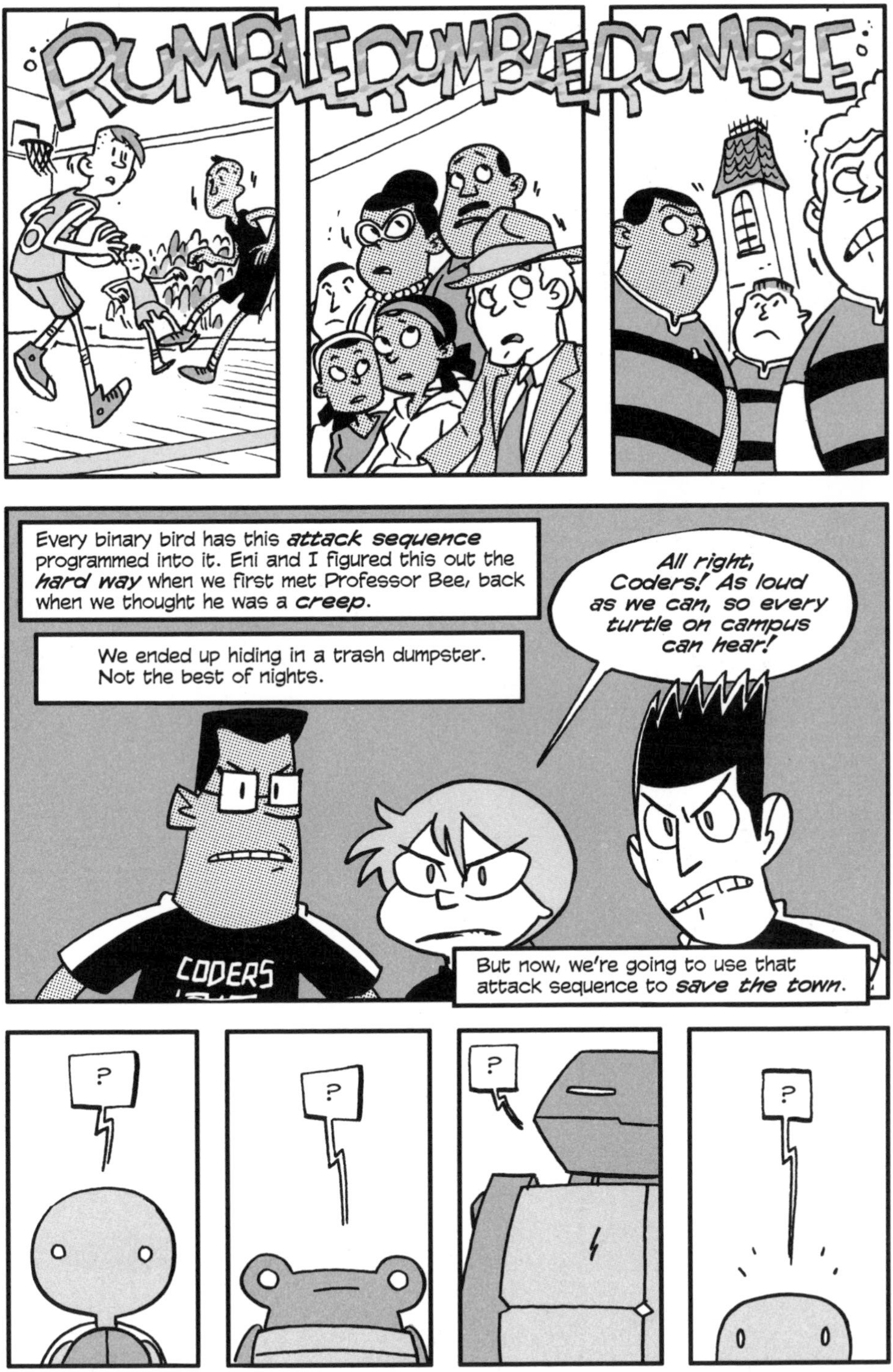
RUMBLE RUMBLE RUMBLE
Every binary bird has this attack sequence programmed into it. Eni and I figured this out the hard way when we first met Professor Bee, back when we thought he was a creep.
We ended up hiding in a trash dumpster. Not the best of nights.
All right, Coders! As loud as we can, so every turtle on campus can hear!
CODERS
But now, we're going to use that attack sequence to save the town.
?
?
?
?

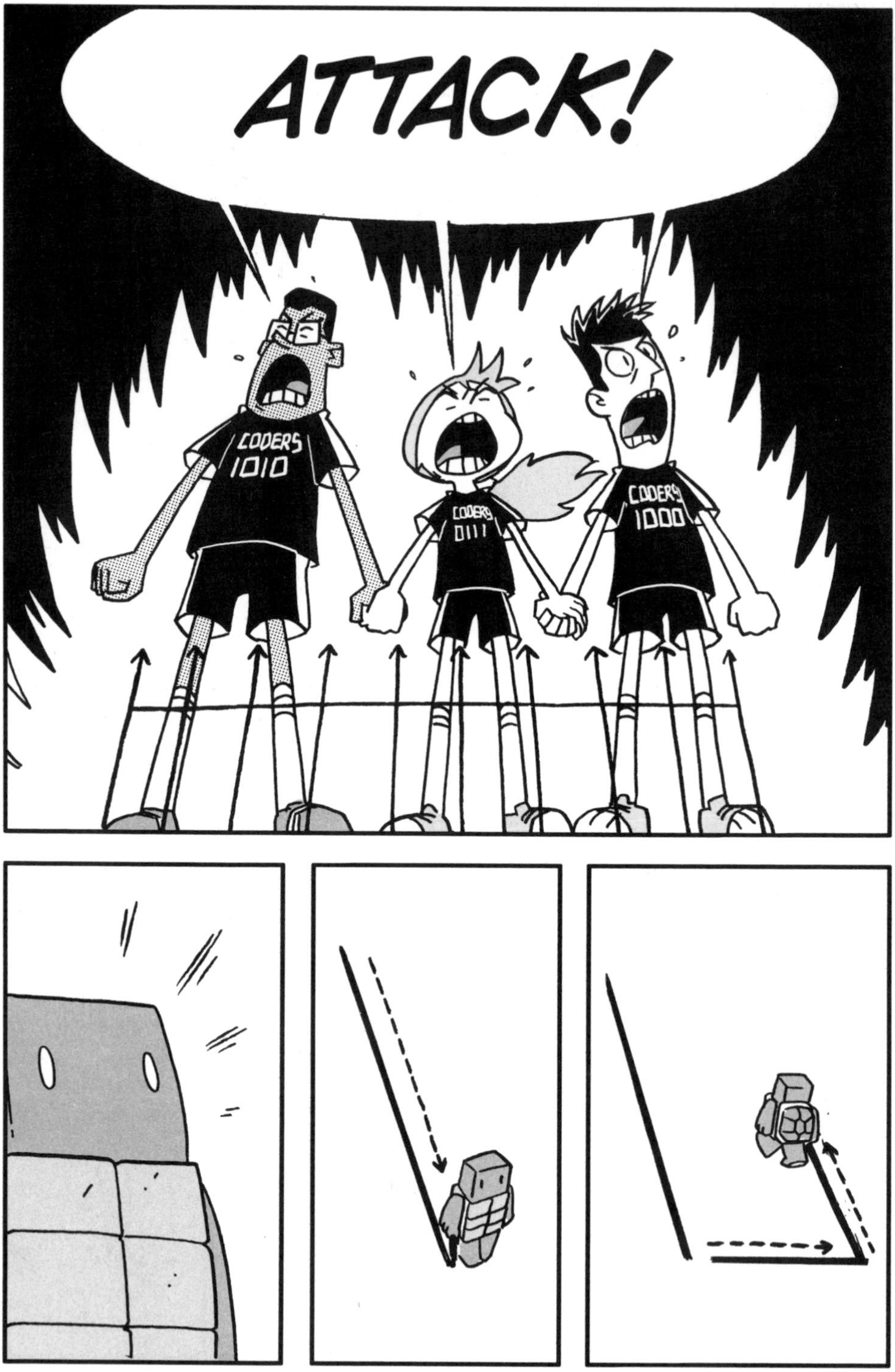
ATTACK!
CODERS 1010
CODERS 0111
CODERS 1000

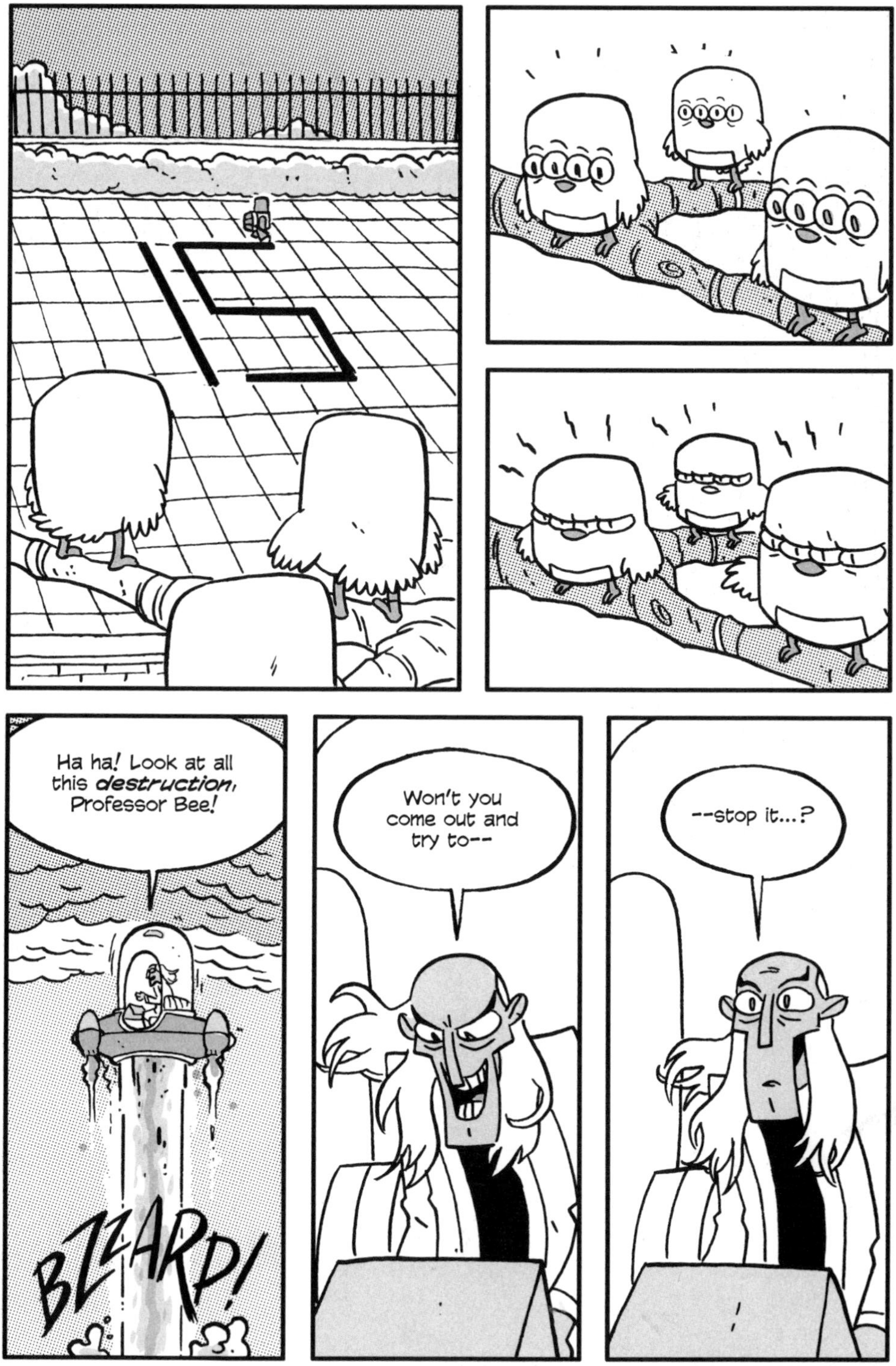
Ha ha! Look at all this *destruction*, Professor Bee!
BZZARD!
Won't you come out and try to--
--stop it...?

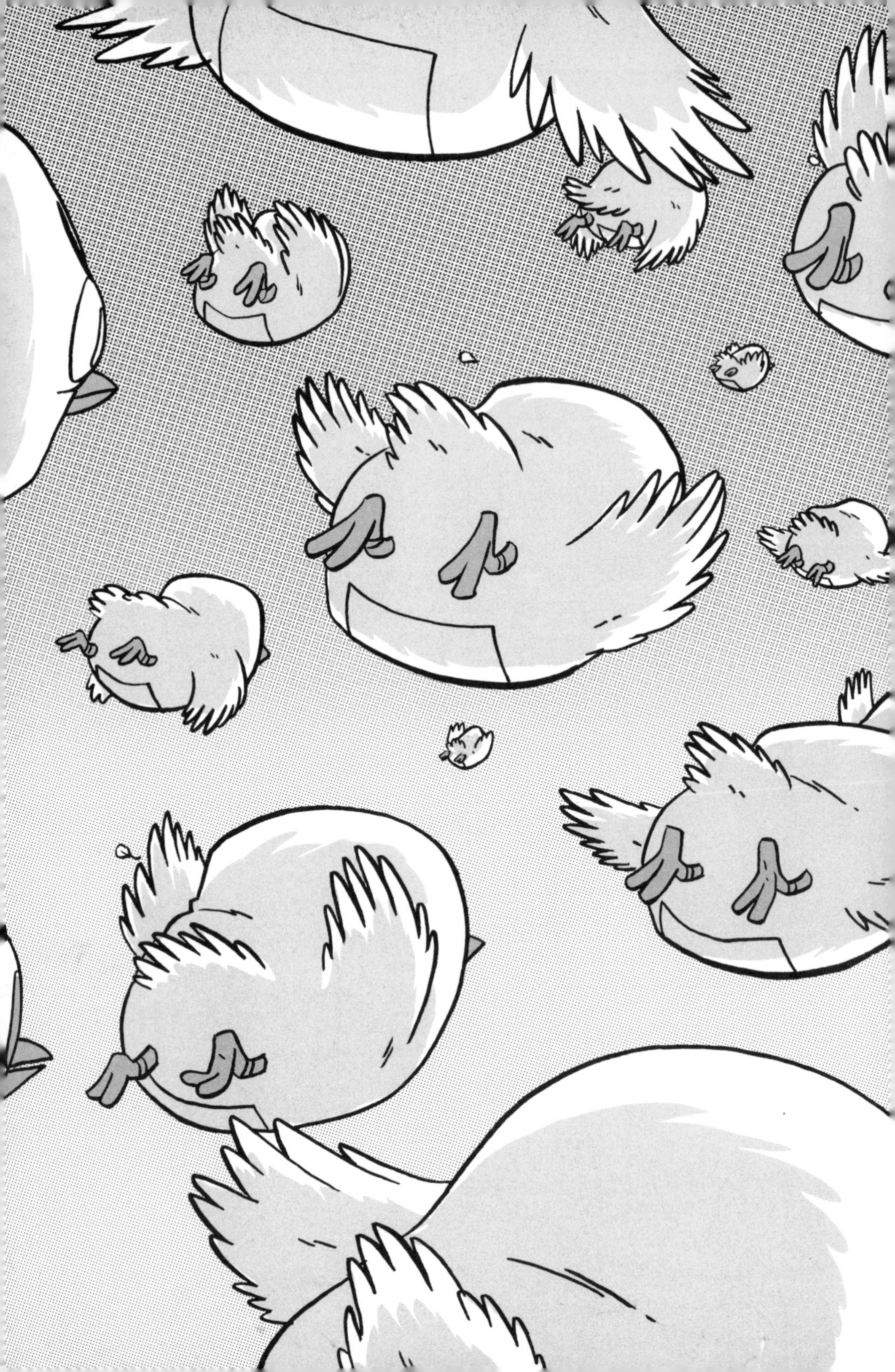

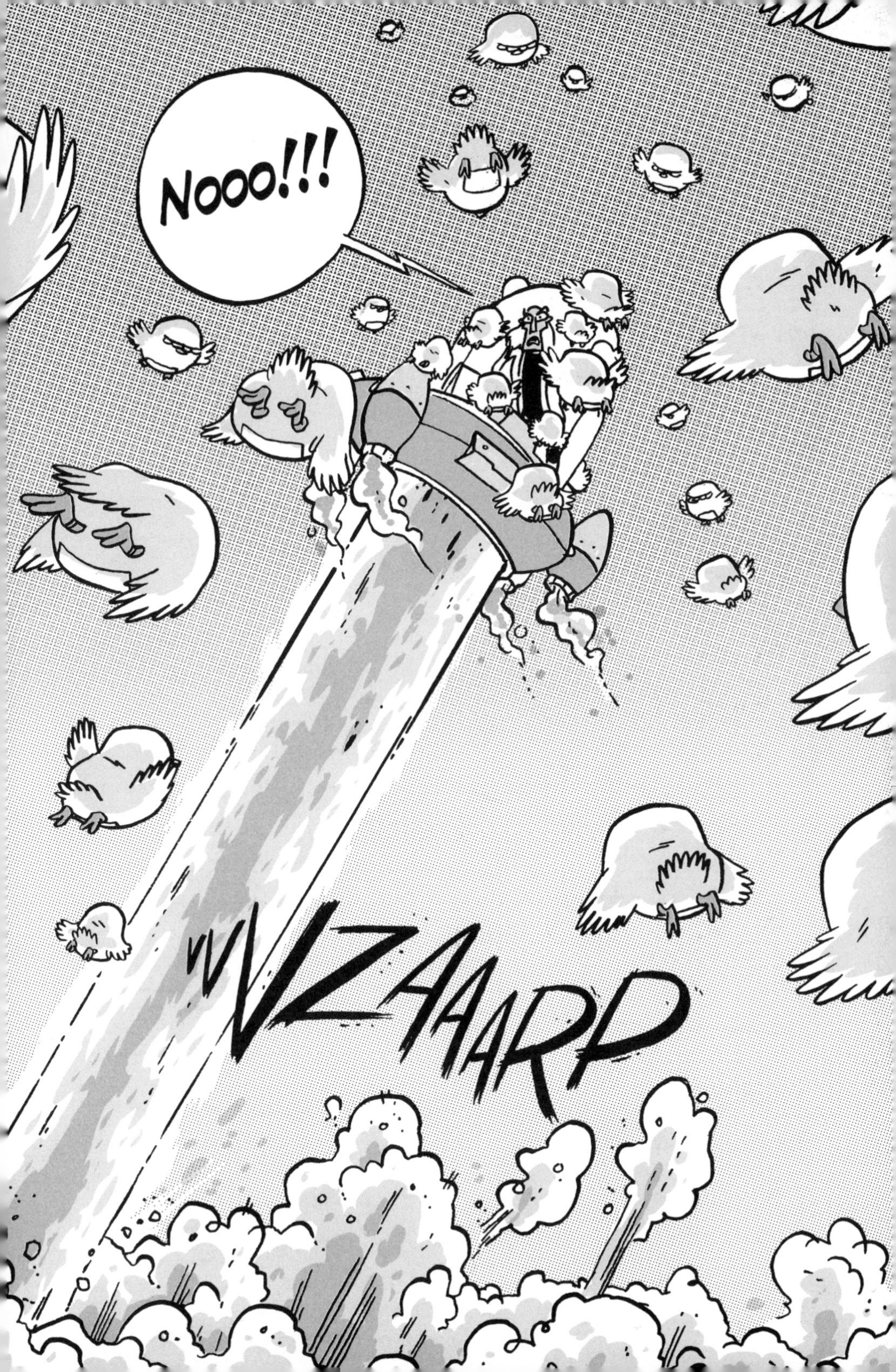
NOOO!!!
VVVZAAARP

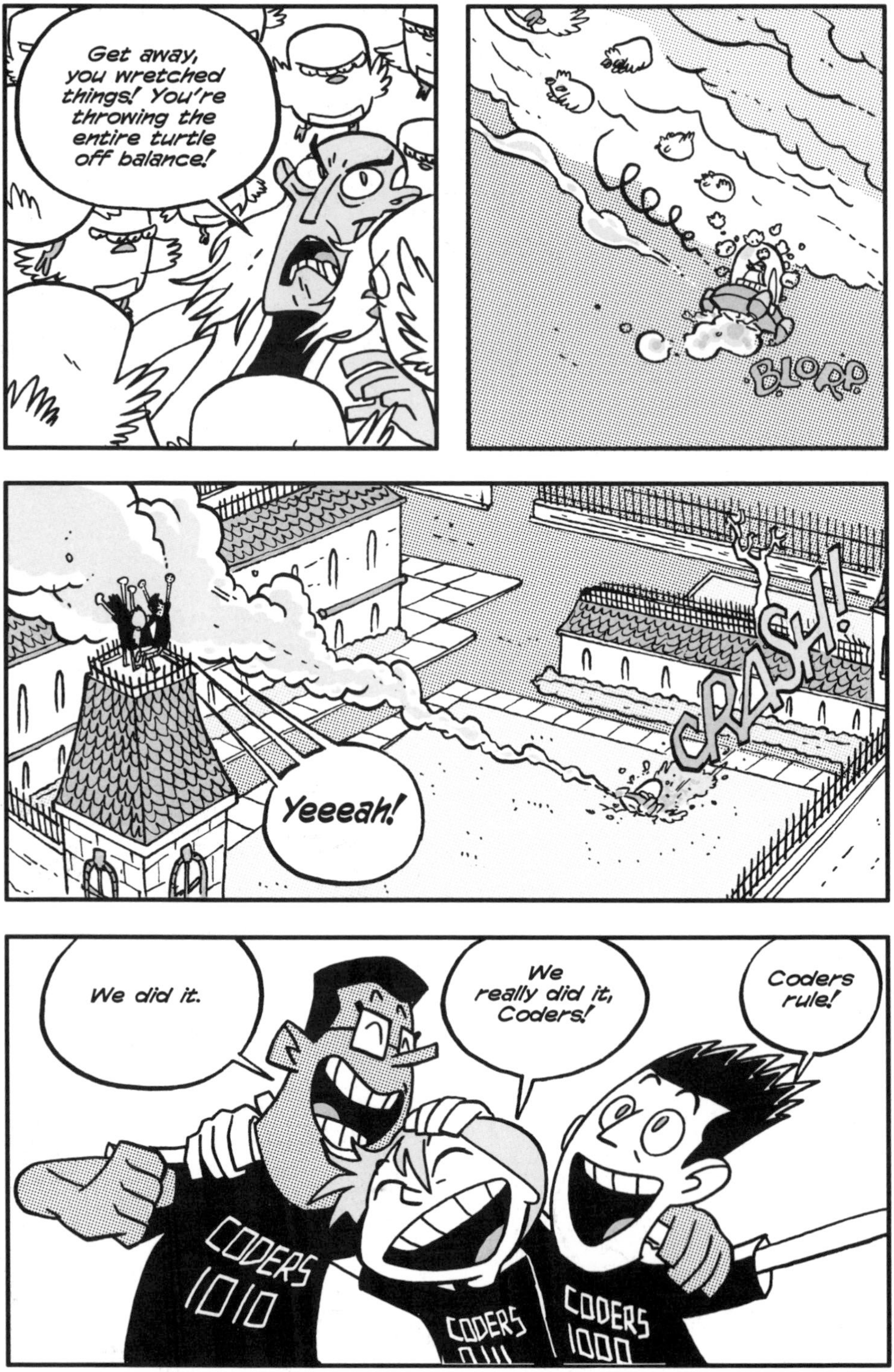
Get away, you wretched things! You're throwing the entire turtle off balance!
BLORP
CRASH!
Yeeeah!
We did it.
We really did it, Coders!
Coders rule!
CODERS 1010
CODERS
CODERS 1000

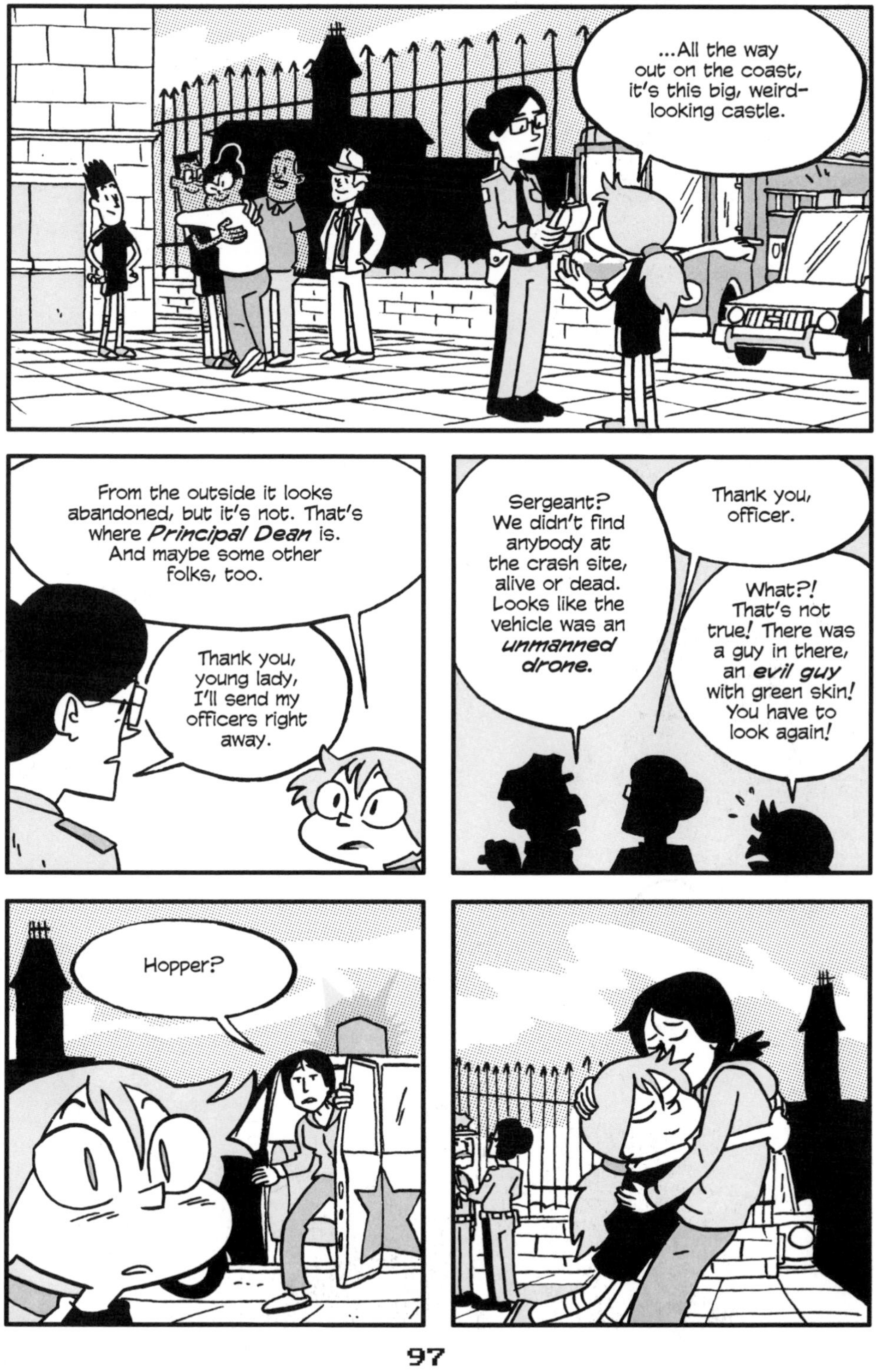
...All the way out on the coast, it's this big, weird-looking castle.
From the outside it looks abandoned, but it's not. That's where *Principal Dean* is. And maybe some other folks, too.
Thank you, young lady, I'll send my officers right away.
Sergeant? We didn't find anybody at the crash site, alive or dead. Looks like the vehicle was an *unmanned drone.*
Thank you, officer.
What?! That's not true! There was a guy in there, an *evil guy* with green skin! You have to look again!
Hopper?

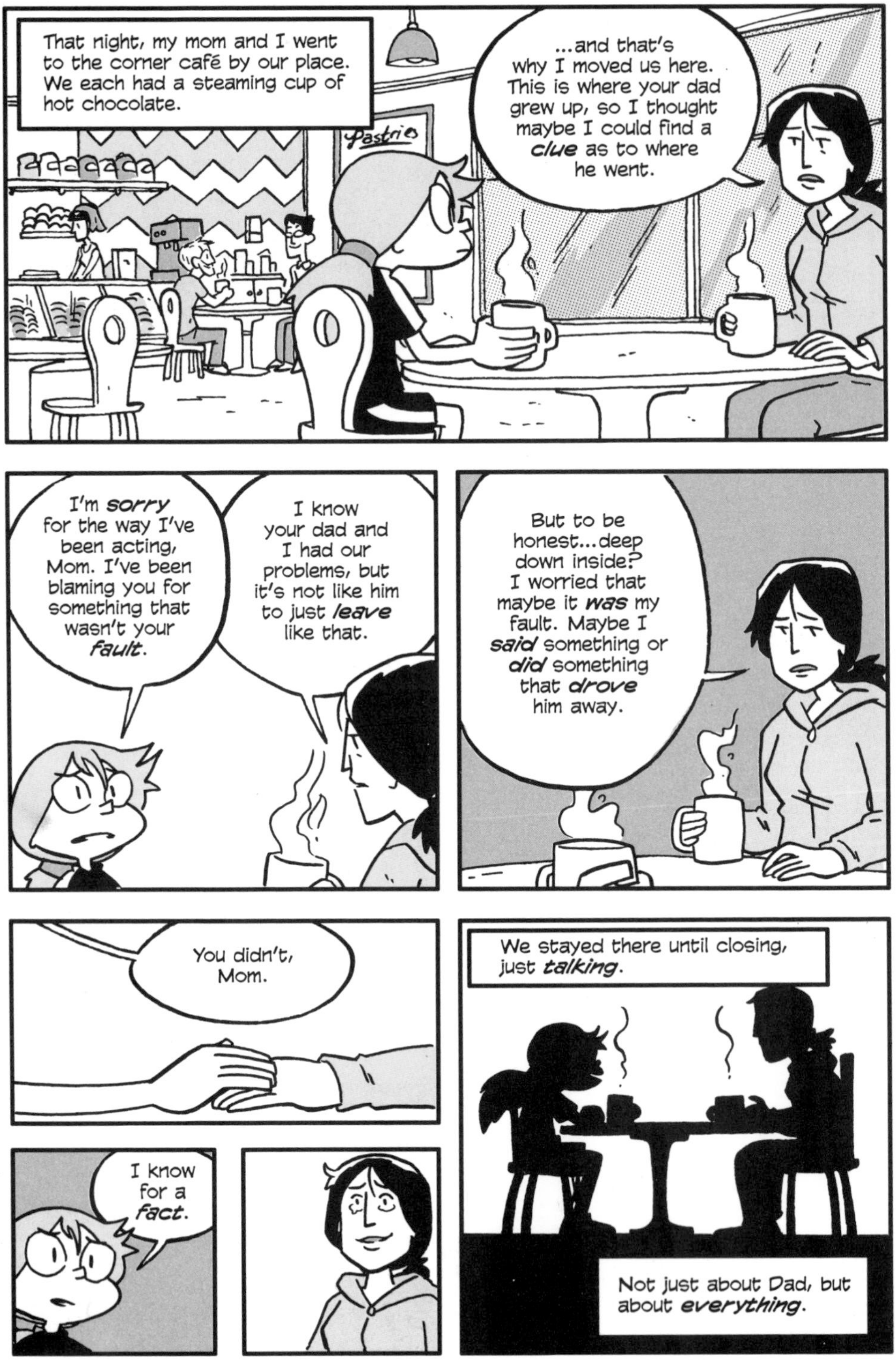
That night, my mom and I went to the corner café by our place. We each had a steaming cup of hot chocolate.
Pastries
...and that's why I moved us here. This is where your dad grew up, so I thought maybe I could find a *clue* as to where he went.
I'm *sorry* for the way I've been acting, Mom. I've been blaming you for something that wasn't your *fault*.
I know your dad and I had our problems, but it's not like him to just *leave* like that.
But to be honest...deep down inside? I worried that maybe it *was* my fault. Maybe I *said* something or *did* something that *drove* him away.
You didn't, Mom.
I know for a *fact*.
We stayed there until closing, just *talking*.
Not just about Dad, but about *everything*.

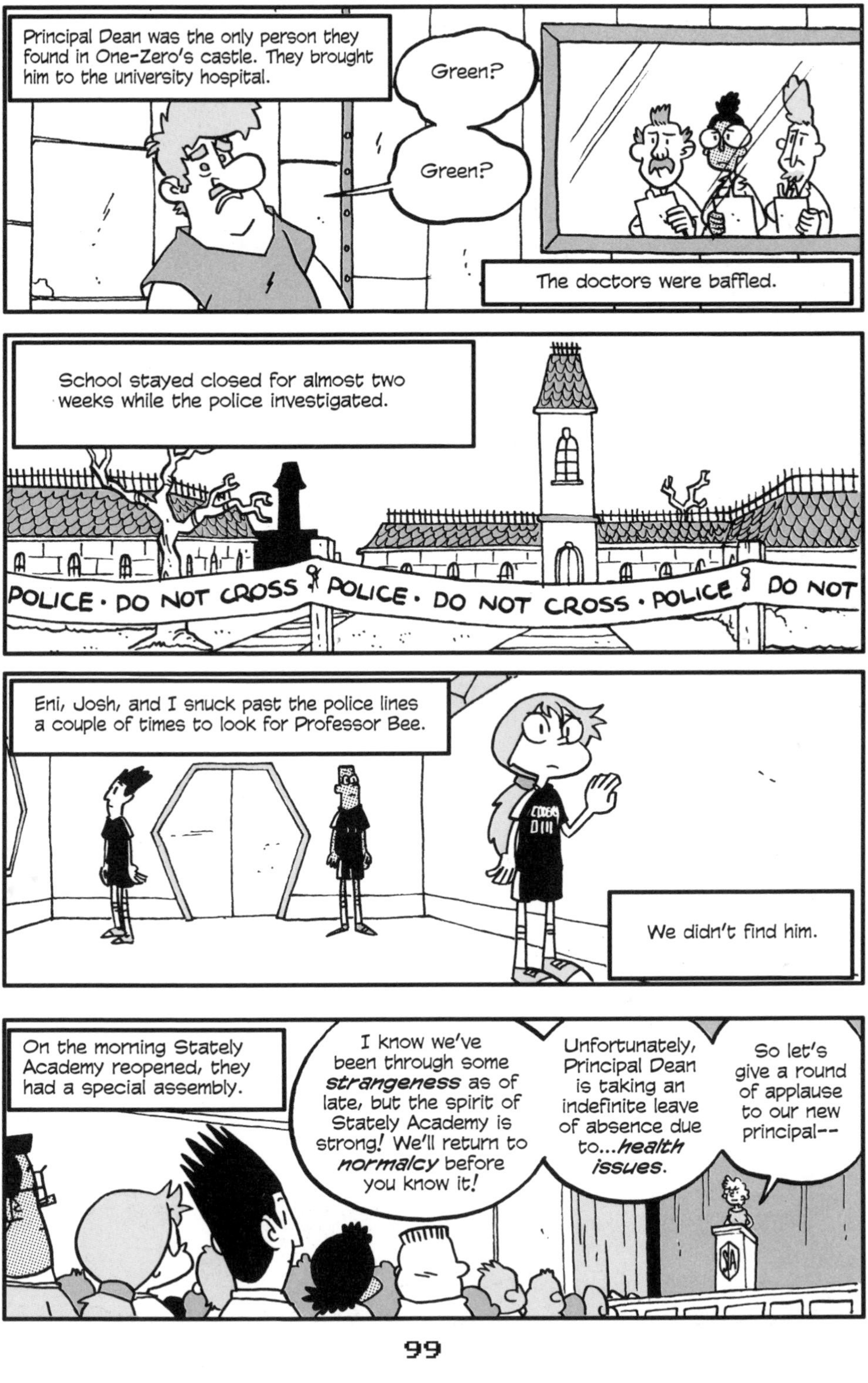
Principal Dean was the only person they found in One-Zero's castle. They brought him to the university hospital.
Green?
Green?
The doctors were baffled.
School stayed closed for almost two weeks while the police investigated.
POLICE · DO NOT CROSS · POLICE · DO NOT CROSS · POLICE · DO NOT
Eni, Josh, and I snuck past the police lines a couple of times to look for Professor Bee.
We didn't find him.
On the morning Stately Academy reopened, they had a special assembly.
I know we've been through some *strangeness* as of late, but the spirit of Stately Academy is strong! We'll return to *normalcy* before you know it!
Unfortunately, Principal Dean is taking an indefinite leave of absence due to...*health issues*.
So let's give a round of applause to our new principal--

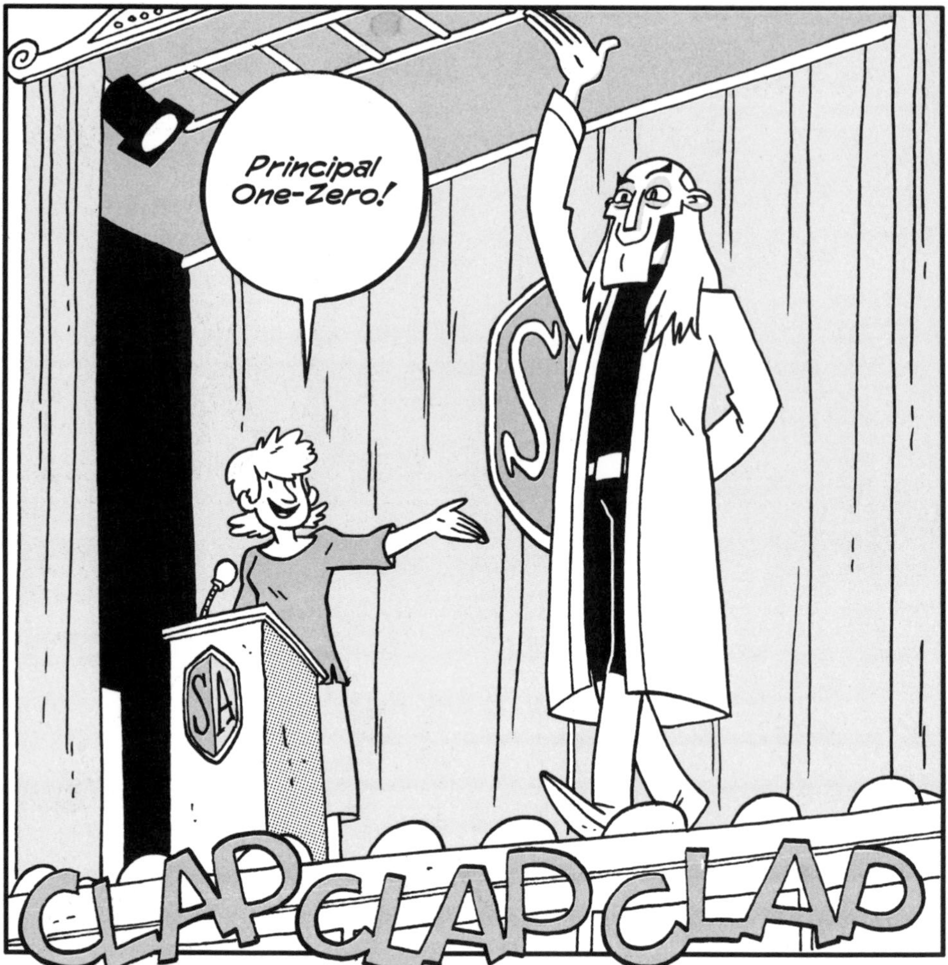
Principal One-Zero!
CLAP CLAP CLAP

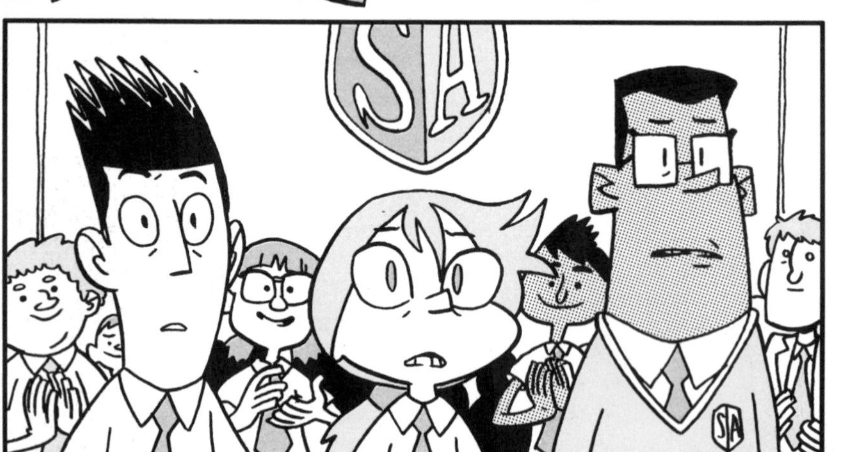

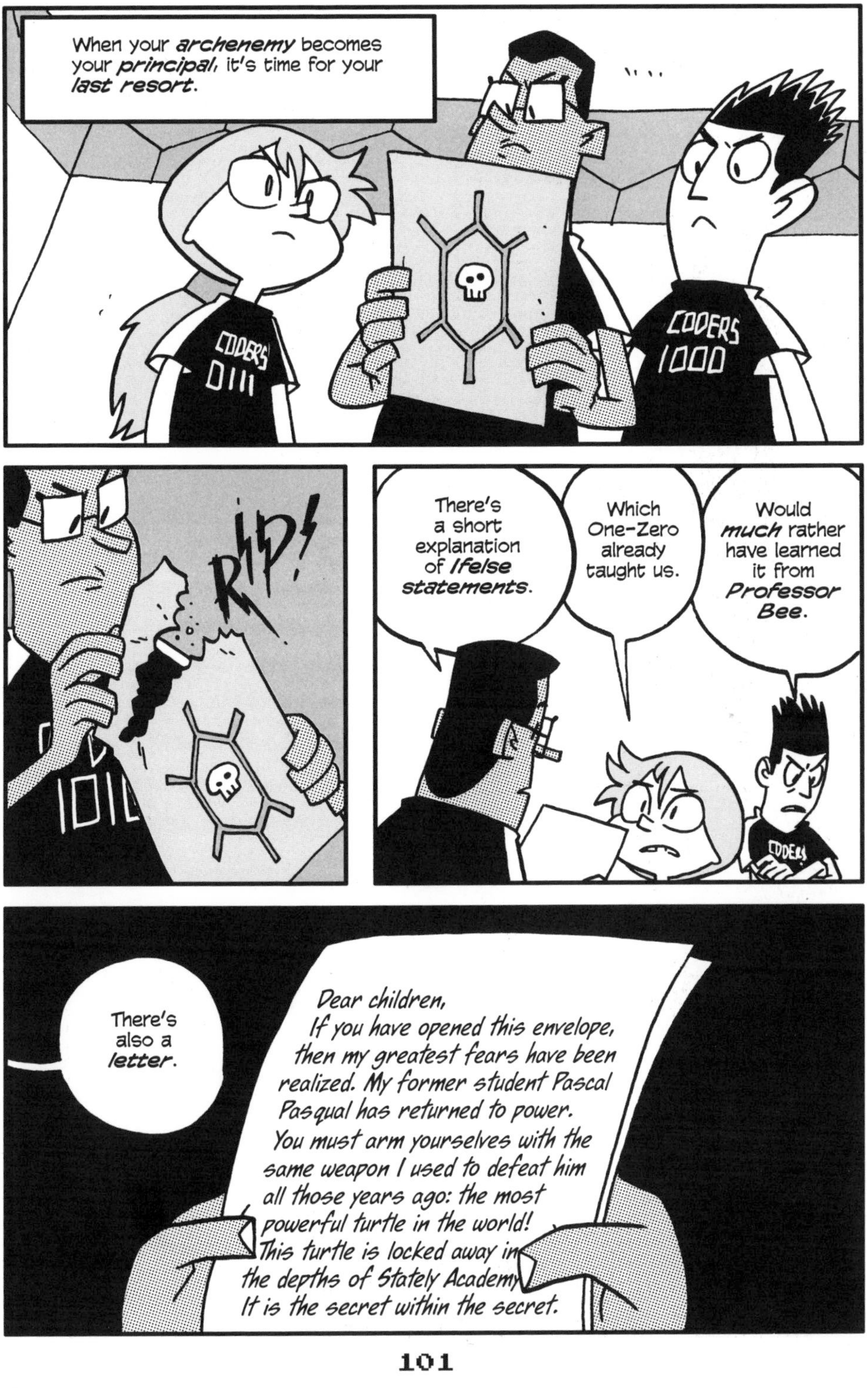
When your archenemy becomes your principal, it's time for your last resort.
...
CODERS 0111
CODERS 1000
RIP!
1010
There's a short explanation of Ifelse statements.
Which One-Zero already taught us.
Would much rather have learned it from Professor Bee.
CODERS
There's also a letter.
Dear children,
If you have opened this envelope, then my greatest fears have been realized. My former student Pascal Pasqual has returned to power.
You must arm yourselves with the same weapon I used to defeat him all those years ago: the most powerful turtle in the world!
This turtle is locked away in the depths of Stately Academy
It is the secret within the secret.

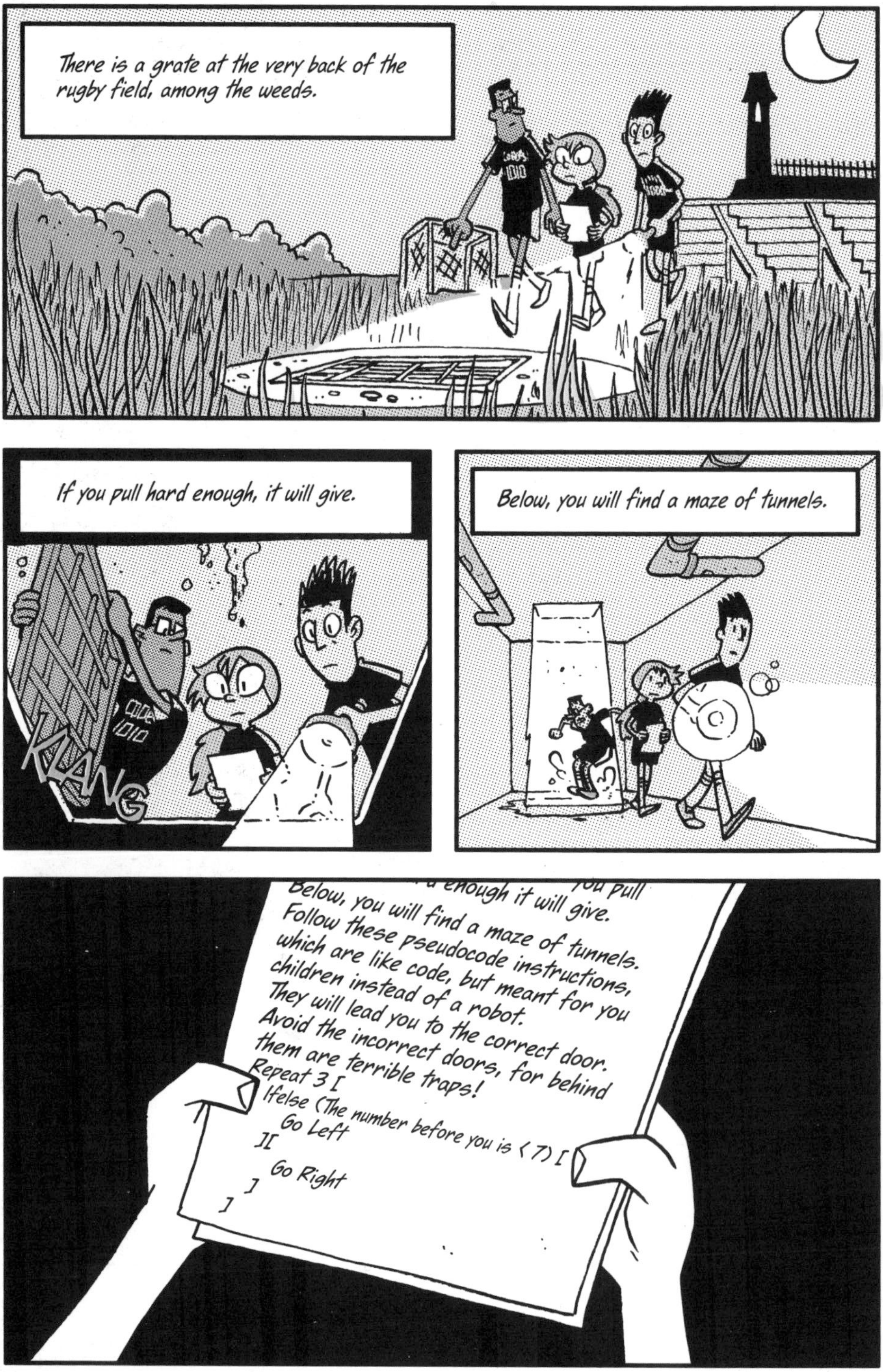
There is a grate at the very back of the rugby field, among the weeds.
If you pull hard enough, it will give.
KLANG
Below, you will find a maze of tunnels.
enough it will give.
you pull
Below, you will find a maze of tunnels.
Follow these pseudocode instructions,
which are like code, but meant for you
children instead of a robot.
They will lead you to the correct door.
Avoid the incorrect doors, for behind
them are terrible traps!
Repeat 3 [
Ifelse (The number before you is < 7) [
Go Left
][
Go Right
]
]

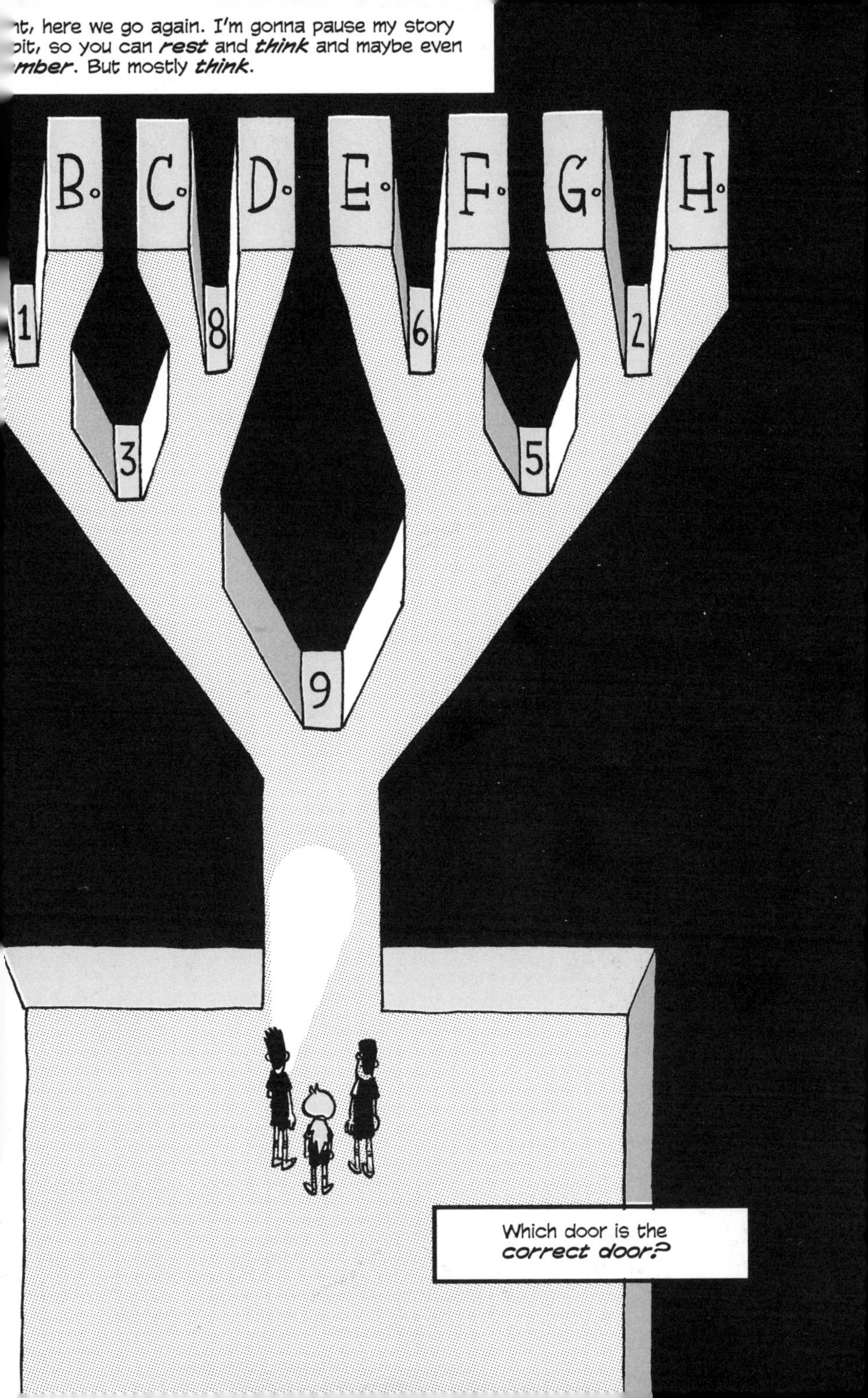
nt, here we go again. I'm gonna pause my story
it, so you can *rest* and *think* and maybe even
mber. But mostly *think*.
B.
C.
D.
E.
F.
G.
H.
1
3
8
9
6
5
2
Which door is the *correct door?*

Continued in

Robots & Repeats

Ready to start coding?

Visit www.secret-coders.com

Check out these other books in the Secret Coders series!

**Secret Coders
Paths & Portals**

This book is dedicated to Cary Matsuoka, my high school computer science teacher.

—Gene

It's so awesome to bring Secret Coders to readers, and I hope everyone learns as much as I did about coding! Thanks to Gene for being a fun teacher (and a terrific writer!).

Special thanks to my parents, Barb and Tom, who encouraged my love of reading and solving puzzles. Thanks to Judy Hansen, everyone at First Second, and every librarian and bookseller who believed in what Gene and I programmed here in these books.

To my amazing wife, Meredith, who helps me realize what comics are capable of.

—Mike

A Secret Message For You!

Install Logo (go to secret-coders.com to find out how) and type in this code for a secret message!

```
PenDown
Repeat 2 [
  Right 180
  Repeat 3[
    Repeat 2 [
      Forward 25
      Right 90
      Forward 45
      Right 90
    ]
    Forward 25
  ]
]
Right 90
Forward 40
Left 90
Forward 70
Left 90
Forward 80
Left 90
Forward 70
Left 90
Forward 40
Left 90
PenUp
Forward 30
Left 90
Forward 20
PenDown
Arc 360 10
PenUp
Back 40
PenDown
Arc 360 10
PenUp
Forward 20
Left 90
Forward 30
Right 90
Forward 45
Left 90
Forward 30
PenDown

Right 90
Arc 90 20
Left 90
Forward 65
Back 20
Arc 90 20
Right 90
PenUp
Forward 20
PenDown
Right 90
Forward 45
PenUp
Right 90
Forward 20
Left 90
Forward 20
Right 90
Forward 90
Right 90
Forward 20
Left 90
PenDown
Arc -90 20
Right 90
Forward 65
Back 20
Arc -90 20
Left 90
PenUp
Forward 20
Left 90
PenDown
Forward 45
PenUp
Left 90
Forward 20
Left 90
FORWARD 45
Right 90
Forward 45
Left 90
PenDown

Forward 60
Right 90
Forward 45
Back 10
Arc 90 10
Right 180
Forward 80
Back 10
Arc -90 10
Left 90
PenUp
Forward 10
PenDown
Forward 50
Left 90
Forward 70
Left 90
Forward 50
PenUp
Right 180
Forward 230
Right 90
Forward 130
Label "HAPPY
Right 90
Forward 20
Label "CODING!
Forward 10
Right 90
Forward 10
Right 90
PenDown
Repeat 2 [
  Forward 50
  Right 90
  Forward 70
  Right 90
]
Right 225
Forward 40
HideTurtle
```